SIGNAL
RED

rimi b. chatterjee

PENGUIN BOOKS

PENGUIN BOOKS
Published by the Penguin Group
Penguin Books India Pvt. Ltd, 11 Community Centre, Panchsheel Park,
New Delhi 110 017, India
Penguin Group (USA) Inc., 375 Hudson Street, New York, NY 10014,
USA
Penguin Group (Canada), 10 Alcorn Avenue, Toronto, Ontario, Canada
M4V 3B2 (a division of Pearson Penguin Canada Inc.)
Penguin Books Ltd, 80 Strand, London WC2R 0RL, England
Penguin Ireland, 25 St Stephen's Green, Dublin 2, Ireland (a division of
Penguin Books Ltd)
Penguin Group (Australia), 250 Camberwell Road, Camberwell, Victoria
3124, Australia (a division of Pearson Australia Group Pty Ltd)
Penguin Group (NZ), cnr Airborne and Rosedale Roads, Albany, Auckland
1310, New Zealand (a division of Pearson New Zealand Ltd)
Penguin Group (South Africa) (Pty) Ltd, 24 Sturdee Avenue, Rosebank,
Johannesburg 2196, South Africa

Penguin Books Ltd, Registered Offices: 80 Strand, London WC2R 0RL,
England

First published by Penguin Books India 2005
Copyright © Rimi B. Chatterjee 2005

Typeset in Sabon by InoSoft Systems, Noida
Printed at Saurabh Printers Pvt. Ltd, Noida

PROLOGUE

Top Secret
Access Code: Red Ten
Priority Code: Alpha One
Report Code: P/1/55-S403
From: Central Control Authority
Re: Current status of Subject S403, principal investigator: Project Trishul, Project Agnivan, Project R30445, Project LDW500, Laser Shield ADP, X-Laser, Advanced Rangefinder & Guidance Systems, Project 045891; contributor to: LADAR, Lunar Probe AX5T, Shikhandi (Stealth Materials Initiative Phase III), Anti-Laser Atmospheric Stealth Blanket, VarGeom Flat Panel Display, Divyachakra Phase II, LH-Max Damage Heuristics, Varuna III Deep Submarine RFGS, Ultralight Weaponized Robots. For list of completed projects where Subject was PI see attached report.

<<Text>>
Assessment of Operative B266: Met Subject soon after verdict of Service Tribunal. Subject saw verdict as failure of system. Primary emotions were rage, betrayal and despair with randomized hostility to authority. Subject reported loss of motivation to work, regretted past contributions to military technology and professed remorse. There was an overblown sense of personal responsibility and aggrandizement of guilt/ shame complex. Subject left without concluding interview.

Assessment of Operative A45: Subject could not give coherent account of his motivation and there did not seem to be any intellectual foundation for his strong disaffection triggered by loss of prospect of 'freedom' with which Subject has been obsessed. Subject is vulnerable, displaying scepticism and paranoia over motives and benevolence of government. There was impaired social function and one lapse into hysterical behaviour.

Actions: Subject considered burnt, removed from all projects with immediate effect. All sensitive documents confiscated. Subject retained within Centre and placed in zero-sensitivity activity. Contact with other faculty members reduced to absolute minimum. Loss of social prestige engineered to discourage fraternizing with former colleagues. All contacts to be logged so long as sensitivity of listed projects persists.

Suitable directives transmitted to Director, CARD. Concerned project handlers to take requisite measures. Subject stripped of security clearance and assigned enhanced covert vigilance.
</Endtext>>

PART I

ANU

CHAPTER ONE

'Anuprabha!' Vidura exclaimed. 'How nice to see you again! Did you get here from the station all right?' She kissed Anu's cheek.

'Yes, the bus was just where you said it would be. All big and bright with "Centre for Advanced Research and Development" on it like you said. It was huge, and I was the only one in it!'

'Oh, the bus goes into town twice a day so the campus wives can go shopping. Here, let me take your bag.'

Anu looked around the spacious sitting room. 'What a lovely bungalow! And the garden, and the grounds! Do you and Gopal really live here all alone?'

'Alone?' Vidura smiled as she led the way upstairs. 'You could say so. But there are 200-plus families on campus, all down the hill. You must have seen them on your way up. It's a little self-contained community.' Vidura threw open the door to the guest bedroom. 'See? You'll have your own view of the garden. The bathroom's through there. Would you like to freshen up before lunch? And then we can have a nice chat over tea. I'm dying to catch up with everything that's happened to you since Cambridge. Why, it's been years!'

'Of course. And I'll want to hear all about you as well.'

'Lovely. I'll just go see to the maids.' Vidura left her to unpack and went downstairs.

Anu opened the screen doors and ventured out onto the veranda. It was hot, but the shade of a nearby pipal tree took some of the sting out of the sun. She had come here from Mumbai, across the Vindhyas to the northern corner of Madhya Pradesh, through landscapes arid like the skin of a deserted planet under the summer sun. Yet here on the grounds of the Centre the grass was green, the flower beds filled with ornamental foliage and hardy flowering perennials. She looked out over the shady lawn fronting Vidura's house and down the neat green slopes bisected by the smooth black approach road. Only an army of gardeners and enough water to supply a small town could have produced that effect. The campus bungalows she had passed on the way up to Vidura's house had been pure white, gracious, scattered along the slopes of the hill. She had noted everything—the children's playground with its padlocked swings and brand new jungle gym, the clean smooth roads, the pretty fences—and taken pictures for documentation. The Centre was not new; Vidura and her husband had lived in this house for ten years now.

When Anu had got down from the bus she had glanced uphill from Vidura's gate to the summit, on which sat the long, low buildings of the Centre itself, just visible within their citadel-like enclosure. She was impressed, and in a way disheartened as well. All this neatness and order bespoke a corresponding watchfulness. Her task was going to be doubly difficult.

She shook off the feeling, bathed quickly and went downstairs. She would have to begin by asking questions. There was no point in anticipating difficulties before they occurred.

Vidura was in the kitchen, supervising the cook and the maids; there were two, Anu noted. 'Almost finished.' Vidura wiped her hands and came out. 'You must be starving. Come, let's eat. It's simple fare; we don't get anything fancy in the local market, but it's good and very cheap.'

'Fine with me. Will Gopal join us for lunch?'

'Not today. Usually he's home for lunch, but today he has

some visiting dignitaries to entertain. He'll eat at the staff canteen in the department.'

After lunch they moved to the sitting room with mugs of coffee.

'Well,' said Vidura. 'Tell me how you've been. What's it like in the big city?'

'Fine. I've got my own flat now. It's on the northern outskirts of the city, but it's big and right now totally empty. I'd like to keep it like that, just have a bed on the floor and a lamp or something.'

Vidura laughed. 'Oh, things will accumulate over time, you'll see. Space tends to get filled up.'

'What about you? You came here straight from Cambridge, didn't you? What was it like, coming to India? You were so worried before you left, I remember. All the Indians were dropping by to give you advice.'

'Yes, I remember. All I knew about the country were the stories Daddy would tell sometimes, about snakes and famines and things. I was terrified. I mean, we left Kenya when I was eight, London was where I really grew up. All those years in Islington and Fulham I never once thought I'd have to leave and set up home in another country. It felt so strange when we made the decision to go. Daddy's friends were horrified. In those days hardly anyone ever went back; I mean, hardly anyone from India *lived* in Britain.'

'As opposed to "went to study"?' Anu asked drily.

'Yes,' Vidura blushed a little. 'At Cambridge when you and Maya and the others said "I'm going home", you meant India, but to us, London was our home, if anywhere was. Everyone predicted I'd have a tough time getting used to it, but the funny thing was once it was decided that Gopal would join the Centre things went so smoothly. They even changed my citizenship for me in London before we came; all I had to do was sign the forms. And Rachel—you remember her, she was the music student who married a Punjabi—took six years to get hers done.

Then we just got off the plane and a government car whisked us straight here. It was almost an anticlimax!' She laughed. 'We stayed at the guest house for a week, then our stuff arrived, and the next day we were installed in this bungalow. Ration cards, gas connection, telephone, everything was provided immediately by the Centre. We didn't have to meet a single official.' She chuckled. 'You could say I still haven't seen the real India.'

'So you're happy here?'

'Oh yes. Where else can one live in such comfort and security in this or any country? Even in London things are hard now. I'm glad Daddy isn't around to see what's happening to England. Only,' she looked a little wistful, 'it does get a little boring at times. The other staff wives are nice, but I'm afraid they tend to find me a bit strange, poor dears. And there's no cultural life at all. I can't remember when I last went to the cinema. That's why I'm delighted you've come to visit.' She squeezed Anu's hand.

'Oh, I've been thinking of coming for a while, I just couldn't get around to buying my ticket, e-mailing you, applying for leave, all that. But I'm really glad to be here. I had no idea the place was so nice.'

'Glad you think so. This bungalow is really home to us now. I've done my best to do it up.'

'It's very pretty. I'd like to meet some of the wives. Do you visit them at all?'

'Sometimes, but the constant gossip is a little wearying. People really don't have a lot of conversation, as you can imagine. And they're all a bit jealous of me, because Gopal's doing so well. They take that sort of thing very much to heart.'

'Really? Is it a problem?'

'Oh no. When I look back I'm so glad that Gopal took the offer in spite of his misgivings. He was having trouble in Cambridge; he couldn't find a suitable research group, and his supervisor had taken on this brilliant young Pole who's done some groundbreaking work since. There are so few openings these days, and the sciences are so specialized. We were in dire financial straits, even with Daddy's help. Then out of the blue Gopal got a letter, and he jumped at the chance. Of course we knew it was defence work—that's why we didn't tell most of our friends in Cambridge, who were sort of pacifist and wouldn't have liked it, and we had to wait six months while the Indian government checked out our backgrounds. The only thing that worried us was that we might not get to see Daddy so often because of the restrictions on foreign travel.'

'Aren't you allowed to leave the country?'

'Oh yes, but we have to apply in advance and it can be tricky. Gopal applied twice but he was refused, and I couldn't face going alone. Then we arranged to have Daddy visit us. It was a disaster.' Vidura's face clouded. 'He spent a month here and couldn't get used to it at all. It's not that he was uncomfortable, it was just . . . I don't know, something in the air that made him uneasy. That was the last time I saw him.'

'I'm sorry.' Anu placed a hand on her arm. 'I'm really sorry, Vidura.'

Vidura blinked. 'It's all right. I just felt so helpless about it all. I think that was the one time I regretted having come here. But Daddy wrote me a letter from the hospital. He said, *you've done the right thing, Eufie* (he always called me Eufie, my middle name's Euphemia). *Your children will have a country they can call their own.* I cried when I read that. I think he always felt himself an exile, under the tailored suit and the pukka accent, and it comforted him to think his grandchildren would close the circle. Except of course that there weren't any grandchildren.'

'Are you sad about that?'

'Of course. You know, it's funny how before we were married we were always so worried, we took such care, and then afterwards we thought, now it's okay, let it happen, but years went by and nothing did. It's hard to realize that you're not getting pregnant when you've spent so long being afraid of it.' She sighed. 'It's probably my fault, my cycle's awfully irregular. A few years ago we went for some tests, but the doctors basically told us there's nothing wrong, try harder. They gave me some medicine to regulate my cycle, but it sent my blood pressure up.' Vidura sighed again and twisted a cushion fringe between her fingers. 'Gopal's always so busy. And so tired.'

'Does he work with chemicals in the lab?'

'I suppose so,' Vidura looked uncertain. 'He works with glass; I suppose that's a chemical. Everything is, isn't it? Why?'

'No, just wondering. What sort of work is he doing now?'

'Something to do with sensors. I don't know really; he doesn't talk much, and I suppose a lot of it's confidential.'

'He doesn't like you to ask about his work?'

'Oh, he's not secretive or anything, he talks about the lab and the people all the time, but the technical details—well, I never ask him to explain unless he does it on his own. I don't want him to have to refuse to tell me.'

'I see.'

Vidura smiled. 'What about you, Anu? You've put on weight since Cambridge. I still remember you in that lovely black chiffon sari at the college ball. Remember?'

'Yes, and falling into the Cam.' They laughed. 'Those geese got the fright of their life!'

'I loved the way you took it off, hung it to dry on Melanie's car and calmly spent the rest of the evening in your blouse and petticoat. That was the blouse with the mirrorwork from Bikaner. Everyone thought it was this high-fashion skirt and top! Actually so did I, at the time.'

'Yes,' Anu smiled. 'Sarah liked my satin petticoat so much she practically forced me to leave it behind. Remember how David insisted we put the sari on for him?'

'I thought he looked quite cute in it. How is Sarah? Are you in touch with any of the old gang?'

'Sarah's at CERN in Geneva. She helps me sometimes with research. And Ravi—you remember Ravi?—he's at the Ambedkar Institute for Social Study, like me, only he's in economics.'

'You read sociology, didn't you?'

'Yes. When I got back I specialized in work environment studies. Lots of corporate stuff.' She made a face. 'So I've run away here for a holiday.'

'I'm really glad you did. And so is Gopal. I've made him promise to come back at least before dinner to see you, but one can never tell with these bigwigs, they might not let him go till eleven at night.'

'Oh dear. What sort of people does he have to deal with?'

'All sorts. Government mainly; this is a state-run establishment, after all. And sometimes visiting scientists who are collaborating with our teams. I told him to let his scholars take them round the labs, but he has to do it himself.'

'How many scholars does he have?'

'He's got one full-time scholar, Agniv Nag. There's another, K.S. Sachdeva, whom he's helping to supervise. They get their degrees from the University of Bhopal, but they do their work here, in the lab. It takes them a long time, eight or ten years, mostly because once they've done their thesis the Centre makes them rewrite the whole thing before they submit—to hide the classified stuff, you know. I feel a bit sorry for them: fancy having to write your thesis twice. Both the boys are new, they've only been here a couple of years, and he spends a lot of time with them.'

'Is Gopal happy working here? Or does he not say anything about it?'

Vidura looked thoughtful. 'I think he is. From what he says I gather there are very few places in India with the facilities to do the kind of work he's doing, and nowhere else where he can do it in peace. He seems contented. He's an Assistant Director now, and he heads his own team. There are seven Assistant Directors, a Deputy Director and the Director himself.

The ADs do the real work, you know. Gopal has twelve people under him. I meet them sometimes at campus functions, but it doesn't do to mix too much with the juniors.'

'Why not?'

Vidura's mouth quirked a little. 'It's not done.' She took the empty mug from Anu and went into the kitchen. Anu followed her and admired the gleaming marble worktops. 'Are all the bungalows so lavishly done up?'

'Yes indeed. The government tries its best to make sure we don't miss the comforts of home. They're always renovating and redecorating the bungalows and the hostels and everything; they fix things the moment you ring them up.' She smiled. 'People have had nervous breakdowns on retirement because they'll have to leave all this and go live in some city. So the Centre has set up a housing scheme near Delhi for retired staff. They deduct payments on the flat from Gopal's salary. I've visited it, it's lovely.'

'So, essentially, if you work for the Centre you're set for life?'

'Yes.' Vidura grinned mischievously. 'Jealous?'

'Green with it.'

'There's a downside, though.' Vidura frowned. 'Gopal never mentions it but I've heard from the other wives that the men can't leave even if they want to once they've been confirmed in their posts. If anyone wants to take up a job, the application has to be forwarded through the Director's office. It's never cleared, so they say. They always find some excuse to refuse permission, or they just lose the file. And I have to admit I've never heard of anyone leaving to take up a job outside. When they retire they get made directors of this and that; I suppose by then what they know is obsolete anyway, so they can be safely turned loose.'

'Why would they want to leave?'

Vidura bit her lip. 'Sometimes . . . I don't know. I've heard of men wanting to quit for personal reasons, because they can't get on with their team or because . . . they have some problems with their work. People don't talk about it much.'

'So Gopal has to stay at the Centre?'

'Yes. I don't think he minds; the Centre is his life.' Vidura got up and turned on the lights. Insects pinged against the window screens, and birds, twittering sleepily, sought the trees out of a darkening sky.

'Are there any women on the staff? Research workers, I mean, like Gopal.'

'A few. They don't mix with us wives, and the wives see them as competing with their husbands and cut them dead mostly. They're a bit traditional, most of the wives; they think the women are taking the bread out of the mouths of the men's families.' She made a wry face. 'I feel a bit sorry for the women faculty, but they're hard to be friendly with; like all scientists they don't much want to talk about anything but science.'

'But Gopal talks about other things.'

'Only because I've spent thirteen strenuous years civilizing him. And it's only skin-deep; if he sees another scientist you can forget about conversation for the rest of the evening.'

Anu, head on one side, studied her deeply. 'Go on, admit it, you *are* lonely.'

Vidura shrugged, smiling. 'When I look at all I've been given, it seems unfair to cavil. Yes, I am a little. The only person I can really talk to is Rahil Vidyadhar, and he's only here for a while.'

'Who's Rahil Vidyadhar?'

'A Sanskrit scholar who's visiting. You'll probably meet him; he drops in from time to time. I think he's a bit lonely among all these scientists as well. And his talk is fascinating; it's a jewel given how inarticulate his colleagues are.'

'He works here?'

'He's on deputation from the Sanatan Sanskriti Parishad. He's working on a set of ancient manuscripts which are thought to contain mystical secrets.' She smiled at Anu's look of surprise. 'You see, one of Gopal's projects concerns a kind of medieval glass that's found only in a particular village in India. In fact, no one knows how it was made, and modern methods have only approximated the quality. All the world's stock of that glass is contained in the storeroom of an old haveli thought to have belonged to a medieval artisan who knew the secret.' She smiled. 'I've seen the glass; it's a lovely deep red. It's called Signal Red. Did you know that once all the red signal lamps in the world were made from that one stock of glass?' Anu shook her head, and Vidura went on, 'The glass is still used to make jewellery. I have a wonderful necklace made from it that Gopal brought me from his last field trip. Remind me to show it to you. Anyway, this set of Sanskrit manuscripts was found on the site, in an old wooden box. They're a series of very lovely poems, but the government thinks there must be a clue to the process embedded in the text, so they've sent Rahil-ji to check it out. He's supposed to be working with Gopal.' Vidura looked a little uncomfortable. 'Rahil-ji's a wonderful person, but Gopal was a bit . . . doubtful when the ministry told him what it had in mind. He even told the minister to his face that science doesn't come out of songbooks. There was a bit of trouble about that, but it's all right now.'

'I see.'

There was the sound of a motorcycle engine outside, revving and dying, then the clink of the kickstand hitting the concrete drive. Vidura opened the door. Gopal Chandran stood in the twilight of the porch, blinking.

He was slim, with a long, ascetic face and a certain boyishness about the ears that many South Indian men have till well into middle age. His hair was just starting to show signs of grey, and as he walked into the light of the central lamp the lines in his forehead were momentarily thrown into relief. He had turned forty a week ago. Now he put his helmet carefully down on a little ledge by the window.

'Hello, Anuprabha. Did you have a good journey?'

'Totally trouble-free. I was stunned.'

He smiled. 'No doubt you'd heard all the stories about the express buses being unsafe. But you needn't have worried. I put the word out that a guest of the Centre was coming, and the Security Force boys kept a watch.'

'Really? You can do that?'

'It's routine. The local people know they're not to bother us. They leave us alone.'

'I wish I'd known that. I hardly slept a wink.'

'Well, now you know.' Vidura smiled. 'It's perfectly safe to come here whenever you want. Just drop Gopal an e-mail.'

'Yes,' Gopal smiled. 'Vidura has hardly anyone to talk to. It's good you've come.'

'Viddy was telling me.'

He smiled. 'I envy you women. You can talk about your lives so easily.'

'Indeed?' Anu raised her eyebrows a little. 'Do you have trouble talking about your life?'

'Oh, Gopal's hopeless at anything like that,' Vidura patted him playfully on the arm as she went to answer the door. It was the maids, back for their second shift. Gopal sat down and began going through the day's newspaper. 'I go to the lab before the paper guy arrives, so I only get to read it in the evenings.' He folded the paper open at the sports section. 'So what do you think of the Centre?'

'I've hardly seen it. I'd love to see a lab.'

'I'm afraid you can't. The labs are only for authorized personnel but you can take a look at the grounds. And of course if you want Vidura can take you to meet some of the other staff families. Apart from that there's not much to do here, but I'm sure you and Viddy have a lot to say to each other. It's been, what, ten years?'

'Yes, Gopal. I'm surprised you remember.' Vidura smiled indulgently.

'Even I can do elementary maths, Viddy. Besides, I'll never forget Cambridge. It was the one great formative experience of my life.'

'Really?' Anu looked at him with attention. 'I had no idea you felt like that about it. Do you miss it? Would you like to go back?'

Slowly Gopal shook his head. 'I'm doing important work here,' he said seriously. 'Very crucial work for the nation.'

'I'd love to go back,' Vidura said wistfully. 'Oh, not to stay. Just to visit for a while. For a change.'

There was a little silence, filled only by the sounds of the maids at work in the kitchen. Then Vidura said brightly, 'I'll just go check on dinner,' and disappeared into the kitchen.

'What sort of work are you doing?' Anu asked in tones of polite inquiry.

'I work on novel glass applications.'

'Oh! So you make . . . new kinds of bottles, windows, that sort of thing?'

He smiled. 'No.'

'I'm sorry, I probably seem very ignorant to you.' Anu looked crestfallen.

'Oh no. Bottles and windows were major technological innovations, and I could go on about how important they were and all the trouble people took to learn how to make them. But glass has moved on since then. For instance, your e-mail message to me was transported along a tiny filament of glass.'

'Fibre optics! Yes, I have this little lamp at home made of glass fibres. It's very pretty.'

'There's no limit to what people can do with glass. You can wear it, look through it, drink out of it, bake a cake in it, make boats of it, send electromagnetic impulses down it. And there are more and stranger things you can do. I'm just looking at some of them. We have projects running on glass nano-wires, photonic computing, various kinds of shields and sensors. But right now most of my work is on flat-panel displays and carbon nano-tubes grown on glass.'

'Tell me about them.' Anu sat forward and rested her chin

on her hands, a look of rapt interest on her face. He smiled. 'Suppose you were walking along a dark alley. It's so dark you can't see your surroundings. Wouldn't you like, say, a pair of spectacles which had a tiny display on their lenses that told you if people were about, how many, in what direction?'

'Oh yes! The alley near my flat is just like that. Can you really make such a pair of glasses? The number of times I've walked down that alley with my heart in my mouth!' She thought for a bit. 'But you're talking about defence applications, aren't you?'

'Yes. Granted that you could use the glasses as I said, to ensure your safety on a dark road, there's not really much chance that people will develop such a thing because you want it for that purpose. Work like that demands big money, so nearly all the time it's the army who gets it first. The defence utility is obvious, isn't it? After it's been tried and tested, then there may be civilian trickle-downs.'

Anu looked puzzled. 'But there are lots of women like me who are dead scared of walking about at night. I'm sure if someone were to market such a product we'd buy it.'

'My dear Anu, the price of that product would be way too high. The developmental costs alone are staggering. Then there's scaling-up, patenting, field trials, manufacture, all sorts of processes to be dealt with. Insecure women on city streets just don't have those resources.

Vidura had come back. 'Oh, he's talking about the goggles again. Ask him what you do once the magic eye has detected the goons. Will the military lend you a bazooka to finish them off?' She grinned. 'I always tell him it would be cheaper and safer to hire more policemen and have them stay awake at night.'

Gopal shrugged and picked up the paper again. 'That's for the government to take care of. I just do my job.'

The maids put the dinner on the sideboard and took their leave. Vidura and Anu laid the table. The doorbell rang, shattering the silence of the evening with a long impatient panicky buzz. Startled, Vidura looked at Gopal who put the paper down and went to the door. Anu got up too and wandered over.

In the space between the open door and Gopal's body she saw a man—or rather he had the height and frame of a young man but on it there still rested the pudginess of a child, as if he was yet in the process of becoming something. He had a broad square face, at this moment very agitated, deep-set eyes of great brilliance and thick hair cut short and oiled so enthusiastically it looked painted on. 'Agniv,' Gopal was saying. 'What's the matter? Is there a problem at the lab? Why didn't you call?'

'It's Dr Mani Sheth-ji, sir. They've . . . they've done such thing! Sir, I cannot believe! You must help, sir. I've just come. I am sorry . . .' Confusion overwhelmed him as he realized he'd disturbed his supervisor at dinner.

'What are you talking about, Agniv? What's up?'

'Dr Sheth-ji, sir! They have made him the in-charge of campus amenities!' Agniv's voice rose into a squawk. 'I heard just now only. They are promoting Mr Kundu into his place to be head of his group. Sir! We must go to Director and plead him to . . .'

'Be quiet!' Gopal snapped. 'Don't even *think* of doing such a thing! Didn't I tell you not to get mixed up with Dr Sheth? I told you it would be madness to work with him. Look, I've known since November that something would . . .' Gopal suddenly noticed Anu's eyes on him, stepped out onto the porch and closed the door after him. His voice became inaudible, but Agniv's harsh adolescent tones could still be heard. 'But he is *good*!' he wailed at one point. 'Can they not see that? What is there if he is bad at talking to . . .' Then Gopal hushed him.

Anu went back to the table and sat down. Vidura was laying out dinner with a worried look. After a while Gopal came back, locked the door and sat down gravely.

'Who was that?' Anu asked cautiously.

'Agniv Nag. My scholar. I do apologize, but he tends to get excited.' Gopal nodded to Vidura, who began to ladle out rice. 'Just a little disappointment. He'll get over it.'

'And Dr Sheth? Who is he?'

A quick shadow of disapproval flitted over Gopal's face. 'A colleague,' he said lightly. 'I worked with him once, on the lunar probe, when we were both greenhorns. Try some of this lime pickle, my mother sends it every year from Palghat. It's divine.'

They spent the rest of the evening reminiscing about Cambridge. Gopal fell asleep in the middle of the conversation as the two women talked. 'Poor man, he works so hard.' Vidura looked at him tenderly. 'Half the evenings he can't keep awake, he's so exhausted.' She nudged him. 'Time for bed, I think.'

Gopal awoke with a start. 'I wasn't asleep.'

'You were snoring, dear. Come on, Anu must be tired too after her journey.'

CHAPTER TWO

'Oh, I'm so sorry, I wasn't expecting anyone to be here so early in the morning.' Anu blinked and took a step backwards.

On the veranda downstairs, where Anu had come for a breath of fresh air, sat a man dressed in dazzling white dhoti-kurta. His plump fair face was set off by the bright red tilak he wore, which still had a few grains of rice sticking to it. He wore gold-rimmed round glasses with amber lenses through which his large eyes peered intensely. But he smiled pleasantly enough and waved her to the deckchair beside him. 'I am the one who should be sorry,' he said gravely. 'I didn't mean to startle you, but I often drop in on Vidura-ji early in the morning on my way back from the temple. If she is not up, I refrain from disturbing her by sitting here on the veranda till she is ready to receive me. You must be her Cambridge friend.'

'Yes, I'm Anuprabha Shastri.'

'Anuprabha? That is an unusual name.'

She smiled gravely. 'My father was a scientist who worked on cosmic rays. He named me. He wanted me to follow him into science, but I chose social science instead.'

'I see. "Atom-radiance". Very appropriate.'

'And you are . . .?'

'Rahil Vidyadhar.'

'Oh, of course. Vidura told me about you. You're working on some ancient manuscripts about glass.'

'Yes, the texts of the Signal Red project.'

'What are these poems like? How do you analyse them?'

'They purport to be descriptions of nature. However, the third in the series enumerates all the "red blossoms of the earth" then known to mankind, and speculates on "the blood-flowers we do not yet know". Another describes the birth of Kali. Yet another deals with the *trimurti,* Brahma, Vishnu, Shiva, in terms that suggest metaphors for chemical processes. The odd construction and metaphor led us to suspect that they were the codified form of some secret knowledge. Unusually the possessors wrote it down, but they disguised its true nature so that the uninitiated would not know. An ancient form of patent protection, if you like.'

'I see. Ingenious.'

He smiled. 'I have come here to study them, and I am to share my insights with the scientists and work with them.' He shrugged. 'That's the theory, anyway. I am sceptical about the possibility.'

'Why?'

'Scientists have such closed minds and they care little for history, not even of their own discipline. Even your friend Dr Chandran told me that science progresses by letting go of the past.' Vidyadhar sighed. 'India has lost her pride in science. Yet we were the source of nearly every worthwhile discovery known to science. We must point out to the world community the debt it owes us. In the meantime, we work to rediscover our traditions. My main role is to inspire a sense of pride in those who work here. If they will listen.'

'I see.'

He half turned in his chair, the better to fix her with his gaze. 'And I am also working on ancient theories of the mind. One of the great mysteries, to those who really think about human nature, is why people wish to do what they do. You will understand that the power to rule belongs to him who can control men's minds. I am merging ancient knowledge in this field with modern research findings. The Russians have done a great deal on physico-chemical techniques for control of the mind. They lacked direction, however, because they did not have access to the ancient teachings, and their moral vision was faulty. Such techniques employed merely in the service of a soulless, godless materialist system can never succeed. There has to be dharma as well as karma, so that what we do is sanctified by a higher power, whether you call it "God" or "Nation". I will shortly be setting up a foundation for motivational assessment and correction. This will help prevent cases where scientists get demotivated and lose the ability to work, as was the case recently with Dr Sheth.'

'Oh. What happened to him?'

Vidyadhar waved a graceful hand. 'He became infected with pernicious ideas. There is much corruption that has entered our mindset because of the unfortunate degeneration of our society in recent centuries and the entry of foreign ideas. Dr Sheth believed he should be free to sell his services to the highest bidder. But knowledge is not a commodity in the marketplace: knowledge is puja, it is bowing before god. I am endeavouring to resurrect this ideal. All these men here should aspire to be *acharyas*. They are the new Brahmins.'

'Haven't we had enough trouble with the old ones?'

A sharp pause, then he slowly shook his head, his gaze fixed on her. 'The time you've spent in foreign lands has warped your ideas, I see. You did not understand what I said. Let me explain. Science is a pure profession. It brooks no second loyalty. It is *tapasya* itself: austerity. Certain men are fitted to work with their minds by nature; they are born thus, but they must reach the adept state through discipline. That is the reason for all this.' He waved a hand at the gardens, the road beyond. 'It is an ashram. Nothing less. You should know this, being a Brahmin yourself.'

'I'm not.'

He frowned. 'Your name is Shastri.'

She met his gaze steadily. 'Not all those who knew the shastras were Brahmins.'

He pursed his lips. 'Your ancestors would never have been given that title if they were not fit for it. To know the shastras *is* to be a Brahmin.'

Anuprabha was silent. Then she said mildly, 'Won't you let me be different?'

'No, because difference endangers society. Uncertainty is the curse of modern man. Society can only have the coherence and beauty of a great temple if we all know our place in it. We Indians need the certainty of birth to tell us who we are.'

'I don't.'

He shook his head slowly, indulgently. 'You are not a lone particle in the void, child. You are part of a society that has made and nurtured you. You owe a debt of respect and homage to that society.'

'But if I believe casteism is harmful for society, don't I harm society if I say nothing about it?'

'Uff, forget all that Cambridge nonsense,' he chuckled, waving his hands. 'The West has taught you a wrong and foolish idea of caste, and so you say it is bad. In any case, are there no castes in Cambridge? Were there not laws, not so long ago, prohibiting you from being there at all, along with Catholics, dissenters and other *shudras*? Why do the Western liberals who make speeches about caste think they have a right to comment on us, who were old in knowledge and wisdom while they were still savages wearing animal skins?' He shook a playful finger at her. 'Be wary of the gifts of Westerners, they give with dirty hands. You will catch contagion from their unclean gifts.'

'If they are unclean because they have castes, then so are we.'

He laughed, suddenly, a bark of delight. 'You argue just like a Brahmin,' he said with satisfaction. 'Yes, you are a true Shastri.'

Anu let a few seconds of silence spin out like a full stop to that observation, then asked brightly, 'Tell me about the Signal

Red project. Are you finding it an easy task? Or is it terribly difficult?'

'I prefer to call it Project Lalitavarna. The *shlokas* require careful reading. For instance, I am working on the idea of the *trimurti*. Do you know that the compound which colours the glass is something called cadmium sulphoselenide? A strange entity. Cadmium the destroyer, toxic to life; selenium the preserver, essential to life; sulphur the creator, spewed from the earth in its moments of creative upheaval. Two metals, one non-metal, married in a complex structure. Shiva, Vishnu, Brahma. Therein lies the essence of the mystic vision. But unfortunately the Arabs ripped our knowledge from us and sold it to the Europeans, all through the age of persecution and ruin by foreigners. Do you know how much of their science is based on the plundered fragments of ours? By looking in the ancient wisdom for scientific short cuts I am trying to redress the balance.'

'I admit that the ancient world owed a great debt to India,' Anu said carefully. 'And that the foundations of much of what is known today were laid here. But if the Arabs hadn't collected and carried our knowledge to the West, could we, on our own, have advanced further? Isn't it better that our knowledge now belongs to the peoples of the world? Can't we also build on what they built? You say the knowledge was stolen. But can one really steal knowledge?'

'Yes, one can,' he snapped. 'Quite apart from the issue of *apatra*, or the sin of knowledge being taken by unworthy recipients, in essence the robbers violated what they are pleased to call intellectual property. Have you heard the term?'

'Yes, but . . .'

'And now they presume to sell it back to us. They have no right. It was ours, ours from the start.' His eyes flashed. 'That is why I find it sickening when they drone on about how Western science was created by Aristotle. Fools! The Greeks too stole from us. That is why I boil with anger when they lay

hands on our ancient birthright. We must mobilize to stop this
raping of our motherland. Had they left our science to us, we
would have done great things. But they took our wealth and
destroyed our industries. That is why I call them thieves,
looters, plunderers, usurpers, colonizers. Dirty foreigners with
dirty minds and dirty hands. It will take us years to clean their
left-behind filth from the motherland, but we will do it. We
will assert, we will *prove*, the purity of our culture. Even the
human filth they have left behind will be purged.'

Anu took a deep breath. Her own emotions were beginning
to interfere with her scholarly objectivity; she tried to clear her
mind and think of the next question. He was looking intensely
at the sky as if contemplating his dream. She practised her
dissociative technique, learned over many interviews with
difficult subjects, of seeing him as a flat plane of colour. He
became a composition in white, skin tones, red, gold, black.
Her heart rate slowly stabilized. She let him slide into focus,
and tried again.

'Do you really think the ancient poets knew the chemical
composition of cadmium sulphoselenide?'

He looked grave. 'I believe they did.'

'But can you prove it?'

'Proof? You talk of proof? Where the violence of the ages
has been at work, only the heart can supply proof. That is why
I do not speak for the ears of the Western historians. I publish
no papers, I attend no conferences, but I speak to the wise and
tell them why they should be proud. Every week in the
conference room of this Centre I meet with them and speak to
them, open their eyes to their duty, their glory. They are doing
great work here. Such work should be done with pride.'

'Hello,' said Vidura behind them. 'Rahil-ji, how are you?'

'As well as god has kept me. Your young friend denies that
she is a Brahmin.'

Vidura smiled. 'Anu's mother, Sorayya, is a Muslim. So she
can be both, or neither, as she chooses.'

This seemed to shock him more than anything Anu had said. 'It's all right,' Anu murmured. 'It doesn't rub off.'

'I see now why you have so many confusions, young woman. And why you feel no pride in yourself.'

'I do. It just isn't your kind of pride.'

'There is no other kind.' He sat stiffly now, head turned away. Vidura, sensing the tension in the air, pulled up another deckchair. 'Come, Rahil-ji, you don't mean to say it bothers you? Only the other day you were discussing Lucknowi Urdu poetry with me like a *shair*. What's got into you?'

'If you write Urdu poetry in Deva Nagari script, it is not so different from Hindi poetry. Urdu is only a name invented by foreigners. And art is different: life is more serious than art.'

'You mean to say mixing ideas is all right, but mixing genes is not?'

He winced. 'If you must be so crude.'

Vidura smiled mischievously. 'When you were discussing Khajuraho sculpture I would never have guessed that you were so finicky.'

'Khajuraho was created by the Chandellas, the lords of Jejabhukti: an ancient and great land of our pride. Have I ever said the *Kama Sutra* is evil? There are good arts of the body, and there are perversions.'

'Oh, come now, surely you don't think Anu here is a perversion?'

He looked at her severely. 'She is an unfortunate victim.'

Anu bit her lip. It would be useless to ask any more questions now. Vidyadhar's eyes behind the amber glasses rested on her again. 'Well, child, you have dedicated yourself to learning, have you not, and that is a Brahminical thing to do. You have responded to the call of your better nature.'

'Nonsense,' Vidura smiled. 'She just happens to be a very intelligent woman.'

'Yes, that's the Shastri side coming out.'

'You're stubborn, aren't you, Rahil-ji?' Vidura said affectionately. To Anu she went on, 'We have the most lovely fights about Indian culture. I don't know what I did with my mornings before he came. He's an education.'

Vidyadhar actually blushed. 'You are too kind, madam Vidura-ji.' He rummaged in his bag. 'I have brought the book on Ramanujam that I said you should read. Anuprabha, you can read it as well. The story of Ramanujam will tell you a great deal about Indian science, and about your Cambridge. You see, Cambridge killed Ramanujam, and killed also India's hopes of outstripping the West in the science of numbers, which was stolen from us in ancient times. It was a conspiracy of the wartime intelligence authorities in Cambridge. Ramanujam refused to work on their codes, so they secretly sprayed tuberculosis bacilli from condemned beef carcasses into his room.'

'Really?'

His eyes flashed. 'Read the book.'

'Yes, Rahil-ji, we'll read it with great attention,' Vidura smiled and shook her head to warn Anu not to speak.

'Numbers are very important. They can tell you everything about the universe. Ramanujam learned his craft from his mother, who was an astrologer of unusual power. Had she not been a woman, India would have had its star mathematician a generation earlier. Her name was Kamalottamal. I have asked the ministry to create an institute in her name, to investigate the power of numbers. For instance, she predicted the exact age at which her son would die. I myself have studied the science of numerology for years, but to be that good—it is a gift from heaven.'

'So women *are* of some use, apart from cooking and cleaning and going to the temple, eh?' Vidura chuckled. Vidyadhar looked offended. 'The highest ideal for a woman is to be a *vir mata*, a mother of heroes. That's what she was. She deserves to be worshipped as a goddess.'

There was a silence in which Rahil-ji gave Vidura a pitying look.

'But do not be disappointed, Vidura-ji,' he said softly. 'Even without sons, you can at least be a *brahmacharini*, a seeker after truth. That too is a worthy objective.'

'And what are you?' Vidura asked a little sharply.

'I? I am god's instrument, that's all. When he plays upon me I sing; when his hands are still I am silent. I am here to do his bidding on earth. And now, ladies, I must leave you. I have a meeting with the Director.'

They watched him get up and walk down the path.

'There goes a cruel man.'

'No, Anu, he isn't cruel, just ruthless. There's a difference.'

Anu looked at her. 'You're quite taken with him, aren't you?'

Vidura shrugged. 'I was so starved of intelligent company when he came here, and he knows so much about so many fascinating things. Listening to him I felt it was wrong of me to know so little about India. There's no proper library for us here, I could never have found out all those wonderful things on my own.'

'Yes, much of what he says about ancient history and culture is sort of true,' Anu said carefully. 'But his interpretation of it . . . I don't think it stands up to scrutiny.'

'Oh, Anu, how thoughtless of me! I'm so sorry.' To Anu's dismay there were tears in Vidura's eyes. 'I shouldn't have told him about your parents. I never realized . . . when we were in Cambridge, I had no idea how you must be viewed in India, like a . . . freak or something . . .'

'No, Viddy,' Anu clasped her hands round Vidura's. 'It's not like that at all. Most of the time no one even thinks about it. Not everyone's like Vidyadhar about it. Come on, stop looking tragic.'

'I mustn't tell the other wives, they'll behave in the same way. How horrid for you. Oh, what am I saying, it'll be all over the place now that Rahil-ji knows.'

'So what? It's not a problem. Look, it's 9 a.m. and I'm starving. Why don't we have breakfast, Viddy? All this will look better after coffee.'

'I'm so sorry, Anu, I totally forgot.' Horrified at her lapse of hospitality, Vidura served them both the eggs and toast that the maids had left on the hotplate, and made two cups of coffee.

'Can we go meet some of the faculty wives today?' Anu asked. 'Might as well try and beat the speed of gossip.'

'Yes, we can go and visit Malti Prasad down the road. Hang on, I'll give her a call and see if she's free. Not that anyone's ever busy around here.' Vidura took the plates and piled them up in the sink for the maids. 'Malti's kids will be at school and she'll be back from the temple by now, we can talk for maybe an hour before lunch.'

Anu nodded, and Vidura made the call. Malti Prasad was indeed free. Vidura called Gopal to tell him where they'd be, filled a tiffin box she was due to return with sweets, and they set off for Malti's house.

CHAPTER THREE

'Sir, may I come in, sir?'

It was Agniv, his broad square face shiny with sweat as he peered anxiously round the door. 'Of course. You're late this morning, Agniv. What's the matter?'

Agniv hung his head. 'I . . . I . . . I saw Dr Sheth-ji, sir.'

Gopal sighed and shuffled the papers on his desk. 'Agniv, sit down. I need to talk to you.'

Agniv sat, fixing his eyes on the edge of the desk. His fingers methodically creased and uncreased a corner of the battered file he always carried. He was wearing the same clothes as yesterday, wrinkled as if he had slept in them. Gopal felt a hint of unease. Agniv was always unkempt and awkward, but now there was a feverish tinge to his gaucheness. He wondered if it was just because of Dr Sheth, or something deeper.

'Agniv, are you afraid I was angry with you last night? I'm sorry if I spoke harshly, but I had my reasons. I know you wanted to work with Dr Sheth on the laser shields very badly, but I told you before that personnel are only allowed to cross team boundaries under exceptional circumstances. I knew that Dr Sheth was in . . . difficulties with the authorities, so I warned you to stay clear. The possible benefits of sharing expertise with him weren't worth the risks. Do you understand me?'

Agniv looked up a little sharply. 'Sir, Dr Mani Sheth-ji is best in doing experiments. Not just best in the Centre, but *best*. You yourself said so. And he wanted me to work with him.

I could have learned his methods. You said you would allow, Director would not object if both team heads give permission. And . . .'

'Agniv, Dr Sheth is no longer the team head. If you want to work with his team you'll have to ask Mr Kundu. I checked with the Director; Mr Kundu is now Assistant Director in charge of the laser team. It's official. No one can change it now.'

Agniv said nothing. He stared at the ground. The only sound was the faint crackle of the file cover giving way under his fingers.

Gopal tried again. 'Agniv, this is the real world. You're not in college any more. Pretty soon you'll be in paid employment, and then one day you'll be sitting in my chair. Look, I agree with you that Dr Sheth is a fine scientist. He's one of the few people I'm really grateful to have worked with. His insights on wide-spectrum stealth alone have put India ten years ahead in the field. But he has no clue how to conduct himself in the real world. I'm one of the lucky ones; he's fought with nearly everyone else in the lab. He can't keep his opinions to himself, and he just won't learn the rules. Do you know why he was due for removal? He wanted to join a company abroad. He had the gall to send in an application and then see the Director and demand that it be forwarded. The Director said what any sensible person would have said. Dr Sheth's headed eighteen of our most sensitive projects, and been involved in countless others. His input is crucial to all of them. He just cannot leave; he's bound by the Official Secrets Act and the Sensitive Information Directive. Everything he knows is dynamite. The Director offered him anything he wanted, money, status, lab facilities, personnel, anything. He wouldn't take less than freedom, he said. The Director said, it's too late, you've been here eleven years. And Dr Sheth threw the application in his face and left the room.'

Agniv's eyes were round. 'He did, sir?'

'Yes. That was bad enough, but it would have blown over; he's not the first scientist to get emotional about this sort of thing. But he moved the Service Tribunal.'

'What is that?'

Gopal smiled. 'Well may you ask. It's the body that's supposed to arbitrate when any of us have a problem with our employers. But you've never heard of it for a very good reason. If a person goes to the Tribunal, they get a fair hearing, all the evidence is examined, and the decision is scrupulously fair. But after that, you can say goodbye to your career. You're finished.'

'Finished, sir?'

'You've rocked the boat. You've betrayed a sacred trust. You're given some ridiculous dead-end post and paid your salary for showing your face every morning. That's it. They'll never let you near a lab again.'

Agniv licked dry lips. 'That is why they . . .'

'Yes. When Sheth went to the Tribunal last year, I knew it was only a matter of time. That's why I warned you not to collaborate with him. You would have been caught in the crossfire and marked out by the authorities as Sheth's man. And I don't want your career damaged, Agniv. You're one of the best students I've ever had. You could go far. You can't afford to take stupid risks. It's my duty to keep you away from risks.'

Gopal studied the boy's face. How could he tell this young man, still so painfully idealistic, why he really needed him? It was not just Agniv's mind he required, it was his eyes and hands as well. He, Dr Gopal Chandran, headed the glass group. His job was to come in to his personal, comfortably appointed office in the morning, push paper, take roll call, give orders, hear reports, allocate tasks, discuss programmes. Then his team would troop out to the labs, leaving him behind, in exile. He was a senior administrator; the lab was no longer his territory and if he went there they would all spring to attention and watch him like a hawk: what is the boss looking at, who is he favouring? If he touched a piece of equipment, god help him, he was treading on the jealously guarded domain of some sharp young technician. There was never any chance of his actually getting to carry out a procedure; to do so was to imply that the person whose job it was was incompetent, and all the others would forcibly move that person down a notch in the group pecking order. When he went in he could feel their gazes on him like laser beams. Why doesn't Mani Sheth invent a shield against dirty looks, he thought wryly. That would have done us both some good.

But Agniv was his alter ego, an extension of himself. Agniv could go anywhere, do anything, and he, Dr Gopal Chandran, Supervisor, could follow. Whatever Agniv's hands touched magically became accessible to him. When Agniv had a problem, he could peer into the window of the vapour deposition machine as if he were the lowliest technician. Agniv's samples were his treasures, Agniv's blotted notebooks his playground. He knew he sometimes pushed the boy too hard, made him work late hours, set him impossibly difficult tasks. It wasn't entirely to make him learn, although that was part of it. The real reason was that he, Gopal, had been locked by time and custom out of his own world, and Agniv was his only key.

He shook himself. Agniv was a bright boy, one of the brightest he had ever taught, but wayward and curiously lacking in a sense of basic self-preservation. He was only barely aware of the other people in the lab, and certainly never thought about them in relation to himself. That wasn't healthy in the long run. He couldn't afford to have his student antagonizing random personnel.

'I am sorry, sir,' Agniv mumbled. 'It was just, I was wondering . . . you know curvature problem Mr Narottam-ji is working on? Dr Sheth-ji said we could solve if we grow tubes of different lengths on same sample. He is too good at making. With variable tilt . . .'

'Agniv, I understand perfectly. Your input on Narottam's problem was invaluable. But you shouldn't have brought Dr Sheth in, even if you had consulted him in private. That causes all sorts of complications. Also, try not to blurt out what you think at the group meetings. There's a way to tell people they're wrong. If you must make a point of it, tell me what you think and I'll tell Narottam. You're lucky Narottam's an easy-going fellow and didn't mind, but others might take offence if you ask them *"Are you blind?"* like that in front of the whole group. Understand?'

'Yes, sir,' Agniv mumbled, crushed.

'Don't let it get you down.' Gopal smiled at him affectionately. 'When I was young I was just like you. It took me a long time to learn not to poke my nose where it doesn't belong. Sometimes it's very hard not to say to someone, *You're doing that wrong, do it like this.* But believe me, not saying it is the best thing you can do.'

'But . . . but . . . sir, we are all here for doing science, sir? We are all part of same team, no, sir? If I see some person working in wrong way, should I not give insight? Means, I am helping them, no?'

'Maybe, but they'll either resent it or take your idea and not acknowledge it. Which would you prefer?'

'Oh, I do not mind if they are taking my idea, so long as they carry out correctly all procedures. It is all for good of nation.'

'*Don't,* Agniv. Because they'll either come back for more, or they'll be afraid of you. This is a very competitive place, Agniv. Just bring your ideas to me and I'll deal with them. I'm their boss, they'll take it from me.'

Agniv stared at him, open-mouthed. 'Why they would be afraid from me?'

'Because you'll make them feel insecure. They'll think you're making a fool of them to test them, and that you want to step into their shoes. You don't want them to think that. Do you understand how you're to handle it in future?' Agniv nodded slowly, doubtfully. 'Good,' Gopal dismissed the subject with a wave of the hand. 'Now tell me about those tests you were doing last night. Did you finish them or were you so upset by Dr Sheth that you abandoned them?'

Agniv looked shocked. 'No, sir. Results are all ready in lab. I was wanting to show this morning but when I came I met Dr Sheth-ji, he was going out. I . . . I walked with him little way. He told to me . . .'

His hands clutched the tattered file again. Gopal said gently, 'Dr Sheth has reason to be bitter, perhaps. You don't have to tell me what he said. It's a hard life working here if you happen to fancy your own independence of mind too much. Independence is the lifeblood of research: don't get me wrong, we need it here. But we have to accept that it must be confined to our work, our technical problem-solving, if you like. There we're free: we can do whatever we like, be as brilliant and innovative as we can. That's where we must fly like eagles, Agniv. But we must know how far that freedom extends, and be careful never to cross the line, because that sort of thing endangers the whole system as well as ourselves. It's a trade-off, you understand, Agniv? We have to pay for our freedom with obedience outside the realm of science, but it's worth it. If you know that and accept the price, then this is the place for you. But you must be certain, because once you've decided there's no going back.'

Agniv swallowed hard. 'That's what he asked me. He asked, "Do you want to rot in this place?"'

'I see. And what did you tell him?'

'I said, I am not knowing what I should want.'

'What's the reason for your doubt, Agniv? Aren't you happy here? Aren't the facilities good enough? Do you miss your family?'

'Yes, sir. No, sir. Means, sir, I . . .' His voice wound down unsteadily; he dropped his gaze and stared blankly at the floor.

'It's all right,' Gopal said gently. 'Think about it. Try to find someone you can talk to. Have you tried discussing your doubts with the other students?'

'Yes, sir, but . . .'

'What did they say?'

'They were laughing only.'

Gopal sighed. 'I'm afraid they're a bit unimaginative. Well, don't brood over it. You'll find that as time passes some things become clear on their own. At least now the question is there for you to answer. And don't hesitate to come to me if you want to talk again, okay?'

Agniv nodded. 'Well,' said Gopal in a lighter voice, 'let's go see those results of yours.'

The lab results were what Gopal had expected. Agniv had set up for him several sandwiches of glass that showed some promise in the direction they were seeking. 'Making these things is not the problem, really,' said Gopal, frowning at the little squares clamped in the circuit board, 'it's getting them to do anything useful. Look at this borosilicate sample. We're getting a fair throughput and a decent glow, but there are too many variations. We're looking for uniform brightness and good controllability. That patch over there looks good, doesn't it? Have you differentiated the field emitters? Okay, try for pure red, then cycle through the colours.'

They watched. 'So pretty.' Agniv's face was rapt. 'I love making these ones. So small you cannot see and yet they are being able to shine. Sometimes in my dreams I am seeing them, like rows of paddy in field.'

Gopal snorted with amusement. 'What a pity you're not a scanning electron microscope, Agniv. The things I could see with you!'

Agniv chuckled.

'Shall we run another batch of these tonight?'

'Yes, sir. But please ask Dr Verma-ji to check template for control circuits, sir. I have suspicion there is some persistent error in gold contacts deposition, which is ruining samples.'

'We talked to him last week about that. You mean he hasn't corrected it?'

'First batch was okay, but this time I got three that did not work. I tried so hard to grow perfect tubes and he has spoiled them!'

'Hush, Agniv. Have you still got the bad samples? Give them to me. This has been happening far too frequently. I'm afraid I'll have to make an issue of it.'

On the way back to his office he pondered Dr Verma. Something happened to scientists when they'd been in this place for five or six years and done at least one major project. It was the knowledge in the back of their minds, he admitted reluctantly to himself, that they were safe. Oh, they'd need to jockey for promotion and do the other fellow down, but they'd never be fired. And by then they probably had a kid or two, who went to school by the Centre's bus and played in the Centre's playgrounds, and their wives were firmly entrenched in the Centre's social hierarchy. Even if they only pushed paper for the rest of their lives, they could live comfortably and with no worries till they retired and beyond, secure that the contents of their heads were enough to keep them in clover with the Government till kingdom come.

Gopal had never been able to understand that attitude. When he had reached that level and faced the little voice that whispered, *You're trapped*, he had thrown himself into work. The life here was not a haven, it had to be earned twice over. He couldn't accept the idea of sitting back and congratulating himself on a cushy deal. That would have bracketed him with the mediocre ones. And he was sure, he could stake his life on the fact that he was *not* mediocre, not by any means.

If I were in a university or a private firm, he thought, *I'd measure myself against others. But whom do I measure myself against here? We're cut off from the world. We censor ourselves; when we go to seminars or write papers, we wring*

*the secret heart right out of our work and present the dry skin
to the public, and then hear them say, 'That Dr Chandran? A
lightweight, just messes around with stuff others have done. All
that's been on the market for ages.' So many fat complacent
university department heads I've heard say this. Don't the fools
realize that we can't afford to be at the mercy of the West for
our weapons systems and machines? What do they know of the
wizardry I must perform to duplicate the West's miracles with
a fraction of the resources and manpower? Do they even have
the wits to care?*

Sometimes the urge to speak was almost unbearable, but he
bore it: discretion was the one job requirement that was non-
negotiable. And of course, there was so much of his work that
couldn't be gutted with safety, so he never attempted to write
it up for publication; it stayed in lab notebooks or got mashed
into reports for the Centre, for the ministry. To the outside
world his output was a fraction of what scientists at his level
did.

*What a lot of work they do, what a lot they write, those
men in universities facing ranks and ranks of students every
day. I can't possibly let myself sit here and feel glad that I
don't have to.*

The phone rang. It was Vidura. 'We're just going to visit
Malti. When are you coming for lunch?'

'Malti Prasad? I thought you didn't like her.'

'Well, she's not a great favourite, but Anu wants to meet
some campus wives, find out how they live, so I thought why
not. Tell me when you'll be back for lunch so we'll have an
excuse to run for it.'

'One, then. But say twelve if she's a bore.'

'Okay. Oh, can you take Anu to the cybercafe to check her
e-mail in the evening?

'Sure.'

'Thanks. Bye, darling.'

He hung up and sat back. It was good Vidura had someone

to talk to; sometimes he felt a little guilty at how bored she must be. And she'd always liked Anu. Gopal himself found her a little disconcerting, but she was okay.

It occurred to him that he'd forgotten to ask what work Anu was doing. No problem, he grinned to himself, and logged on to the Net. He could wow her with how much he knew about her; she was an academic and there was bound to be stuff about her on the Web: seminars, papers, abstracts. He keyed in her name; most days he spent odd moments net-surfing—some sites were blocked but he had access to most of the important things—it relieved his boredom and took his mind off the team and its squabbles.

He had expected only a couple of hits but got more than twenty. He raised an eyebrow. A high-flier, our Anu. The first match was the entry on her Institute's website. Not very informative; it just said her area of interest was work environments and techno-scientific culture. He began browsing through the rest.

The third one was a seminar paper, headed 'Ethics in Science'. He skimmed through the text, then did a double take. With a growing sense of disbelief, he read:

. . . the scientist working in very advanced fields is by and large employed by the state. As such, his/her work is most likely to be used in defence. This inevitably brings with it the ethical question of killing people. To work, the scientist must be convinced that it is right to kill in certain moral and political circumstances . . . The scientist, while enabling the state to act, has no say in the actual deployment of weapons. Hence only if the scientist trusts those in power to use these new capabilities in a morally responsible way, can he/she be reconciled to the loss of responsibility.

He stared at the screen. What was all this? Since when was

Anu an expert on defence scientists? A tiny clutch of apprehension
squeezed his heart. Why on earth had she asked him all those
questions about his work? Something wasn't quite right here.
He read on, hoping for answers.

The more evolved scientist (MES) knows that he/she
cannot afford to withhold cooperation from the state.
However, the MES watches governmental aims as they
appear to him/her, and carves out a certain amount of
autonomy without going so far as to refuse to work
outright. For instance the instrumentation and control
systems supplied with a particular technology; may be
designed to preclude what the MES considers immoral or
unethical uses of the technology. Of course such fail-safes
can be perverted or worked around, but the scientist can
feel at least that he/she has provided the means to use
the technology ethically . . .

Tell that to Dr Sheth, he thought. That sort of idealistic
rebellion did *not* work in the real world. Anu had more to say
on the lower moral orders. He skimmed through.

The less evolved scientist (LES) gets around the problem
by not thinking about it. The LES uses a number of
psychological mechanisms to do this. The least advanced
of them is the justification through putative herd. The LES
reasons thus: if I do not develop this technology (about
which moral doubts may be raised) someone else will do
it. This is morally untenable; it is like the soldier saying,
if I had not raped the girl someone else would have done
it. In ethics one cannot be responsible for another's action
or inaction, only for one's own.
    The second argument is 'everyone is doing it', which
is not very different from the first. It is notable that both
these arguments tend to appeal to those who are

mediocre or see themselves as mediocre; they are afraid
that others are more competent and will replace or get
ahead of them if they refuse to please the state on the
grounds of 'wishy-washy' moral considerations. They see
science as impersonal and unstoppable, doomed to
progress forever . . .

Of course we're all replaceable, Gopal thought irritably.
*None of us does original science; the military intelligence
people and the ministry set the problems for us. We read about
what the West does in the intelligence reports and copy it in
our labs. We're just glorified technologists; none of us will ever
get the Nobel Prize.*

The slightly more evolved scientists (SES) in the continuum
of the morally clueless, have a paradoxical view of
themselves as 'helpless'. This view depends on a sweeping
failure to examine their own state. The SES look at the
'big picture' that indicates that they require heavy funding
and infrastructure to work, and for this they must pay the
price of moral autonomy. In their depressed moments they
tend to think 'we are no better than slaves'.

He scowled at the screen. Anuprabha seemed to be reading
his mind. Now she was probably going to explain how
misguided and foolish he was for holding such an opinion.

This sounds irresponsible to outsiders because these
'slaves' work in rigorous and demanding fields. No one
can be driven into doing such work; a great deal of
personal dedication is required. An essential factor in
slavery is that all slaves are interchangeable. In actual
fact, given the degree of specialization in science, it may
be quite hard to replace scientists at the drop of a
hat . . .

She's right about the personal dedication, but she seems to have a very noble view of the intellectual side of what we do. If only she knew, he thought. The rest of the paper was a brief historical account of the evolution of science from magic and mysticism and an analysis of scientific dispassion. He opened the next link.

Restrictions on scientists' freedom to speak about their work tend to spread over their other interactions also. They live in enclaves, where they are made to feel special and aloof from the herd. They believe in a vague sort of way that the public cannot understand their complex and difficult work, and that the best science flourishes away from the public gaze. In such an atmosphere getting one's name in the newspapers (unless for something like the Nobel), writing a textbook, or generally becoming famous for non-scientific achievements, tends to attract the suspicion and distrust of other scientists.

He killed the window. Affronted anger and a certain suspicion were beginning to form in his mind. He opened the next one, called 'The Case for the Defence'.

Ask a scientist about ethics in science, and he/she will immediately assume you are talking about the integrity of data, and inviting him/her to condemn the (rare) researcher who 'massages' data for gain or glory. For most, the issue does not go beyond this, and to the general public such an attitude appears solipsistic and selfish.

Furthermore, most people see science and mathematics as 'hard'; they assume they will not understand the scientists' work or concerns and they express this opinion in a self-deprecatory tone. For the scientist this may inflate his sense of being a species apart (and above) or it may deepen the feeling of isolation and loneliness in society, the conviction that the ethical issues the scientist is facing are not interesting or debatable in the public sphere, and that he/she must struggle with them alone.

His suspicion was almost confirmed. If she knew so much about science and scientists, why had she done the little-girl act at dinner and asked him such ingenuous yet pointed questions about his work? What was her game?

To do what no other scientist has done, to find or accomplish or create as never before, is the one sweet sovereign joy of science, and the scientist has been fabricated like a smart bomb to seek that joy and none other. That this never-done-before thing may be ethically suspect is something the scientist is vaguely aware of, but he/she has never been given any positive reinforcement to recognize this, whereas the goal of excellence has been positively reinforced all his/her life.

I'm certain now, he thought. *She's come here on some sort of mission and her motives, I'll be bound, are highly questionable. This has to be stopped. I can't have a house guest of mine going around snooping. And if, god forbid, she publishes anything about the Centre, I'm in the doghouse. What is she after?*

Oh, god, they've gone to Malti Prasad's. But she can't do much harm there, can she? And Vidura is with her.

Nevertheless, he felt a profound unease. This was a problem he didn't know how to deal with. For a wild moment he considered calling up the Director and telling him about his suspicions. But he resisted the impulse: there might be nothing in it, and Vidura would feel betrayed if he got the military police to haul her friend off for questioning.

I'm supposed to take her to the cybercafe. Then I'll get to the bottom of this. What was it the Director said yesterday to

*the man from the ministry? 'As far as the public is concerned
we hardly exist.' He's right: better that no one bothers us, or
bothers about us. I've got to make her promise not to name
or indicate the Centre in any way. Why is she talking to our
wives? Prasad doesn't get on with his wife, I know that. Few
of us do, this place is killing for women. Thank god Viddy's
so understanding, but I don't mind admitting I feel bad for her
sometimes. Is that what Anu's after? How much has Viddy in
her innocence told her? And if Anu goes off and writes some
half-witted exposé everyone here will point fingers at me. I've
got to make her promise to lay off or leave, that's all. If I
appeal to her as a friend, surely she'll see my point of view?*

Resolved at last, he settled down to go through Agniv's
notebooks.

CHAPTER FOUR

'I had no idea there was no e-mail on campus. I thought my message came straight to you, you were so prompt in replying,' Anu said.

Vidura shook her head. 'No, we don't have access from within the campus; for security reasons mail sites are blocked. As for your mail, Gopal saw your message at the cybercafe in the town. He checks my account and whenever there's anything for me he rings up, reads it out and types my reply.' She looked a little apologetic. 'We're not very connected. Gopal will take you to the cybercafe in the evening.'

'Thanks, Viddy.'

Malti's husband worked on 'something to do with nano-powders, whatever those are', according to Vidura. He had worked with Gopal and Mani Sheth on the team that had helped put India on the moon, eight years ago. 'Nobody thought we could do a moon-shot so cheaply,' Vidura said. 'But we showed the world.' Since then, Anu gathered, the three scientists had drifted apart; Vidura was vague about the reasons.

As for Malti, she had studied economics in college and sometimes gave tuition to the campus children. She could sing well, and often sang at the rare campus get-togethers. But she wasn't much interested in anything outside her life, which revolved around the temple just outside the campus gates. 'She's a pretty representative sample.'

'Down the road' had been an understatement. They had to go down the hill quite a way and pass a number of bungalows before they reached Malti's house. Vidura explained, 'After Gopal was promoted to team leader we rated one of the bigger bungalows further down, which the senior wives like because you don't have to climb so much. But I couldn't bear to leave this house and the view, so Gopal applied to retain it. The authorities grumbled a bit, but they let us stay. The downside is it's a long way from anyone I can visit.'

'Why? Oh, don't tell me, it's the pecking order again.'

'Yes, not that there's really anyone among the seniors whom I'd like to visit regularly. People tend to stick to people who come from their place, speak their language, understand how they grew up, their food, their customs. Like everyone else, I suppose.' She smiled, but without much gaiety.

Malti's bungalow was larger and more sprawling, but as they entered the marble-paved veranda a certain sameness in the wall paint and the door fittings diluted its grace a little. It might be a grand residence, but it was also produced from a template, and would be grand and imposing regardless of who lived in it. Anu found herself wondering how these people felt, spending their days on a stage once filled by past actors who had lived and died and fought and loved in these same rooms, knowing that they too would vanish and strangers take their place. Now she had some understanding of what Vidura meant by people having nervous breakdowns when they left. These walls held so many tender memories, wedding nights, children's birthdays, moments of comedy and tragedy, only to be brutally abandoned at last as the inalienable property of the state.

Malti, a short, plump woman in a shiny red sari and permed hair, received them and led the way to her sitting room, which was huge. There were low Gurjari wooden seats with cushions all along the sides, which gave the room the impersonal look of a meeting room. A large mat was spread in the centre, sprinkled with a few cushions. There was no other furniture. Malti began to lead them to the central mat, then changed her mind and made them sit in a corner. Vidura made the introductions. Malti namasted gravely. 'Anu-ji, will you take tea?'

'Yes, please. No sugar.'

'Vidura-ji?'

'Only if it's no trouble.'

'Oh, don't do such formality. After so many days you have come to my house. Phulmani!' A maid appeared. '*Bina chini do chai lao*! So, Anu-ji, what do you think of our campus?'

'It's lovely,' Anu said sincerely. 'How happy you all must be to live here.'

'Oh, it is good, it is good,' Malti ran her eyes along the pure white walls. 'Happy? Yes, only sometimes little boring. We have only each other, no? And god.'

Vidura coughed gently.

'Vidura-ji, Rahil-ji has started taking prayer meetings, you know? He said it was disgraceful we had to go outside campus to worship god. So now by rotation some of us are hosting. Yesterday I had, that's why . . .' she waved a hand at the arrangement of the sitting room. 'So lazy these maids are. This morning I said, *sab theek karo*, but they have done nothing.'

'I wasn't aware of this,' Vidura said reluctantly.

'Oh, but you must come. Next one is in Kiran-ji's house. I am going to lead in singing bhajans. After so many years I am singing regularly. Rahil-ji is so good. What did we do before him?'

Vidura looked a little startled. 'Yes, hmm, indeed.'

Malti looked at her slyly. 'He used to see you almost every day, no? Reva Mausi would see you talking on your porch. But now he comes less often. That is because he is so busy with the prayer meetings! You did not know, no?'

'What else do you spend your time doing?' Anu interjected innocently.

'Oh, I used to give tuitions, but now few children are wanting. All want to study science. And why not? My own two, they are sons, no? Best career for boy.'

'What about the girls?'

'Oh, yes,' Malti looked grave. 'Big problem, so far from home, how to arrange. So difficult to get boy's parents to come and see. Thank god I am not having to worry.' She perked up. 'And yourself? How many childrens?'

'None, Malti-ji. I'm not married.'

Malti's hands flew to her mouth. 'Oh! So sorry! But you must be Vidura-ji's age.'

'Didn't find anyone suitable, I guess.' Anu contrived to keep her face straight. *Come on, woman, bite the bait.*

'Oho!' Malti looked pleased. 'Where from you are?'

'Mumbai.'

'Shastri, no? Hmm. Ah, here is the tea. *Bewakuf larki! Bhujia le ao, aur do plate.* Now,' she turned back to Anu. 'You are from which state?'

'Well, my father was born in Lucknow.'

'Good, good. Vegetarian, of course?'

'Yes.'

Vidura looked at Anu in surprise.

'Good, good,' Malti closed her eyes and muttered to herself. 'Which *gotra*?'

Vidura expected Anu to say *Pardon?* But instead she said, '*Bharadwaj.*'

'Hmm, hmm.'

'What sort of people live here, Malti-ji?' Anu's tone dripped innocence.

'Many many. All very learned, good families, bright prospects. But sometimes lonely. Community is small, relatives far away. We have only each other, no? Like Mr Acharya, poor man, lost his wife three years ago. Very sad.'

'I remember that,' Vidura said. 'Ectopic pregnancy, wasn't it? They couldn't get her to the hospital on time. I'm afraid the medical facilities here are rather basic.'

'No, no,' said Malti in an affronted tone. She made a complex signal to Vidura with her eyes, which Vidura completely failed to understand. Malti went on, 'No children, very nice man. Hometown is Allahabad, vegetarian. Parents are living with him. Only forty-two.'

'Could I get to meet him?'

Malti looked a little disconcerted, then said, 'Why not, why not, at your age . . .' A suspicion assailed her. 'You are not widow or divorcee, yes?'

'No, not at all. But tell me more about the campus. I'm dying to know all about it.' She ignored Vidura's gaze boring into the side of her head.

'Well,' said Malti, 'it is best place to live in all of India. No worries, no problems. Only small difficulties, like for marketing, you can get nothing, and there is no good cinema, but who needs now with video CD? Also, less of cultural activity. But children are having good schooling, husband is well paid, every so often we can go to Delhi to shop, and then we stay at Centre guest house. It is like that thing which butterfly makes—cocoon.' She said the word again, emphatically, circling her hands to enclose a tiny space. 'Coc-coon.'

'It sounds wonderful,' Anu said, smiling. 'What about your husband? Is he happy here?'

'Oh yes. Best place in all India, he says.'

'He must have a lot of work on his hands.'

Malti hesitated. 'Yes, he is very busy.'

'When does he usually come home at night?'

'Sometimes at ten. Sometimes when very big job, he does not come. All night they are in lab, doing god knows what all work. Or he comes late and goes away again in early morning. It is because he is team head like Gopal-ji. But Gopal-ji I hear does not spend so much time in lab. Vidura-ji is lucky, no?' She smiled archly.

'It must be so hard to manage everything on your own,' Anu

said sympathetically. 'What a sacrifice you all must make for your husband's careers, and for the nation.'

'Oh yes. No one knows how much sacrifice we pay for nation's security. But when there is war, then we see the fruits. Without us where India would be?'

Vidura looked at her watch. It was already twelve, but Anu showed no sign of budging. She sat and listened raptly as Malti described in detail her typical day. Vidura knew from experience that Malti could keep this up indefinitely, and she couldn't see why Anu suddenly had this all-consuming interest in it. And what was that hocus pocus about *gotra*? People only talked about that in relation to marriage, right? What did Anu think she was playing at?

They were all taken by surprise when Mr Prasad walked in. Malti sprang to introduce her new friend. Prasad greeted her gravely.

'Malti was telling me about all the interesting work that you do,' Anu said. 'It must be so exciting to work with nano-powders. The possibilities are astounding.'

Prasad looked at her as if she were a clever child who had recited, quite by accident, the laws of Einsteinian mechanics. 'Yes, indeed.' He turned to his wife and asked unceremoniously, 'Is lunch ready? I'm going to have my bath.' He strode to the door leading to the rest of the house, then paused on the threshold, struck by a thought.

'Are you a scientist?'

'Yes,' said Anu.

'What's your field?'

'Sociology.'

'Oh!' he chuckled. 'That is arts.'

'It's a social science, sir.'

'Nonsense!' He leaned negligently in the doorway, holding the top of the frame with both hands. 'I will tell you why. There was this article by some sociologist in the papers yesterday on marriage. It said the mean age of marriage for middle-class

probabilistic v. deterministic

girls in India now is twenty-five years. But nearly every girl who has got married from this campus has done so even before graduation. How do you explain that? You can't call it a science if there's no predictability.' He smiled as if challenging her to understand the question.

'Social behaviour is underdetermined, sir. Humans have free will. That's why social science is probabilistic, not deterministic. I would say there are other communities in India where the age of marriage is considerably higher. That would affect the average, and of course you have to see if the curve is skewed. We learn to think in terms of trends, not laws, sir. Like quantum mechanics,' she finished coolly.

He burst out laughing. Malti looked uneasily from one to the other.

'Well, this is very interesting. You must tell me what you "scientists" really do, some time.'

'We ask questions,' she said quietly, but he had disappeared inside.

It was evident that Malti had no further taste for gossip and wanted to go in and see to her husband's bath and lunch. They took their leave. They were hardly out of the gate when Vidura said, 'Well!'

Anu grinned. 'Sorry, Viddy, but I had to give the old bat the wrong idea.'

'Whatever for?'

'As a counter-story. If people hear two conflicting accounts they believe the one they're comfortable with. If Rahil-ji's a less efficient gossip retailer Malti's version should overtake his.'

'Why on earth should you want them to think you're vegetarian? Anyway, the maids will have reported what you had for lunch. Everyone will know by now, and in any case we're one of the few "non-veg" households around.'

'Damn. Didn't think of that. But it'll be interesting, don't you think, to see the suitors queuing up?'

Vidura frowned as if to scold her, then burst out laughing. 'You've always been a thorough imp, haven't you? But be warned; people are terribly earnest here. They might not see the joke. You could have a frustrated widower pursuing you all the way to Mumbai.'

'Oh, I know how to deal with them. How do you think I survived into blessed singlehood? Anyway, they're much more likely to run a mile when they hear who I really am.'

Vidura chuckled. 'I suppose I ought to get on my high horse and tell you to stop making a spectacle of yourself,' she said. 'Gopal certainly would; he's a lot more like the people here than I am. But it's only a bit of harmless fun, and they could do with their earnestness punctured a bit. Okay, go ahead and gold-dig, baby. It'll be more fun than a Jane Austen remake.'

They were giggling together like schoolgirls as they came in through the gate. Gopal had already arrived; his bike was under the shade by the porch. 'How was your day, darling?' Vidura asked him gaily.

'Horrid. And yours?'

'You always say that,' she said affectionately. 'I don't believe you for a moment.'

'How's Malti?'

'The same. Arranging marriages for everyone on campus, including the cats and dogs. Thankfully she didn't talk about that guru of hers; she was too busy telling Anu all about campus life.'

'Really?'

Gopal had let the maids in, and they had set out the food on the sideboard. The three of them sat down to lunch. Vidura served them. 'Yes, indeed. In fact I think when she heard Anu's unmarried she was trying to sell her the concept of living here permanently.'

'Good god. And were you sold, Anu?'

Anu grinned. 'It's a tempting idea. The social whirl, the nightlife, the cultural ferment; I would fit right in.'

'We met Prasad as well,' Vidura went on. 'He crossed swords a bit with Anu.'

'What for?'

'Well, he didn't seem to think Sociology's a science. But Anu stuck up for herself.'

Gopal chuckled. 'I see.'

'We didn't get a chance to talk about his work,' Anu said. I'm really interested in what people are doing here. Not the technicalities, but what it's like for them as people. Why they do it, how they feel about it.'

'Indeed?' Gopal raised his eyebrows. 'Well, I'm afraid you'll find very few people willing to discuss that. Motivation's a very personal thing, especially to a scientist.'

'I quite understand. Nevertheless, sometimes it can be liberating for the individual to get a chance to discuss personal things.'

'So you think we need liberating?'

Anu shrugged. 'It's in the nature of human beings to want to feel their motivation is understood and shared by those around them.'

'And what do you think my motivation is?'

'I haven't a clue,' she said frankly. 'You'll have to tell me.'

'Yes, do,' said Vidura playfully. 'What's it like to be a hot-shot scientist?'

'It's a very responsible position.'

'Of course,' said Anu. 'You must find it quite a burden at times.'

'Not at all.' He said slowly, holding her gaze, 'No one can be driven into doing such work; a great deal of personal dedication is required.'

'And what's the source of your personal dedication?'

Gopal shrugged. 'Maybe I'm part of the continuum of the morally clueless.'

Vidura gave him a slightly puzzled look. After a pause, Anu asked, 'Do you really feel that way?'

'I'm just quoting expert opinion.' He nodded at her. Now Anu looked puzzled. Sensing a conversational hole, Vidura stepped in. 'Tell us about your work, Anu.'

'Yes, do. What's it like to be a hot-shot social scientist?'

Anu gave him the same cool look she had given Prasad. 'It has its rewards.'

Gopal said, 'If it's really a science, then aren't you treating people as things? Isn't that unethical, to reduce human life to laws and equations? Isn't it an insult to everything that makes us human?'

'That's not what we do. There are no laws and equations in sociology. There are trends and tendencies, yes, and there are models. But they are only probabilistic. They don't tell any one individual what to do and how to do it.'

'Then what's the point?'

Anu smiled. 'The point is in the modelling. Probability tells you what a group does, and lets you make predictions of how strong the forces are on any one individual. If your society favours early marriage, there may be a 60 per cent chance you'll marry early. But you, the individual you, might equally well marry late, for a number of very valid reasons. Nevertheless, you will have fought the magnetic pull of that 60 per cent chance. If you were to spend a hundred lives, exactly the same except for your age at marriage, you would be below a certain age forty times, and above it for the rest.'

'That's ridiculous. People only marry once.'

'Yes, but that's not the point. For every forty who marry late, there are sixty who don't. If you were, say, a marriage bureau manager, you'd want to know what the prospects of a particular client were. But you could only say that your client can't marry over this age if no one in recorded history for that community had ever done so. Even then, she might do it, and you'd have to change the model. So there'll always be a margin of error. All probabilistic social models have that.'

Gopal merely looked at her and said nothing. She continued,

'Look, people who don't think tend deeply to believe in something called the law of averages. They think if they toss a coin and get four heads in a row, the next throw will produce a tails with a four in five probability. That's rubbish. It doesn't matter how many times you toss the coin, the next toss always has a probability of 50 per cent heads or tails. People confuse the statement "the likelihood of getting five heads in a row is vanishingly small" with the statement "the likelihood of getting a head after four heads is very small, and therefore it's bound to be tails". It isn't. The likelihood of getting a head or a tail on that toss is exactly the same: 50 per cent. Generations of gambling houses have fleeced people because of this expectation. Do you follow what I'm saying?'

'Somewhat.'

Anu went on, 'But people aren't things: they don't play fair. Once a company asked me to evaluate whether the redecoration of their offices had boosted productivity, and the employee who had urged the company to redecorate in the first place left because the office didn't feel the same! Caprice is a uniquely human quality, and the one great headache of all predictive sociologists.'

'Very philosophical,' Gopal said drily. I'd love to hear you tell me all about how people should think, but I'm already late for the afternoon's work, so I'll take my leave. When do you want to check your e-mail?'

'Oh, any time that's convenient for you.'

'I'll pick you up at six, then?'

'OK.'

Vidura yawned. 'This heat is killing. Are you tired, Anu? What say we sleep for the afternoon while Gopal sits in his nice air-conditioned office?'

'Sure.'

Gopal left, and Vidura and Anu retired upstairs.

CHAPTER FIVE

Anu chewed thoughtfully on the end of her pencil. Vidura was probably asleep by now; the buzzing afternoon brightness lay everywhere like a glass-wool blanket, deadening movement and sound. She was in her room, and she'd risked some time to take out her papers and work on them while the day's encounters were still fresh in her mind. She looked at the page in front of her. At the top of it was printed 'Husband's Personality Profile'. Next to this she pencilled the letters 'GC'.

She ran her pencil down the list of options. After some thought she ticked, 'I find it hard to talk about emotional issues'. Then, 'I subscribe to an elitist view of my professional community', 'I have a strong need to conform and excel within my community', 'I have a strong sense of commitment to the nation-state', 'I do not welcome discussion of my motivation'. She turned the page over and ticked 'Number of hours spent at work: more than eight', 'Number of children: none', 'Sympathy for wife's concerns: fair', 'Egalitarianism within relationship: fair', 'Communication with wife: poor', 'Waking hours spent together per working day: less than six', 'View of gender division of labour: conventional.'

She took a 'Wife's Personality Profile' sheet, wrote 'VC' on top and scowled. Vidura talked readily about her life and emotions, but she was more of a mystery than Gopal. When Vidura described her life in such glowing terms Anu got the feeling that there was another voice talking that she couldn't hear. Did Vidura hear it? Or did she sincerely believe she was happy and contented? The daily business of looking after her household used only a portion of her mental resources. The rest couldn't simply evaporate, to materialize when needed in times of crisis or enhanced load. Was Vidura aware of this? Anu recalled that Vidura had been an extremely bright student. She had read history and done her thesis on the French Revolution. To coop such a mind up in an artificial version of a provincial town and set it to supervise two maids twice a day was, to put it mildly, unfair, but Anu knew quite well that the first person to deny such an interpretation would be Vidura herself. How then could she describe her? Should she take Vidura at her own valuation, or should she voice what she, Anu, suspected about her state of mind? *I might be dead wrong*, Anu thought. *I may be guilty of putting myself in Viddy's place and imagining how I'd feel. But I'm not Viddy. Am I justified in extrapolating my feelings to her?*

No, she decided. *Record how Viddy sees herself. Then make a note of your own suspicions. I'm probably bothered about it because she's my friend. So much for scientific detachment.*

She turned back to Gopal's page. Was she transposing her feelings about Vidura onto him, seeing him too harshly because subconsciously she blamed him for what she saw as Vidura's stagnation? She searched deep in her mind. *No,* she concluded slowly. *I think I'm free from bias. I do like Gopal, he's so serious and dedicated. But what came over him at lunch?*

She tapped the end of the pencil slowly on the sheet. She knew enough about scientists to expect a certain amount of hostility to questions. She had to swallow that, not react or try to preach to them. She smiled to herself a little wryly. She shouldn't have needled Vidyadhar, or Prasad. But habits of outspokenness died hard. It was tough, playing the little woman round-eyed with wonder and hero worship, just to get them to talk. She snorted with suppressed laughter.

'Amusing story you're reading?'

Anu jumped.

'Oh, you're writing, I see. How interesting.' Gopal was standing in the doorway. She spread her hand on the paper. 'It's only four-thirty,' she said plaintively.

'I thought I'd surprise you.' He strode in and sat down in the chair by the desk, snatched the paper out of her hand and read it slowly. She dug her nails into the pencil. 'Please give that back, Gopal. I can explain.'

Gopal said nothing. He read both sides of the paper, then methodically tore it to shreds. He took the whole bunch from her, tore it up and placed it carefully in the waste-paper basket. Only then did he look her in the eye.

'Have you no shame?' he asked.

'You mean you feel I've abused your hospitality.'

'You're damn right that's what I mean.'

'Gopal, I haven't come here under false pretences. It's just that I'm a sociologist. If you were to visit a lab, wouldn't you take notes? I'm just . . .'

Gopal's finger stabbed savagely at the full basket. 'Those are printed papers. You came here prepared. And, madam, you're going to explain just what the hell you're playing at.'

'I'm not playing at . . .'

'Who are you kidding? Prasad rang me just after lunch. He said, "That woman, she thinks she's so clever." Why did you tell them you wanted to get married? And all those lies you fed to Malti? Why?'

'I didn't . . .'

'You think it's all a game, don't you? You think we're all morally clueless idiots who don't know a questionnaire when we see one? You've come here to spy on us, haven't you?'

'You've been reading up on me on the Web,' Anu said slowly. 'Now I recognize that line. Gopal, why are you so angry? You read my pieces on the Web. Did they seem so alien to you? Forget for a moment it's a sociologist and a woman who's writing. As a scientist, aren't you glad I said some of those things, about ethics and science and how they're all in a tangled mess that no one knows how to sort out? Don't they need to be said?'

Gopal glared at her. 'What makes you think they're not said? Are you privy to our meetings, that you know for sure we never talk about them? I'm constantly discussing ethical issues, especially with the young scientists. But you, madam, have no right . . .'

'I've done nothing illegal.'

'Why did you sneak in here? Don't you know this is a defence lab? What information have you already accessed?'

'For Pete's sake, Gopal, I just wanted to question the wives, find out if they're happy, whether their husbands are happy at home, what sort of social fallout their work generates for them. Look, do you think I'm unaware of how hard it must be for you all, what sacrifices you make? Malti was right about that. Shouldn't the world care about the price you pay for your work? Shouldn't it be . . .'

Gopal gave a short dry cough of laughter. 'Price? We're the best-paid scientists in the country. If you factor in all the stuff we get free, we've got a lifestyle the average person can't imagine.'

'I wasn't talking about money. Gopal, do you ever think about what happens to the things you make once they leave the lab? Do you ever wonder about what they are used for? Doesn't it trouble you?'

'Constantly. I'm always meeting the military to look at field test results.'

'I didn't mean that.'

'I know what you meant. You meant, "Gopal, do you ever hallucinate that you are Oppenheimer and wake up sweating in the middle of the night, afraid you've given birth to a Frankenstein that will destroy the world as we know it?" The answer, thankfully, is no. I have no qualms whatsoever about my work and its use on the field of battle, and I've thought it all through, thanks very much. In any case, I am a scientist, madam. I just say, under certain conditions of temperature and pressure, in the presence of this, that and the other, certain materials behave like this. What's so ethically monstrous about that?'

'But you're not just a scientist. You also develop technologies.'

'Same thing.'

'No, it's not the same thing.' She had to talk now, it was her only chance to get through to him. 'Technology is never value-free. Values are always embodied in technology, because technology needs us. It's . . . it's like a child, it needs inputs and care and maintenance, spare parts, a certain way of being used. It doesn't step in like a god, the god of the machine, and magically solve the problem or perform the task. That's why so many technologies fail when they're taken out of the society that made them and transplanted somewhere else—it's like a child with a family that doesn't speak its language. They don't know how to play with it, educate it, care for it. Every aspect of a machine tells you something about the values of the people who made it and use it. I'll give you a small example. I have a fridge in my flat in Mumbai; it's an old Westinghouse from way back in the '50s. The way it was built, half the fittings inside can't be removed for cleaning, and the front panel has this grooved decorative chrome plate that must have been very bright and shiny when it was new. That plate has to be cleaned once a week with soapy water and a toothbrush.' She was losing him; he was turning away. 'Listen to me, please. That fridge was created in a time when having a shiny front panel was considered more valuable by its creator engineers than the time and effort the housewife would spend in cleaning the machine. Since then we've had the sexual revolution. Women now have most of the say in buying refrigerators, and they want low-maintenance convenience models. Wait. There's more. The fridge brings with it a whole new way of cooking and eating. My grandmother refused for the whole of her long life to eat anything that came out of it; we cooked twice a day for her until she died. When she was young, a good wife cooked twice a day; doing anything else was lazy and bad. The fridge allowed my mother to cheat; she cooked only every other day. Do you see what I'm saying? Her time became more valuable because of the fridge, or perhaps the values themselves changed. We never read Betty Friedan, but she came to us wrapped up nice and snug in that Westinghouse fridge. Gopal, are you listening?'

'That stuff might happen,' he said stiffly, 'in kitchens and things, but not in defence. There's only one value in defence. You said it yourself: killing people. So what's the point of discussing it?'

'No, Gopal, there's also preventing people from getting killed, as you know. Both can be necessary; it's easy to imagine situations where it might be right to kill. But that's not the point. You'll agree there are so many ways to kill a person. Some of them just do the job and go away, but others go on killing long after the target and the quarrel and the entire generation is dead. That's why nuclear weapons and land mines are evil. Human conflicts die a natural death in the course of time, but these weapons inscribe hate on the land so deeply that it outlives both the haters and the hated. So it generates new haters and new people to hate. When all we had were swords and guns, we trusted in the ability of ordinary people to forget, to grow wheat on battlefields among the skulls. Where will they grow wheat among the landmines? If you make a new pathogen and impregnate a powder with it, and spray it over the fields and homes of the enemy, how can you get the epidemic to neatly kill off only enough of them to resolve the conflict? How can you be sure only the necessary pain will be inflicted? How do you save your own life? No smart bomb has been or will ever be that smart. It takes people to decide when justice has been done and we can all go back to our ploughshares and forget about it. Can your pathogen

powder guarantee that? How would you put the demon back
in its bottle once you'd let it out?'

'No one would be stupid enough to do that.'

'Oh? Then what is Prasad working on?'

He stared at her.

'Don't look at me like that. I got to see his research papers
before I came here. I know scientists who don't think like you.
They found the references, even sent me offprints with their own
glosses. Those papers don't say enough to give anyone a map
of how to do it, but it's obvious what he's talking about. He's
written them impeccably; no terrorist would ever work out his
method. But I'm not a terrorist, I'm a citizen. I don't care how
he does it, only that he does it. That's what scares me: that
these things are being done in my name as a citizen.'

'I'll repeat what I said: no one will ever use it in actual war.'

'Do you know that?'

'I believe it with all my heart.'

'Then why is Prasad making it?'

'Insurance. As a weapon of last resort, if we are destroyed
by non-conventional weapons, if all else fails.'

She laughed throatily. ' "Non-conventional weapons." That
phrase always cracks me up. As though those bombs are just
a bit eccentric, don't know the social etiquette of frying people
to death and killing their children with cancer. Why are you
sure that it'll never be used, Gopal? On what do you base your
certainty?'

'No government, no general would sanction it. It would be
too risky for the troops, let alone the civilians. It would only
be used if the ground force was completely decimated.'

'They have assured you of this?'

He made a brusque gesture. 'It's common sense.'

She looked at him steadily. 'Zyklon B was a pesticide. Its
maker won the Nobel Prize. It was meant to usher in a new
age of food security. Do you know what it was used for?'

'No.'

'Gassing the Jews.'

'So? I could take you downstairs and kill you with a kitchen knife. Would that make the maker of the kitchen knife guilty?'

'No, it would not. The kitchen knife has what I've called open values in one of my articles. So does Zyklon B. Open values can be used either way, good or bad. What other use can society get out of your pathogen powder?'

'None, but the method used to deliver that pathogen could also deliver life-saving drugs or French perfume.'

'But it's secret, isn't it? Are you going to licence it out?'

He snorted. 'The method would never have been developed without the defence grant and the huge infrastructure we bought with it. You have no idea of the kind of resources involved in such work.'

'Are you saying all that money and equipment has been used to develop a technology that will probably never be used and which all of us fervently pray will never be used? A tool for revenge? Something that will probably kill off all our last survivors as well?'

'Nonsense, the pathogen is self-limiting and the delivery system has been very carefully engineered. I know you're dying to scaremonger about this, but I'm sorry to disappoint you. That technology is foolproof. You print anything about this, any unfounded speculation about Prasad's work, and I will personally see that you and your career are buried alive.'

'And so we reach Section D: the threats,' she murmured.

Gopal quietly pounded a fist on the desk in an agony of frustration. 'Look, woman, will you get off my case if I tell you that money was not wasted?'

'No, Gopal. That isn't the point.'

There was silence. His eyes bored into her face. 'You win,' he said quietly. 'You're not open to discussion at all, are you? You've come here with certain preconceived notions about how scientists think and you will validate those notions if it kills you. You don't care about Vidura, you don't care about me, you just want some cheap notoriety and your name on yet another putrid liberal bleeding-heart website. You haven't a clue what people will think, have you? The whole Centre knows you're my house guest. They know you think too much of yourself. And when you write up your little escapade and the public in the form of journalists descends on us and demands to know how frequently we sleep with our wives, everyone will know it was me who let the wolf in. Have you thought about that?'

'I was going to say that all this information is confidential and that no names will be named.'

'If you're so squeaky-clean, madam, why didn't you apply through your Director to come here and carry out a study? You're funded by the government as well, aren't you? Why didn't you send in a letter "through the proper channels"?'

'I discussed it with my Director. He said there wasn't a hope: the ministry would give a blanket refusal on principle. So I didn't pursue it.'

'Instead you sneaked down here and presumed on poor Viddy's innocence to prey on her and me?'

'Gopal, stop being emotional. I did nothing of the sort. I keep telling you, I'm on your side. Aren't you disturbed by the ease with which the world takes for granted the most horrible prospects in war these days? Don't you want to do something about it? Won't you stick your head out of your lab for one minute and really look at the world and the people who control it? Have you ever really sat down and talked to Rahil Vidyadhar?'

'What's he got to do with it?' Gopal asked uneasily.

'Everything and nothing. I take it that you haven't. Try it some time.'

'He's just a conceited idiot. The Director seems to find him amusing. I can't for the life of me work out what Viddy sees in him.'

Anu said nothing. Then she began slowly, 'If I promise not

to refer to what I've learned here, nor to write any article that could be construed as being based on any facts associated with the Centre, will you allow me to spend time here, talk to people, just for my own benefit?'

'Just to learn about the behaviour of the species?' he asked bitterly. 'How can I stop you?'

'You could ask me to leave.'

'I'm tempted, but Viddy would be heartbroken.'

'Please, Gopal, tell me in reasonable, cool-headed terms why you hate the thought of me asking questions.'

'I told you. Security.'

'Don't be silly.'

'Look, if anything goes wrong I'm the one who will be under a cloud. You don't understand this place. It's like a fortress. It's not because of laws or anything, it's the . . . I suppose you'd say it's the culture of the place. We're not supposed to exist for the public. Very few non-specialists know about us. It's just because we have to have families and things that there's a campus at all. Otherwise there'd just be the labs.'

'You're describing an insane world. A world where it's hardly possible to be human. Why? Is your world really like that, or do you have a deep investment in believing it to be so?'

'I don't expect you to understand,' Gopal said coldly.

She sighed. 'We're not getting anywhere, are we? I'm sorry. Let's not talk about it any more.'

Gopal rubbed his hands over his face. 'It's five-thirty,' he said at last. 'Do you still want to check your e-mail?'

'If it's no trouble.'

The cybercafe was in the centre of Sitarampur, the little town that provided the campus with its goods and services. Gopal checked his own mail, then waited outside for Anu to finish. He looked down the street at the houses and beyond, to the low rolling hills that surrounded the area. Sometimes, especially on dusty days in May, he missed the green lusciousness of his native Kerala. But since coming here he'd returned only twice: once on the death of his father, once for his sister's wedding. He had been welcomed like a returning hero and Vidura had been treated like a queen, but within a few days in the middle of it all, festival or mourning, he had always fidgeted to come back here, to the lab and to work. He remembered the last time he had visited, when he had begged his mother to come and stay with them. But she had been wiser than Vidura's father; she had refused.

He went back into the cafe and e-mailed his cousins in Palghat, asking after his mother, the family, the affairs of the household. When he came back out Anu was waiting for him. He took her back to the bungalow without a word.

CHAPTER SIX

'Hello, could I get some tea here?'

The two young men looked startled, then one of them scrambled to his feet. 'Yes, ma'am.' He called the canteen boy and ordered tea for her.

'Oh, that's very kind of you. Is this your canteen? It's very nice.'

There were a few young people having breakfast in the long white refectory on the ground floor of the student's hostel. As she waited for her tea, Anu cast her eyes along the table. There were fewer students than she had expected, but perhaps they hadn't all come down yet. They were a nondescript lot, they did not look too well off or 'smart', and most seemed preoccupied. She judged that many of them had been working late; breakfast was obviously not a fun time. Then she heard a familiar harsh, impatient voice: Agniv Nag.

He was in a little knot of students at the other end of the table, earnestly listening now to what someone was saying to him. She picked up her tea and went to join them.

'Do you mind if I sit here with you? My name is Anuprabha Shastri. I'm staying with Dr Chandran for a few days.'

They were startled at her arrival. She realized she had crossed some sort of social line in coming to the hostel, and they were a little at a loss as to how to behave; they had all taken on the stiff, shiny look of students in the presence of authority. 'Yes, ma'am, please sit.' They squeezed up on the bench and introduced themselves. Sachdeva—that must be Gopal's other student, Anu thought—a tall, curly-haired young man in a faded T-shirt and corduroys frayed at the bottom. Agniv, looking as dishevelled as before. Shweta, a shy, neat-looking girl in a dark blue salwar kameez. Namrata, round-faced and rather stout, in a drab khadi kurta and jeans. Rahul, a thin, pale boy with heavy glasses and a mop of hair.

'How do you like it here? Do they make you work all the time or do you get time off to enjoy yourselves?'

'We work very hard,' Shweta said sincerely.

'But sometimes we bunk and watch a movie,' Sachdeva put in. 'That is, when we can get Agniv out of the lab.'

Agniv scowled. 'Too much movie is not good. Once in a month is OK.'

She turned to him. 'You're Dr Chandran's student, aren't you?'

'Yes, Aunty-ji. Sachdeva also is half-student. Other supervisor for him is Dr Rajguru.'

'I wish I were as lucky as Agniv,' Sachdeva sighed. 'Getting Dr Chandran all to himself.'

'Do you like him?'

'He's the best teacher. So patient. He'll explain again and again till you understand, in different ways too. He takes trouble over us.'

'Is that unusual?'

'Oh yes, everybody is so busy.' They all nodded solemnly.

'What do you think of him, Agniv?'

'Oh, Agniv *ka* hero *hai*, *na*? He won't even breathe without Dr Chandran's permission.'

Agniv blushed darkly. She turned to him. 'Agniv, didn't you come to Dr Chandran's house yesterday? I thought I saw you.'

'Yes, Aunty-ji. I am very sorry. I should not have disturbed.'

'You seemed very upset. Was anything the matter?'

There was a short pause. Agniv shook his head mutely. She noted that the others glanced at him and looked uneasy; she felt the edge of something, some emotional storm that had only just died down. 'Never mind.' She turned to Namrata, who was nearest. 'What are you working on?'

'I am from mathematics. I am helping Mr Prasad make some models.'

'I see.' One by one they described their work. Sachdeva was designing control software, Shweta was working on computational fluid dynamics for aircraft. Rahul said vaguely that he was studying microwaves. Agniv said proudly, 'I am helping Dr Gopal Chandran-ji make displays.'

'That must be very interesting.'

'Oh yes! Very, very small displays. Dr Gopal Chandran-ji says that one day we will be able to make artificial eye for people who cannot see. There will be small camera and embedded display linked to optic nerve. Whole thing will fit in eye socket. But that is much far off in time now. Now there is only pilot stage. You have seen flat TV? Picture is not so good, no? If we can make our new displays properly, you will look at TV and think it is window of your house. It will be thin like paint and fill one entire wall. You will be inside the TV programme.'

'Amazing.' The others continued to eat. They weren't listening. Perhaps they'd heard it all before.

'Also we can make many types of instruments with computer interface in front of eye only. No need to look at anything else. Like for weapon sights or any kind of controls, we could mount whole thing in helmet. And we can make gun rangefinder control respond to tracking of eye: you just look at target and press button and boom! It is shot. Already this type of system is there but mostly they are big and heavy. If there is so much to carry, how the soldier will fight? Smaller and lighter is better. Also then more things can be set for him to operate through integrated control. Essential problem is that . . .'

'*Arre chhod, yaar*,' Sachdeva drawled. 'Don't bore Mrs Shastri, Agniv.'

'Oh, I'm not bored,' she said quickly.

Agniv broke off, looked down at his plate and said nothing.

'We call him Agniv the Nag because he only talks about work,' Namrata announced. 'Never anything else, no, Agniv? Always nagging us to work and work.'

'But it's really fascinating to hear about your wonderful new ideas. You must all be doing such important work.'

The others looked pleased, but Agniv's eyes stayed fixed on his plate as though it filled the universe. His shoulders were hunched and his body unnaturally still.

Sachdeva said, 'Yes, defence work is very exciting, ma'am, but the pressure is very much and sometimes we feel we are doing much more than other students in institutes and universities are doing. There they just do their thesis and that's it. Here they make us work. There are so many projects, all very much labour-intensive, and sometimes we feel that's what we are— just labourers.'

'All rubbish,' Agniv muttered.

'Oh, *you* don't think so. Sir asks Agniv to do four tests, Agniv does eight. He's something else.'

'You are never thinking when you work.' Agniv's eyes flashed. 'Only mechanically you do as sir says. If you would think, you would say, what will happen if I do like this? How if I change this, add that? Then you learn.'

'You can do that, Agniv, because Dr Chandran never says anything. If I change what Dr Rajguru tells me to do, I get hell. Only the other day he chewed me out just because the vapour deposition had a few imperfections.'

'Why there should be imperfections? You were not careful with preparing sample?'

'Hey, look, Agniv, cool it. Normal people do make mistakes, you know.'

'Yes,' said Shweta timidly. 'We can't all be like you.'

Rahul snorted. 'It's too early in the morning for all that. Relax, can't you? Morning is for chit-chat.'

Agniv began scrabbling at his bag. 'I am going to lab,' he announced. 'You all can sit and have more tea.'

'*Arre yaar*, wait no. We'll all go.'

He shook his head and stomped out of the hall. The others stared glumly after him.

'I'm s-so sorry,' said Namrata, flustered. 'Agniv is so . . .'

'It's all right,' Anu smiled. 'Don't worry, I quite understand. Well, good luck with your work, all of you. It's a pleasure to have met you.'

When she came outside Agniv was wrestling with the lock of his monstrous bicycle.

'Hello, Agniv?'

He straightened up so fast the cycle almost fell over. 'Aunty-ji! I am sorry.' He caught the handlebars and hauled the contraption upright again. 'I am too much careless.'

'But not when you're working, I'm sure.'

'No, when I am working then there is only work.'

'Agniv, I'm a social scientist. I study how people work, and why they work. Do you mind if I talk to you?'

For the first time he looked her full in the face. 'You study how people work? That can be done?'

'Of course. Why not?'

'How can you do experiments?'

'Oh, that's easy. If you want to find out the effects of a particular factor on people's work, you can change their work conditions and see what happens. Like, how much they're paid and for doing what, how many hours they work, who tells them what to do and how, whether they can do things on their own or not. And you ask them questions: how do they feel, what do they want. Then you put it all together and make a picture of what makes them work well and what doesn't. Companies do it all the time.'

'Ah, ah.' He stared, rapt, into the middle distance, as though he were watching the model assemble itself in the sky. Then he frowned. 'But different people desire for different things.

Some will want a lot many money, some will want freedom only. What then?'

'You're right. Organizations have to strike a balance. And they might need to devise different systems for different categories of workers. It can be tough finding the right solution. Sometimes you have to settle for a compromise.'

They began to walk up the tree-lined road, Agniv wheeling his creaky bicycle.

'What a lovely campus you have.'

He looked around as if seeing it for the first time. 'It is okay.'

'Are you happy here, Agniv?'

'Dr Gopal-ji is a real genius. I am glad to be working under him.'

'Do you feel he's an inspiration to you?'

'Oh yes. He interviewed me when I applied to here. He asked me what I wanted to do. I said, sir, I want to be best. And he said, then you belong here.'

'That's wonderful.'

'He never leaves me to be satisfied with anything. When I do it well, he says, go on, do better. So I go. And then I find one thing that I never thought was there, and he says, now you are real scientist.' His eyes glistened.

'I see.'

'You have seen our labs?'

'Well, Dr Chandran is so busy that I hesitate to ask him to take me. And now he's gone into town so there's no point.' She sighed. 'I so wanted to see where you all worked, but I suppose there won't be a chance now.'

'Oh.' He perked up a bit. 'But I am here, no? I think perhaps we are not running any work right now; there is no reason why you cannot come and see lab if I take you. When we are working of course it is not possible, but now it is okay.'

'Won't Dr Chandran be angry with you?'

'But we are having visitors at all times. Only you must stay with me as I am authorized person. You really should see our lab, Aunty-ji, it is one of most advanced in country. And sir has configured it so well.'

They walked a little bit in silence, accompanied only by the muted creaking of the bicycle. Then he said gravely, 'If everyone in lab was like sir, I would be only too much happy.'

'Aren't they?'

'I wish for that. But I think maybe my expectation is too high. Sometimes sir is angry with me, and I am sad. Or sometimes I am angry with the other sirs, and my sir is scolding me. I think perhaps I have lot to learn.'

'Is it hard to get used to working with them?'

'Sometimes. After I finish work and I say, look, look, this is great, is it not great? But some juniors who don't care for advancing knowledge, they laugh and say, why so fast? Today we cannot work, we have this, that to do, very important. You go and watch movie. And seniors, they do one experiment, then they have ten meetings and make us write fifty reports.'

'I see.'

Agniv shook his head. 'No, it is not that. I am wrong to talk like this. They are saying for my good only. Also . . . sometimes the other sirs who are under sir, they are saying, why is there no war? Let there be war, let men go to war field and try our things. Then we will know results. They are not satisfied with field tests, even though my sir tells them, look, we have done rigorous tests, no war will be hard like this. But they just shake their head and say, we want to make contribution. Meaning: we want to shed enemies' blood. But . . . but in my village in three families there were jawans, brave men. We were so proud. Last war, only one came back home. For months we saw tears in our and other's eyes, so many tears. Those families, they got nothing, only bodies to burn, even their land they had to sell in spite of promises from government. One of them, my friend's family, they all of them went away to city with empty hands. God alone knows where they are now. So sad, so shameful.' He rubbed his hands fiercely over his face.

'When I think of them I ask, should I also want war? Which of my friends will I not see when I am in village again? These big doctor-ji people, their relatives never die in war. They can talk big. How can I say like that?'

'But aren't you helping to prevent deaths also? Aren't you protecting soldiers?'

'That is what sir is telling me. But I am thinking, without death how can there be war? Some people must die, otherwise it is not war, it is only joking. And if soldiers don't die, then other people will die. Simple people in villages and fields will die.'

'You have been thinking deeply about this, haven't you Agniv?'

He nodded sombrely. 'Aunty-ji, you are educated person. Tell me what is right.'

'Right in general, or right for you?'

'Both.'

'Agniv, do you believe there can be justified war? War that has to be fought?'

'Yes,' he said slowly. 'I can think of such war.'

'You wouldn't mind helping to fight such a war?'

'Oh no. I would work day and night to make weapons.'

'But you would not want to work for an unjust war, is that right?'

'Yes, Aunty-ji.'

'Are you sure your work will only be used to fight a just war, one that you would want to work day and night to win?'

He was silent for a long moment, so long she feared he would not answer. He frowned at the rusty handlebars curving between his fists. Then he said quietly. 'I am not sure.'

'What would make you sure?'

'I cannot think.' He bit his lip. 'I am certain that sir knows what is a just war. He would never, never, thousand times never, fight for wrong things. But . . . the other sirs, about them I am not sure. Sometimes what they say makes me afraid.'

'Why does it make you afraid?'

'I do not know. But there are more like them than there are like sir. As long as sir is there I am safe. I know I will stay here. But afterwards . . . what I will do then I don't know.'

'Do you think the Centre will recruit you?'

'Oh yes, sir wants me to work here. All time he is saying.' Agniv looked acutely unhappy. 'But I do not know if that will be right.'

They had reached the gate of the Centre. The security men asked her for identification. She produced her driving licence. 'Authorization?' they queried.

'Aunty-ji is with me,' Agniv declared. 'I am taking her.'

'Sign here.' They gave her a badge to wear and she followed Agniv in.

The inside of the Centre was a bit of a disappointment after the grand bungalows. The foyer was lined with clapboard partitions sloppily painted and covered with corkboards on which a slew of notices had been pinned. From there a warren of passages with tarnished brass plates on the doors led off into various sections. Agniv led her to 'Nano-Tech (Glass)'. There was a little black lens set into the door, which Agniv peeped into: a retinal scanner. The door opened automatically, and he held it for her. As they walked through the cluttered rooms she caught a glimpse of the locked door to Gopal's office, then they crossed a courtyard to the long low barracks beyond. 'The labs are here,' he said. 'We have cubicle with computers for writing up results.' They were in a little anteroom; a door off it led to Agniv's cubicle. As they entered a thin man in a wrinkled grey bush shirt with tea stains on it came out of the inner door, smoothing his sparse hair with a hand. He went to a flask on a table and unscrewed the cap. Agniv said, 'Hello, Dr Raja-ji, sir, are you working now?'

He turned and saw them. 'Who's this?' He squinted with interest at Anu's badge, at an angle to her chest that made her slightly uncomfortable. 'Madam, you must be Dr Chandran's visitor. I am R.S. Rajguru, his second in command.' He reached as if to shake her hand, but she namasted quickly. 'Has Agniv offered you tea? I'm afraid the staff have gone to lunch in the canteen, but there may be some left. I apologize for the cracked cups, but we don't stand on ceremony here.' He looked a little puzzled. 'Is Dr Chandran back, by any chance?'

'No . . . er . . . I'm with Agniv.'

'What do you think of our campus, Madam?' he said, handing her a tiny misshapen cup full of brown liquid. 'Is this your first visit? Agniv, just go and see how the others are getting on and report to me. Where do you live?'

'Mumbai.'

'Oh, excellent. I have many friends in Mumbai. And what does your husband do?'

'I'm single.'

'Oh, yes of course, Prasad mentioned it, how silly of me to forget.' He grinned lopsidedly. 'And when did you graduate?'

'A year after Vidura Chandran.' Let him work that one out.

'So you were in Cambridge together?'

'Yes. And you, sir? What do you think of the campus?'

He was a little taken aback. 'It . . . er . . . it's home to us all, of course. Very comfortable. We are quite satisfied with it. Although our wives are always complaining about the shops and the cinema.' He laughed deprecatingly.

'What does your wife do?'

'My wife? She's visiting her relatives. Just can't stay here for three months on end. Says it bores her stiff. But I get bored in Agra, so she's stayed on without me.'

'Does that happen often?'

'Sometimes—more often than you'd think.'

'Don't you find it a little difficult with the children?'

'Oh, they're all in boarding school. Four girls and a boy. It's quite an expense, you can imagine. But my wife used to teach in a residential girls' school, so they give us a concession on the girls. She goes to stay with them sometimes. Keeps her out of my hair.' He laughed again.

'I see. I guess you must spend a lot of time in the lab, then.'

'Not more than I can help. After all, this is a government job.' He winked at her.

'I really must be going,' she said, putting the cup down deliberately. 'It's late, and Vidura will be wondering what's become of me.'

'Oh? Doesn't she know you're here?'

'Actually I came to see the lab, but if you're working . . .'

'The lab? By all means. But you'll have to go through the changing room; the dust lock, we call it, and wear a bunny suit—that's one of those whole-body outfits—and cover your hair and all that. You could borrow my suit; I have a spare,' he offered gallantly, taking her arm. 'Although it's a bit difficult to wear it over a salwar kameez. Come, maybe I can help you . . .'

'It's all right, I think I'll leave it for now. Agniv, I'd like to go now. Thank you, Dr Rajguru.'

'My pleasure. Perhaps another time?'

Agniv escorted her back to the gate. 'So sorry you could not see lab. Maybe tomorrow?'

'Certainly, Agniv. Thank you. Oh, by the way, could you tell me where I can find Dr Sheth?'

Agniv opened and closed his mouth a few times. Then he said in a small voice. 'He is at guesthouse, at bottom of hill. In-charge of campus amenities. But . . .'

'It's all right, I'll find it. Thank you for all your care, Agniv. I'm glad to have met and talked with you. Here, take my card. If you would like to discuss your problems further with me, don't hesitate to send me a mail or call, or send a letter. I'll be very willing to help you, okay?'

'You are very kind, Aunty-ji.'

'I'm concerned about you, Agniv. Dr Chandran is right; you're a very intelligent person and you could be a great scientist. But I don't like to see you so troubled. If there's anything I can do to help, you'll ask, won't you?'

'Yes, Aunty-ji.'

'Bye then.'

Agniv stood by the gate, the card in his hand, and watched her disappear down the hill.

She walked briskly. She knew where the guesthouse was; it wasn't far from the main gate. As she turned into the lane for it, she saw Gopal go by on his bike, headed uphill. She hoped he hadn't seen her.

The guesthouse stood in its own garden, lovingly tended and resplendent even in comparison to the gardens of the bungalows. It was a horseshoe-shaped white building; the rooms had individual balconies. It drowsed under its shady trees; the foyer was cool after the heat of the sun.

The receptionist was reading a highly coloured Hindi paperback. He put it away as she leaned over the desk. 'Could you please tell me where Dr Sheth may be found?' The receptionist pointed to a door leading off the foyer. When Anu knocked on it, a pleasant voice said, 'Come in.'

She entered. A fair roly-poly man about Gopal's age sat at a desk. 'Excuse me, are you Dr Sheth?'

'Of course I am. Do you wish to book a room?'

'No, I . . . I'm staying with Dr Chandran.'

'Aha, the lady from Mumbai. Yes, now I can place you.' He grinned. 'And how may I help you, Dr Shastri?'

'Er . . . could I talk to you for a while?'

'Certainly. My time is at your disposal.' He waved at a chair in front of his desk. She sat down.

'Have you been looking after the guesthouse for long?'

'Since yesterday. Why?'

'What were you doing before that?'

'I was working up at the Centre. I've just been assigned new duties. Is there a problem?'

He was looking at her with good-humoured interest. She had a disturbing feeling that she had made a mistake. Was this the same Dr Sheth everyone was so worried about? Were Gopal and Agniv wrong somehow? He was watching her; she could not fathom what his faint smile meant.

'No, there's no problem as such, it's just that I was speaking to Agniv Nag a little while ago, and he seemed to think, well, that there was. A problem, I mean.'

'Agniv? Yes, I met him shortly after my transfer, he wanted to work with me but of course it's now out of the question. He was a bit excited about it.'

'I see. Sir, may I ask you a personal question?'

'Go ahead.'

'Are you happy here?'

'Certainly. Under the circumstances, I'm as happy as I could possibly expect to be. What about you?'

'Er, well, I'm only a visitor. I'm trying to understand the people here and I don't mind telling you I'm not having much success.'

'An honest confession. Yes, I gathered as much. Prasad and a few others were discussing you in the market. I passed them on my cycle, all sitting on their scooters in the middle of the road with their shopping bags and yakking. Sometimes they behave as if they own the town as well as the Centre. Well, it's impossible to talk discreetly while sitting on an idling scooter, so of course I overheard their conversation, which they thought important enough to insert into their morning chores.' He shook his head. 'You haven't been having any success at all, I'm willing to bet.'

Mystified, she asked, 'I'm sorry? They were discussing me? What were they saying?'

'Now *that*,' he chuckled, 'would be indiscreet to reveal. But I can tell you that they have totally misinterpreted your motives. One group thinks you're out to hook a husband, and the other wants the military police to take you in for questioning. You have got them thoroughly puzzled.'

'And you have correctly interpreted my motives, I take it?'

'Of course. That fool Prasad wasn't listening. You're a scientist, of course. You've come here to study us.' He grinned again, revealing *paan*-stained teeth. 'Am I right?'

'Absolutely.'

'But you must know, the scientist (my kind, that is) builds his whole life around the concept of being the *studier*, the unobserved observer. It turns the whole universe upside down if he becomes the *studied*. It's like something is suddenly looking back up the microscope at you. Not a nice feeling, and one likely to evoke violent reactions. I can see why you would want to keep your quest a secret from them.'

'You're right, sir. I knew that before I came here. But I can't think how to make them talk to me. They either cite security and clam up, or they dismiss me as a meddling woman who isn't capable of understanding. Is it hopeless? Should I stop?'

'Oh no,' he said. 'Please keep trying. I ask this because the benefits to ourselves are far greater than anything you might get out of this project, as anyone with half a brain can see. I'm only sorry that I no longer have a passport to the inner realm that I can lend you. As you may have heard, recent events have rendered me *déclassé*.'

Suddenly at a loss for words, she looked carefully at him, trying to read him. He smiled. 'Ask me anything you want. As a vain example to my brothers in lab coats, I promise to try and answer to the best of my capability. It's the least I can do.'

'Sir, do you feel that the system has betrayed you?'

'Hmm.' He considered this for a long time, his head cocked a little on one side as he watched some inner panorama unroll itself. 'I used to. I went through a period of hating everything and everybody. I admit I was angry as hell when they told me I was a slave, but that was unjust. I knew the rules when I joined. If anything, *I* have betrayed the system. I lost my confidence in it, so I could no longer operate in it. And in this business, if you don't have faith, you have nothing.'

'What made you lose faith in the system?'

'It was a cumulative process, with many elements. Of course, when I worked it all through, which I think I only managed adequately last night, when my wife and I sat down and talked over our lives here, I realized I had no option but to accept the state of things. We went to bed at four in the morning, but we were satisfied. We finally understood.'

'What were you trying to understand?'

'Essentially, my own distress. I had to find why it hurt so bad to go on doing science here, why it was tearing me apart. You see, I have two treasures. One is my belief, regardless of the motives and beliefs of my masters, in humanity's essential goodness. The other is my faith in my own competence. I realized that if I were to continue, the second would destroy the first. If I did well in the work I had here, I would have to accept that I had aided human nastiness. But it was my wife who opened my eyes. She said, "I get up every morning before you do and run this household; I am skilled at that. But if I were to do something else: run a company, teach a school, I would do that competently as well. I know it. Why do you think competence has only one face?" And I realized she was right. There are many ways to be competent in life. I've only explored one of them and left the rest to gather dust. Why should I think that the way I've followed all my life like a man possessed is all that matters? There are things to do I've always wanted to try, all ways of making the world a better place, whereas the science I did was producing more and more ways of the other kind. Why not start on these things now? I'm thirty-nine. My best years as a scientist are probably over. Most people in my line who are my age know that; they live through their students. But I don't want a second-hand life. I thought to myself, what about all those sportsmen who know that they're on the scrap heap at forty? How do they live? Do I see any of them committing suicide? Then why me?'

'What will you do now?'

'Just what I'm doing. I'm really glad they've put me in charge of the campus. There's a lot of work that needs doing. The sewage system is a disgrace; I'm going to redesign the whole thing. The Director's promised me a grant to upgrade that and the water supply. There are fallow plots all along the perimeter; I'm going to get Horticulture to cultivate vegetables and herbs for the campus. My wife's a classical singer and dancer, she wants to record an album. I'm going to take time off to help her do it. The Director has promised me all the leave I want, provided I don't make trouble. Why should I make trouble? I've seceded from their world. I don't belong there any more. Nalini's thirty-eight years old; I want her to be able to make a name while her voice is still strong.'

'What about the work you've already done? Do you feel troubled that you've put it in the hands of your masters?'

'That was a hard one to swallow. Yes, I agonized over the part I played in their little theatre of cruelty before the penny dropped, but of course no one was going to put the genie back in the bottle. I can't undo my past mistakes. But they were honest mistakes; I made them when my work was my life. Not any more.' He smiled. 'I was blinded for a while by my conviction that all I could be was what I had been. But that's not true. Yes, I regret leaving science, I love it and I wish I could do it. But that's just the old me speaking. Science has given me a lot, and I treasure those memories. But life goes on.'

'Won't you miss it?'

'At the moment, I do. But I'm studying the music industry now. I think I could be a good manager. Music's always been my second love. Nalini and I met because of it, and it's always been a bond between us. My daughter too is a good singer. Who knows, we could stage family concerts. Would you like to hear?' He sang a few lines. 'That means, "Allah, dear one, you have set me afloat in the stream of life. Guide me to the land of loving hearts and sparkling eyes, where truth and love rule every living thing." My wife sang that to me last night, and suddenly everything fell into place.'

'I would like to meet your wife. Would that be all right?'

'Of course. We'd love to have you, and Vidura and Gopal as well, if they want to come. Gopal took it badly, I know. I tried to explain to him, but I'm bad at talking about these things, never developed the habit. I told him I'd like to get inside the heads of the people who read my reports, take a look at the nasty clicking efficiency of their minds churning out plans to finish off all the people they think of as garbage. I said, don't kid yourself that these weapons are aimed at enemies; enemies are just neighbours on a bad day. Gopal doesn't like that kind of talk; he very politely ran away as he would from a raving madman. That was a little upsetting. And he wasn't the only one. I quickly learned to keep my metaphysical observations to myself.' He sighed. 'As I said, I can't introduce you to the other Centre staff now, because they're all behaving like I have leprosy, but I can tell you in retrospect about my work here. What would you like to know?'

She paused, searching for words, but failed to find any. She shook her head. 'Maybe you could start by telling me what is it that makes you see things differently from . . . from Gopal and the rest.'

He chuckled. 'All right, I'll explain. People here are locked in the same box I inhabited for so many years. However, I was an uneasy prisoner: Nalini ragged me mercilessly about it. She never let me believe the Centre was everything. Once when I was being really fatuous she physically rubbed the newspaper on my face and said, read, read what your wonderful inventions are doing to the real world. If it wasn't for her, I'd have turned into Prasad years ago!' He laughed uproariously at the thought. 'And Gopal, who I suppose has been your archetype during your trip, is even more locked in than me. He's a sensitive and clever man, and so he can't tell the really dangerous people to take a hike. Now I have the sensitivity of a brick, and

Nalini's always telling me how dumb I am, so I'm sort of insulated. If I see something or someone I don't like, I shoot my mouth off, and they think, well, there's no percentage in co-opting this one, he's a troublemaker. So such people with their ideas and their programmes steer clear of me—you've met that scumbag Rahil Vidyadhar? Ah, thought so—but they can weave subtle webs around people who behave like gentlemen and don't want to hurt anyone's feelings. People like Gopal.'

'I know.'

'Also, I laugh; I can't help it. I used to go to lab seminars and spot the passages of nonsensical jargon people had padded their papers with. I'd give them marked copies of their handouts. You can imagine how mad that made them. After a while people would shout me down every time I opened my mouth, so I either stayed away or snored in the back row.' He chuckled deliciously. 'One paper which was just mathematical formulae was so hilarious I took it home and set it to music! Nalini laughed so hard she got hiccups.' He coughed. 'I'm sorry, I think I'm a little delirious. It's all this sadness and happiness and questions and answers at once, as well as lack of sleep. We've been wound up for months really, Nalini and I, and it's such a relief to be out of it all. I'll try to make better sense.'

'It's all right. Maybe I should talk to you later. You've helped me understand a lot. Just the contrast between you and Gopal is so illuminating. I think I can see now where I have to attack.'

'You're a sharp researcher. I wish I had your skills. Maybe I'll come and take a course at your Centre, if I'm ever in Mumbai.'

'I'd be delighted.'

She took her leave; he got up and shook her hand enthusiastically like he was in a Charlie Chaplin film. 'He's only a couple of years older than I am,' she thought, 'yet he's rearranging his life like a rebirth. What sort of person can do that? He's laughing about it, but it must have been a terrible wrench. I guess he always was a square peg in a round hole, and that saved him. And whatever he may say, science has been a casualty in his life. Gopal would never accept such a bereavement.'

That thought sobered her up a bit. It was very definitely lunchtime. She hurried up the hill, anxious not to be late.

CHAPTER SEVEN

The campus was full of the sounds of cars reversing into the porticos, playing a discordant medley from *Jingle bells* to *Vande Mataram* as the staff came home for lunch and parked by the front verandas of the great white bungalows. Gopal's bike was not there; Anu hurried inside. The maids had just finished and Vidura, in a cool blue sari, was setting the table. 'There you are,' Vidura said. 'Do you want to have a wash before lunch? It must be boiling hot out there.'

'Afterwards. Isn't Gopal back yet?'

'He called to say we should start without him; he's in a meeting.'

They sat down to lunch. 'Do you know Mrs Sheth, Vidura?'

'Nalini? We were quite close once. Nice woman, very quiet, but with a mind of her own,' Vidura smiled. 'Why?'

'I talked to Dr Sheth this morning. He said we could visit some time. That is, if it's okay with you and Gopal. If not, I'll pop down on my own.'

'Why shouldn't it be okay?'

'I don't know. Dr Sheth seemed to think Gopal might have a problem.'

'I don't see why he should object to a social visit. In fact, I was thinking of going over myself. Whatever's happened between Mani Sheth and the Director shouldn't be a reason for everyone cutting them dead. That would be most unfair on Nalini, and so silly.'

Somehow this was a sentiment that Anu couldn't see Malti Prasad agreeing with. Vidura had made a lemon soufflé for dessert. 'Yum,' said Anu. 'You still do a wicked soufflé, Vidura. I wish I could cook like you.'

'Oh, I'm still no good at Indian food,' Vidura laughed. 'I'm hoping you can teach me that. We have to rely on the maids so much. I wish I could do your *murg masalam*.'

'OK, let's have *murg masalam* for dinner then.' Excited at the thought of cooking together like in their long-ago student days, they went to the kitchen to see if they had all they needed. Vidura opened cupboards and inspected jars of this and that, while Anu helped her identify the spices by smell. 'I'll get the maids to make *parathas* for us.' The doorbell rang. 'Gopal's back.' Vidura went to the door and let him in. 'We've already finished, Gopal; that was some meeting . . . but we'll keep you company. Anu's in the kitchen, she's going to cook *murg masalam* tonight.'

'So she's back from Sheth's, is she?'

'Yes. Gopal, can we go and see them? The Sheths, I mean. I haven't seen Nalini for, oh, it must be more than a year now. And especially now, with all this . . .'

'It wouldn't be a good idea.'

Vidura raised her eyebrows. 'I hadn't finished,' she said, slightly bemused at his tone. 'I was going to say I thought we should set an example for the rest of the community by going to see them. People are so narrow-minded here.'

He grunted, and sat down at the table. Vidura hovered. 'Can we go tomorrow, Gopal?'

'Since when are you a leader of the community?'

Vidura gave an exasperated little 'Ha!' 'All right, Crusty; finish your lunch, then we'll talk about it.' She left him alone at the table and went into the kitchen.

'I don't want you to fight about this,' Anu whispered. 'He'll think I put you up to it.'

'Don't be silly, darling. Gopal's a lovely man, but I don't

mind admitting there are times when I could give him a right ding across the ear. Honestly, he's such a *conformist*! You stay out of it; this is between him and me. I know how to persuade him.'

They finished their inventory of the spices and went back to the table. Gopal was eating the last of his lunch. Without a word, he went into the kitchen and put his plate in the sink. 'I'm off back to the lab.' He fixed Anu with a look. 'You'll be busy cooking all afternoon, I hope?'

'Actually I was planning to go for a walk.'

'It's far too hot. I can't be responsible if you collapse on the road. I strongly recommend you stay at home.'

'We'll both go for a walk,' said Vidura.

'Don't needle me. You must understand I'm saying this for your good.'

'Don't be ridiculous. We're not babies. Honestly, Gopal, you're too much. We'll take umbrellas, and only go a little way down the hill.'

'Where will you go? I don't think you should visit anyone with Anu. It wouldn't be wise.'

'Gopal, what on earth do you mean? Why shouldn't I take Anu to meet my friends?' She stared at him. 'What do you mean, it wouldn't be wise?'

'Trust me, I'm telling you the truth.'

'We'll jolly well go and see Nalini. I know she never sleeps in the afternoon. Really!'

'Are you doing this deliberately to provoke me? Anu, was this your idea?'

'Gopal!' Vidura burst out. 'What's the matter? Why are you behaving like this?'

'Nothing's the matter,' he said deliberately. 'I'm just making sure it stays that way.'

Anu said, 'It's okay, Vidura, I know why he's mad at me. Don't fight it.' To Gopal she said, 'All right, I'll stay home. Don't worry about me.'

Vidura stood in the middle of the room, her hands on her hips. 'Just what is going on here?' she asked in a dangerously mild voice.

'Gopal's angry with me because I went to see Dr Sheth and visited the lab with Agniv. Don't be angry with Agniv, Gopal, it wasn't his fault. He was just being kind.'

'Yes, it wasn't his fault. I should have known what you'd do and given him express orders not to talk to you.' He turned to Vidura. 'Viddy, do you know what this friend of yours is here to do? She's here to dig up dirt. She came here all prepared with a bunch of insulting questionnaires, ready to take our lives apart and hold them up to ridicule. You should see the stuff she's written on the Web. She thinks scientists are a bunch of comic-book villains out to destroy the world. All this while she's been taking notes, provoking people to talk without their knowledge. She's not here to be your friend, she's taking advantage of you for some cheap publicity stunt. Take it from me, I . . .'

'You are the most complete idiot I've ever seen,' Vidura said coldly.

There was silence. Gopal said, 'So you knew as well.'

'I did *not*! How can you say such a thing? Do you think I'd have kept you in the dark if I'd known? But that's not the point. I'd like to know since when have we, the people of the campus, been living on another planet? Why shouldn't people outside read about our lives and know about us? What harm could Anu possibly do, poor thing? She's just doing her job. Anu, you should have confided in me. I'd have helped you. For a long time I've felt that people here need to talk to other people, be exposed to the wider world a bit. Their perceptions are so skewed. I'd have helped you gladly.'

'Vidura,' said Gopal with excessive patience, 'have you any idea what this will do to us when it gets in the papers? Do you know how the ministry will react? That sort of thing is just not an option. I'm sorry, darling, but you're the one who's living on another planet. We're part of defence whether we like it or not. How do you think the army would react if some woman came around asking the officers' wives about their marital relationships and what they thought of their husbands? Would they sit back and let the media posture and comment and make them a laughing stock? Of course there are problems, there are bound to be. Every community has its oddballs and misfits, and if it has any pride it keeps them under wraps and focuses on the good people. But we're not just some isolated township, we have to remember we're part of the might of the state and we can't have people poking around, even in non-classified areas. If you think there are issues that need addressing here on campus, I can take them up with the authorities on your behalf. There are channels to address these things without making a song and dance and posturing for the public. That's all.'

'That's the stupidest speech I've ever heard in my life.'

'It's the unpleasant truth, I'm afraid. We're not some village of artisans or a cross-section of urban India. We are *not* material for some sociologist to earn brownie points over. I can't stress this enough. You're out of line, Anu. I said you could talk to the *wives* if you like, so long as you don't publish anything, but work and the workplace are strictly out of bounds. Now everyone knows you were at the lab. Everyone knows you were not with me. They know I've let my house guest roam around, poking her nose in everything. I've already had people asking what you thought you were playing at. I won't repeat what else I heard. And what possessed you to talk to that madman Sheth?'

'You didn't expressly forbid me to do either.'

'I thought your sense of decorum would prevent you. I thought you'd have some consideration for us as friends. I don't know how you've managed to brainwash Vidura'—Vidura snorted—'but I want to make it clear that you have betrayed us.'

'And I want to make it clear,' Vidura's voice was suddenly high with anger and the beginning of tears, 'that you are a beast.'

Anu winced. Vidura's sobs were the only sound in the silence till she turned and fled upstairs. They heard a door slam.

'I think you should leave,' Gopal said quietly. 'This has gone far enough. It's out of my hands now, and I've got a lot of explaining to do to certain people. It'll be better if you're not around when I do it. I'll come by at three-thirty with your ticket to Mumbai. You can take the Centre's afternoon bus into town and the overnight service to Bhopal. Go and pack. We'll say nothing more about this.'

'I agree with you,' Anu said in the same tone. 'I see there's no point in arguing. I am sorry.'

'Try not to upset Vidura. Living here is hard enough for her. I think you understand why I'm doing this. I have nothing against you personally, I hate the system as much as you do, and I believe you when you say you think you're on my side. But you can't fight it by talking; that just makes you a target. The things I've been hearing have convinced me of it. I'm really sorry I'm having to do this.'

'Don't try to justify yourself.'

He made a sharp movement, then controlled himself. 'It's two-thirty now. I'm going to the ticket counter in town. Be ready when I get back.'

He left. Anu waited for the roar of his bike to recede, then went upstairs and knocked softly on Vidura's bedroom door. 'Come in,' said Vidura's shaky voice. She was lying on the bed; she sat up as Anu came in. 'He's gone, hasn't he?'

'To get my ticket. He wants me to leave.'

'No!'

'Relax, Vidura. It's all right, I don't mind. I don't think I'd get any more answers anyway. Don't be too hard on him, he's just doing what he knows. We mustn't try to fight it.'

A fresh storm of tears forced Vidura to fling herself back

on the bed. Anu sat by her and rubbed her shoulders. 'It's okay, baby.' She laid her head on Vidura's and pressed her cheek into her hair. They lay like that for a long time, until Vidura stopped shuddering. Anu helped her sit up and silently fetched her some tissues from the dressing table. 'He was so beastly to you,' Vidura sniffled. 'I can't believe it.'

'I don't blame him. He's afraid for himself, and who's to say he's not justified? I don't have the right to make him go through this.'

'But he was so *rude* to you. I never thought he'd behave like that. I couldn't stand it. Oh, Anu, you're so strong. How can you face that sort of thing so coolly?'

'I've interviewed abusive people in the past. Like when I was doing this study of a company that was laying off workers, even senior executives. The men were so frightened, as if the world had collapsed on them. They felt like everything threatened them: their wives going out to work; the people still in the company, especially the women; the CVs that came back rejected; even the buses and trains they had to take now that their company cars were gone. They'd just lash out blindly, with words or with their fists. You know, three of them committed suicide just after being laid off; they met for coffee for the last time at the company canteen, laughing and joking, then they went home, deposited their severance pay and took the poison they'd given each other in little paper twists. That was when the company panicked and called in the Centre to see what could be done to help them. You see, their jobs made those men who they were. They weren't the lazy ones; the types who never worked and just shrugged when they were laid off. These men had fought to gain respect and status and wealth, free holidays, expensive schools for their kids, club memberships, kitty parties for their wives, and suddenly they thought they were nobody. One of the men got so mad while I was questioning him that he tried to attack me physically!'

'Oh god.' Vidura's clasped hands twisted around themselves,

as though trying to escape into each other.

'It was my tactlessness; I'd asked him if he felt like "downsizing" was another word for "castration". He was devastated that he could react like that to two little words; he said right there, "You can't punish me more than I'll punish myself for this." I didn't report it; he seemed so gentle otherwise that I felt sorry for him. He blamed the whole world for betraying him. And he was right, the world *did* betray him. He used to be proud that the company valued his contacts, his ability to fix things, but they dropped him first, ahead of shop floor workers and salesmen. He just couldn't accept that, couldn't find anything that could help him become someone else. He was a company official and that was that.'

'That's . . . that's horrible. What happened to him?'

'I don't know yet. We're doing a follow-up study next year.'

'Anu, how do you deal with such pain, when people tell you their stories? How do you stand it?'

'It's hard. But I always tell myself I'm helping them to understand and deal with it. And I write it up in reports—that helps to take it away from me. Then when I publish it, people like you read those stories and those statistics, and they think, my god, what those people must be going through. Then I know I've done my job, I've given them a voice. And maybe someone somewhere will read it and extend a hand to them.' She shrugged. 'That sounds idealistic, I know, and people would certainly say that my academic reputation is based on their suffering, but nevertheless, I have to believe that they're better off for my work than without it.'

'Is that what you were trying to do for Gopal and his colleagues?'

'Yes. Scientists are especially disenfranchised in modern society. But it's like conservative housewives slamming their doors in the faces of feminists. You get told a lot, "We don't need your help." For them, asking for help means rocking the boat and they could sink before someone throws them a life preserver. Or bails out the boat.'

'But what is Gopal so scared of? He's at no risk of being like those men. Is he?'

'No,' she said slowly. 'It's more subtle than that.'

'What do you think is the reason?'

'I didn't know till I met Mani Sheth. I got the feeling that he must have felt like those men in my study, at some point . . . but he's worked his way through it. Seeing him made a few things clearer to me. Now I think Gopal is wearing self-imposed blinkers: he doesn't want to look at his work and the system because he's afraid he won't like what he sees, and then he'll be left helpless, unable to work with conviction, yet forbidden to do anything else. That for him would be hell. So he'll avoid at all costs anything that might make him examine the system.'

'But is the system really going off the rails?'

'I don't know. I was hoping to find out. But the fact that people won't talk makes me suspicious. That they're working doesn't mean they're happy with things; people can go a long way while in denial. But talking about it precludes denial; you have to face facts if someone, an outsider, asks you questions. Avoiding speech: that's the danger signal. And if they tell you very raucously that they're happy, or they treat you as a threat and behave aggressively, that's even worse. If it's a woman investigator, men sometimes just behave crudely to get rid of them; that's what some people are doing here, I think, and Gopal is hurt by that as well; he thinks I've done something to provoke it and he can't bear to be associated with that sort of thing.'

Vidura frowned. 'You know, I've lived here so many years and I've never really thought about the system. I thought the way people behave here is normal in this culture. But now I'm not so sure.'

'I ought to go and pack,' said Anu. 'Gopal will be back any minute now.'

'You're not really going?'

'Vidura, if I stay things will just get worse. Let it blow over. Then maybe you can come and visit me in Mumbai. Get a taste of the real India.' She grinned.

But her poise evaporated when she went into her bedroom and saw the still full waste-paper basket. One of Vidura's tissues was clasped in her hand; she knelt over her half-packed suitcase and cried silently till the tissue was in shreds. It was not merely the disappointment, it was the wholesale rejection; all of her was in that waste-paper basket, shredded to bits. For a moment she longed to see Mani Sheth's cheerful fat face again. But he seemed to belong to a different universe. *Good for you, Sheth,* she thought as she finished packing. *Have a safe voyage down the stream of life.*

Vidura met her as she came out of the bedroom, suitcase in hand. 'Vidura, could you do me a favour? Only if it's no trouble.'

'Yes, darling. What is it?'

'Could you make my apologies to Dr Sheth? He'll be wondering why I haven't come to visit him. There's no hurry, we didn't fix a date, but still I feel bad about promising and then not showing up.'

'Of course I'll tell them.' Vidura wiped her eyes again. 'No *murg masalam* tonight, then.'

'I'll make it for you in Mumbai.'

They heard the bike come up the gravel drive. 'All ready to go?' Gopal asked cheerfully. 'I've told the bus station manager to give you dinner. They do a good tandoori chicken.'

'Okay,' Anu said gaily, desperate to salvage the social moment. She hugged Vidura. 'Write to me,' she said.

'I will.' Vidura bit her lip as she watched the bike disappear down the drive. It seemed to her that she stood there, transfixed, for a very long time as the stillness of the afternoon closed over the absence of Anu like a scab over a wound. What she saw, what she heard in the intervening time was only a function of her senses; the essence of her mind was buried in a dark place far beneath. It was only when the maids arrived that her reverie broke. Mechanically, distractedly, she set them to work. Then she sat down in front of the television, not registering the patterns of colour and light that shifted and changed in tandem with meaningless sounds. Somehow she felt she had failed. Some word she had not spoken, some idea or connection she had not grasped, was haunting her at the edges of her field of perception. She felt as if she had taken a step forward and what was under her advanced foot was only air. Would she find only a step down if she let go or would it be an abyss?

Why did I spend so many years being happy? she thought. *What sort of a fool am I?*

She shook herself. *This was silliness,* she told herself robustly. *Yes, I worked at my happiness here like a project; what else was there to do? No point sitting around and feeling ill-used. I had to make the best of it. And I've been given so much. But maybe happiness isn't something you can work at. Maybe it's bigger and harder than that. Oh god, all this is so unfair to Gopal. He does his best, he really does, he's so much better than all these other men. Why can't I be grateful?*

Where is *he?*

It was seven in the evening when Gopal turned up. 'We missed the Centre's bus. I took her into town and made sure she got in okay to the bus terminus.'

Felt guilty? she wanted to say, but she just sat there, pretending to watch television. He came and sat beside her. 'Vidura,' he said softly. 'Are you angry with me?'

'No dear, what would be the point of that?'

'Anu's . . . she's not one of us, darling. She doesn't understand. Of course *you* can visit Nalini whenever you want. I don't care what the others say. God knows there are too few people here you can talk to. I'm . . . Vidura, I'm really sorry this had to happen. If only Anu had told me before she came here, I could have arranged it better, avoided all these misunderstandings. My position is delicate, you know. People know I was friends with Sheth. They'll think I'll be the next to go off the rails. I have to show them I'm safe.'

'Safe?' she asked in a small voice.

'Reliable, you know. That I'm not about to go cuckoo. I brought *murg masalam* from the restaurant in town. It's in the fridge.'

'I'm not feeling well,' she said. 'I think I'll skip dinner.'

He looked concerned. 'Shall I mix you some salts?'

'No, no, it's all right.'

He put a hand on hers. 'Don't worry, Vidura. We'll go and visit Anu in Mumbai, away from all this. I know you feel cooped up here; so do I sometimes. But we have to grin and bear it. You know I came here for you, so you'd have the kind of lifestyle you were used to and wouldn't have to live in a dirty Indian city and fight for a place on the bus and all that. You were so pleased when we came here and I carried you over the threshold—remember that? It was such fun in the early years. Let's try and hold on to that.'

He went upstairs to change. She stared at the TV screen, the remote control held limply in her hand.

PART II

VIDURA

CHAPTER EIGHT

'*Jai Shri Ram.* My dear friends and brothers, today I will deliver the last of my series on the true basis of science. From next week I will be presenting five lectures on the nature of truth. These will elucidate many of your confusions on what is the truth of the heart as well as the mind, and present for you the wisdom of the rishis and munis on this very important subject. You will find that this vision of truth applies not only to your work but also to life itself. Work after all is embedded in life. First slide, please.' Rahil Vidyadhar clicked on the laser pointer. 'Here you see a *mandala* of the cosmic forces. Notice how earth, the black square, is in the centre. As we radiate outwards, the colours pass through the spectrum of the elements, until at last there is white, *akasha*, the pure ether, what you might call the Michelson-Morley radiation of space. These two, earth and *akasha*, only have meaning when they are connected. That's why man from earliest times has longed for the purity of space. In space the Brahman, the Supreme Being, has his *lila*, his cosmic play. As modern physics has shown, we cannot hope to control or understand that play. We should not see this as our failure, but rather as the manifestation of the might of Brahman. We can only watch it and hope to be part of it through our realization of Brahman within ourselves.

'Ancient Indian science connected earth and space in various ways. The artisan, the craftsman, stood in the square at the base of the system. The learned Brahmins, who always wore white, interrogated space and the nature of the universe. But the Mughals and the British sundered that connection between earth and space, between the artisan with his common-sense wisdom and the Brahmin with his knowledge of *Brahma lila*. Science in the hands of the colonial masters became alien, even though it was our own knowledge disfigured. This state of affairs must change if we are to advance as a great and strong nation and take our rightful place in the world. Next slide, please.

'This is the great sage Aryabhatta, who foreshadowed many of the important discoveries of modern science, including the solar system and celestial mechanics. But he founded no school, as unfortunately happened a great deal in ancient times, because we did not know then that our nation was threatened with great peril. Had we known, we would have guarded our knowledge and enshrined it in lasting institutions, such as this Centre. You have seen how the West locks up its knowledge in patents and secrets, have you not? It is dangerous in science if the exchange of knowledge dries up. And while the sages lived alone in their forest retreats, the craftsmen lived imprisoned by the Mughals, who forced them into slavery and killed or maimed them to prevent their progress. Next slide, please. This is the famous, or should I say infamous, Taj Mahal, a monument built on the destruction of many of our artificers. This is well documented by the Mughals themselves.

'Next slide, please. The Mount Abu temples. This should be the ideal of our science today. The youngest recruit, when he enters the great pursuit of science, should be able to look up and see the cumulative achievements of his elders vaulted over his head like a great temple, an edifice to which he can add his tiny part. I say this especially for my young friends who are seated in the audience today. They must inherit what we build. And in order to build, we must leave individualism and become that temple, for it is not the individual who creates progress, but the elite. The individual is subordinate to the elite. The individual may falter, but the elite goes on. This is the essence of the ancient concept of *jati*, wrongly interpreted as "caste" by the West. To save our science, we must refurbish *jati*. In ancient times, men earned their *jati* by knowledge and penance. That is what we must strive for in the modern *arya bhumi*. "*Arya*" itself means "noble". We must become the abode of nobility. Next slide, please.

'Oppenheimer, when he beheld this mushroom cloud, uttered words from the *Gita*. He said, "I am become Death, the Destroyer of Worlds." Because he was a foreigner he could not access the rest of the consoling message of the *Gita*, which would have solved for him the problem of action in the modern world. Next slide, please.

'Here you see Krishna and Arjuna. Krishna is expounding the message of the *Gita* to Arjuna, who is turning away from battle. First Krishna shows him the full panoply of his might as god, as Ramachandra Purushottama. Then he tells Arjuna, "Submit to the will of god. You are not the agent, you are only the instrument. You must fight your brothers and deprive them of life because god requires it. With god as your charioteer, you will go forward, for god guides you. It is not your place to judge, only to do your duty." Arjuna lets Krishna guide him through the battle; he shoots his arrows under Krishna's guidance. God smooths his path for him, just as lubrication smooths the action of a machine. Scientists too need the lubrication of faith. They are the Arjunas, and the wise ones who are to rule them are the Krishnas. Next slide, please.

'This guidance is what I call totalitarianism with a human face. Here you see the swastika, symbol of well-being, stolen from our science by the West. We must have faith in its true meaning. Next.

'And at last we return to the *mandala*. This particular *mandala* is a *yantra*, an instrument for measuring the World Spirit, the *Brahmatma*. Even modern science today has failed in all its attempts to quantify the *Brahamatma*, yet the Vedic sages knew how to interpret and study it. We must endeavour to reach again that level of expertise. We cannot do this through soulless Western science, we must also look to our great spiritual resources to guide us. Last slide, please. Acharya Jagadish Chandra Bose, who found the Upanishadic life principle in all things, living and non-living, yet was mocked and spurned by the Western scientific establishment, and saw his greatest achievements stolen and enslaved to the Western pursuit of pleasure. Thank you, my brothers. Would anyone like to ask questions? I am at your disposal.'

Gopal sat in the back row, holding in his hand a sheaf of smudgy photocopies. He had found it this morning in his locker, and he had spent an hour reading and rereading it. It was a fairly innocuous paper describing the design of a power supply. The shock had come at the end, where a few sentences detailed what the power supply was for and what it would be part of. On its own it was nothing, but the implications of it left a hollow pit in the depth of his stomach. He had heard hardly anything of Vidyadhar's speech; now he was dimly aware of people asking questions around him. He looked up, wondering what to do about the paper. The two names on it were members of Sheth's group, now Kundu's. He didn't care to speculate on who had put it in his locker. Out of the corner of his eye he saw Kundu raise a tentative hand.

'Maharaj, I did not understand what you said about *jati*. What is its difference from caste?'

'None, in practice. But the idea differs. The "caste" invented by the colonizers was rigid, unbending and mechanical. But in our true social scheme, a man could lose caste if he did not act righteously as required of him by the rules of his caste. For instance, it is the task of Brahmins to seek and preserve knowledge, yet some of them became businessmen and farmers. In truth they were no longer Brahmins, but Vaishyas. Similarly, a man from a caste just below Brahmin (but no lower) could become a Brahmin through learning and penance. But the colonizers came and recorded all castes for all times. That was wrong.'

'So who should I marry my daughter to?' someone murmured in the back row. No one laughed. At last the interminable questions ended and people began to file out. Gopal cornered Kundu. 'Do you know anything about this?'

'What?'

'A paper by Suryavanshi and Batra. I found it in my locker this morning. Tell me, Kundu, what on earth are those two working on?'

Kundu looked shifty. 'How did you find it? It is not connected with your group's work.'

'Nevertheless. Can you tell me what it's all about? Then I'll shred it.'

'I have no idea,' Kundu said distractedly. 'After all, I have only just taken over.'

'But you were in the group before . . .' Kundu had gone. Exasperated, Gopal looked around. The Director had remained behind, chatting with Vidyadhar as he tidied up his slides. Gopal wavered. He could just walk away, burn the papers, and no one would know or care. But he couldn't. He had to know, to be reassured that he was seeing shadows. 'Sir, could I have a few moments of your time?'

'Certainly. Don't you think that was a wonderful talk? I always say Rahil-ji is like a fountain of pure water. Like Gangotri!'

Vidyadhar smiled indulgently. 'Gopal. I have not seen you for some time. And Vidura-ji? How is she? I hope she is well now.'

'Well?' Gopal asked stupidly.

'Oh, some time ago I dropped by, but she said she was not keeping well and did not wish to talk. After that I am afraid I have been very busy and could not inquire after her. I am so sorry. Here, please give her a copy of the speech I made today; I would welcome her comments.'

'Oh. Ah . . . yes, she is better now.'

The Director showed no signs of budging; he was asking about Ayurvedic medicines for his back. Gopal tried to contain his impatience. At last Vidyadhar sorted out his slides and left. Gopal followed the Director into his office.

'Now,' the Director said expansively, sitting down and pressing the buzzer for his peon. He was a very fat man and fussed with his chair every time he sat down, heaping imprecations on the allopathic doctors who could do nothing for his back. Gopal let him finish the finicky ritual and order coffee for two from the peon. 'How are you getting on, Dr Chandran? No problems, I hope? I have been reading your reports with care. We should see a breakthrough soon, no?'

'Oh yes, we have had some promising developments, as you know. We are still refining the control software, and we have found a way to make the tubes very uniform and well aligned. Our success rate is shooting up with the new method. The resolution and colour shading we have achieved is very promising. Soon we will upscale to prototype level. I will prepare a comprehensive report for the authorities when we're ready.'

'Excellent, excellent. Your group has been doing wonderful work. Defence is very interested in downstream developments. Once your displays are in prototype they will approach us for control systems for a number of new weapons. The electromagnetic focusing work has been forging ahead as well. We will have to marry the two technologies soon. I will give you the relevant specifications when their work is ready for instrumentation.'

Gopal felt slightly dizzy. 'Sir, actually I wanted to talk to you about something to do with that. But sir, first I must request you to keep this absolutely confidential.'

'Oh, of course, that goes without saying, Dr Chandran. You need not stipulate.'

'Sir, what I meant to say was, this is not exactly a technical matter. I mean . . . it involves questions of a . . . wider nature. I have been deeply worried and puzzled by this information that I want to share with you,' Gopal took a deep breath, then raised his hands above the desk and put the sheaf he had been clutching on the desktop. 'I . . . found this paper today morning, sir. I read it with care. I am not sure if I understand the import. You will say I do not require to understand it or its implications, but . . . nevertheless, if you allow me, I would like to ask you a few questions about it.'

The Director peered at the paper. He leafed through it, raising his eyebrows. 'Dr Chandran, I'm afraid I must know how you got hold of this.'

'I don't know, sir.'

'You don't know? What . . .'

'I mean, someone just dropped it in my locker. I found it when I got in this morning. Perhaps they made a mistake.'

'Yes that must be it.' The Director swept the papers off his desk and into a drawer. 'Forget you ever saw it.'

'Sir . . .'

The Director frowned. 'Yes?'

'As you no doubt are aware, sir, that paper describes a power supply, a very powerful one, for a klystron, a microwave source. And there is a paragraph at the end that describes how the source will be fitted with a high-k dielectric ceramic reflector. I did some calculations, sir. That microwave source will be more powerful than anything we have at present, and it will be *focussed*. Sir, you don't need to be an engineer to know that this . . . thing, will be able to . . . to destroy living tissue.'

The Director looked at him without blinking. 'That's what weapons do, Dr Chandran.'

'You're not telling me, sir, that this is seriously meant for use as . . .'

'Dr Chandran, you are entirely mistaken. I do not presume

to impugn your science, but you have blown this out of proportion. It is only a little private thing Suryavanshi and Batra are doing out of their own interest, as a personal challenge. You need not worry about it.'

'Sir, I wish I could believe you. But the resources that would be involved in such a project are not inconsiderable, far too great for them to have made much progress without help. Yet they've tested a working model, and they're talking about the other components as if they've already been developed. And . . . sir, I went to the library and looked up the effects of microwaves on living tissue. This . . . thing . . . would make people's veins and organs explode on the inside. "Destroy" doesn't describe it, sir; the damage would be monstrous, inhuman. And the radiation's invisible and leaves no marks: people won't even know they've been hit. You could just focus it on a crowd and reduce them to meat in a few seconds.'

'You have a picturesque imagination, Dr Chandran. It's not a good thing for a scientist to have. Why this squeamishness all of a sudden? The Jews have this weapon; the Russians have had it for years. The Americans have the most sophisticated version, even the British are developing their own. Our neighbours are rumoured to possess several and are thought to be working on a miniaturized version that looks like an ordinary handgun. The next war fought anywhere on earth will see this weapon's first trial in a real theatre. In fact, unconfirmed reports say it has already been used by Greater Israel against Al Ayyarun and by the United States of Pacific Japan against the Mindanao Network. The beauty of this weapon is that it does not destroy materials, only flesh. The user can commandeer the opposition's resources with minimal loss, and of course where terrorists take control of civilian areas no infrastructure need be blown up. We cannot afford to be without it, Dr Chandran. It is crucial to the war effort.'

'I see.'

'I hope you are convinced. I am sorry you came across this

paper. It is classified, of course. But I trust your discretion. Please bear in mind,' he finished with heavy emphasis, 'that this has nothing to do with you or your group, and you need not concern yourself with it.'

'And what sort of control systems are you going to want designed for it?'

There was a silence. Then the Director said heavily, 'That awaits further progress. But yes, I had thought that if you were to achieve success with your panels it would be a good thing to draw on your expertise for this. However, information is controlled in this Centre on a need-to-know basis; I don't need to remind you of that. You do not need to know about this weapon to draw up the necessary control system; I would have given you a report containing only the relevant facts. It is unfortunate that you have stumbled upon this paper. I can see you are disturbed by it. Nevertheless, the job must be done. It would reflect badly on the Centre if we were to produce astounding results on one part of the contract and fall down badly on the other. You seem to have scruples about this; but reflect. What will India do when this weapon is deployed against our people? We cannot leave ourselves unprotected. Besides, it is a scientific challenge that I thought you would appreciate.'

Gopal wanted to say: couldn't we bomb their portable microwave oven to smithereens; why do we have to do it back to them? But he clenched his teeth. Anything he said now would only get him deeper into this morass.

'Sir, I appreciate what you say. I . . . it was just a bit of a shock, seeing this and then realizing what it meant. Of course I will . . . you can trust my discretion.'

'Wonderful. Then if you have no further questions . . .?' But as he was walking out the door, the Director asked, 'Do you have any idea who put this in your locker?'

'No, sir.'

'He committed a gross breach of security. If you find out

who the culprit is, don't hesitate to tell me. You should certainly see it as your duty to do so.'

'I'll keep that in mind, sir.' Gopal went back to his office.

★

Dear Anu,

I'm sorry it's taken me so long to write, dear, but after you left, for a long time I didn't want to do anything at all. I just stayed home and watched TV, I don't know why. Just getting out of bed and dressing seemed like such a great effort. What I would have done without the maids I don't know; they kept the house running and put food on the table. I did my best not to worry Gopal, and that wasn't hard because he's been very busy and I've hardly had a chance to talk to him. I suppose I missed you, and maybe I was a teeny bit angry with Gopal for having behaved so badly. He tried to explain it all to me, but I'm afraid it didn't make much sense; I felt like he was speaking a different language. It's probably my fault; Gopal's right when he says I've been living on another planet. I've realized that just like all the other people here I have my prejudices and viewpoint through which I see everything. Why should I criticize them? I just feel bad because no one else here shares *my* viewpoint. Silly me.

Well, I've been trying to come out of my shell for the past few weeks, without much success, I think. Last week I got my courage up to go see Nalini. Dr Sheth was there too. He remembered you fondly; you seem to have made quite an impression on him. Nalini's going to be giving a concert next month in Mumbai; she wants to send you tickets. How many would you like, and which address would you like them sent to? I gave him your e-mail id; was that all right? It was such a relief to talk to the Sheths. You know, I had been feeling like Robinson Crusoe, marooned on an uninhabited island. I'd almost forgotten that there were things that didn't relate to labs or departments or committees or perks. That's all they talk about here, that or the maids and the groceries and the children's tuition. Dr Sheth's been writing poetry and songs; he sang some for us. They were lovely. I really wish Gopal could have come with me, but of course he was at the lab, and in any case as you know he's very uncomfortable around the Sheths. I wish he could have seen how happy Mani and Nalini are.

Well, after that visit I decided I'd sulked for long enough, and that I had to get back to life. I'm trying to develop a hobby; I've bought some wool from the market and am teaching myself to knit from my Simplicity books. I've got four months to make Gopal a sweater for the winter, but it's heavy going. And the trouble with knitting is that the mind wanders, and then I find I've been sitting and staring at the needles for minutes without moving. At this rate it won't be ready till next winter!

Another thing has been bothering me a little. After I decided not to sit around moping, I got Gopal to bring his students for dinner. The dinner started off well. Sachdeva is just the opposite of Agniv; he's always talking and laughing, so Agniv gets a little eclipsed whenever he's around. To try to get Agniv to talk I asked him what he thought of the World Cup (you know how cricket-mad these boys are). Well, he said something that Sachdeva disagreed with, and Sachdeva said, "We need to teach them a lesson" and Agniv suddenly started shouting. Gopal made them stop, but the evening was ruined. Afterwards he said Agniv's been behaving strangely in the lab. He'll be working, and suddenly he'll stare off into space and not respond even if someone yells at him. Gopal thinks he needs to see a psychiatrist, but to me he just seemed terribly angry and terribly sad about something, and I feel powerless to help the poor boy.

I really miss you, Anu. You seemed to have had it all figured out. I feel so confused sometimes. I keep feeling there must be answers, but I don't even know what questions to ask. I wish I could shake off this feeling and get back to my life. Perhaps I should attend one of Rahil-ji's prayer meetings, at least then I'd feel connected.

Oh, well. Take care, and do write when you have the time. I know you must be frightfully busy. Tell me all about your work in the city. It'll help me get my mind off things.

Love,
Vidura

purpose / aims / control / glory

CHAPTER NINE

The hill was a network of lights in which the twin stars of a car's headlights traced a live circuit. There was an abstract, designed beauty in the setting of the clusters of bright rectangles that marked out houses along the well-lit roads, climbing at last to the long, low striations of light that signified the offices and labs at the summit. A satellite dish was a shield of gold, a communications tower a lance of silver. The captive power plant twinkled with ruby points of brilliance, cadmium sulphoselenide letting only red rays through. Good gatekeeper, cutting the seamless continuum of light into freed and absorbed, escaped and imprisoned. To the lens, there was only red and not-red. There were no other questions, no other categories.

Gopal sat astride his bike and watched. Here, a hundred metres down the approach road from the town to the campus gate, he could appreciate the cold schematic beauty of it all. This complex in the middle of nowhere was the child and citadel of science, clean and limpid in its stark organization, its grid layout, its lit streets and planned bungalows. He could not think of those spaces as containing people. From here it was only infrastructure, a valued and valuable asset to the nation.

Entered in the account books of the republic: so many crores of rupees, so many man-hours of labour invested. Purpose: national security. Aims: laudable. Control: absolute. Glory: unlimited.

This is a machine for killing people.

He gunned the bike and bounded forward as if he were going to burst through the gates. But he braked at the security post and identified himself. Then he went on up the hill.

His own house was dark. Vidura must be asleep by now. It was close to midnight; he had gone into town after dinner, ostensibly to do some shopping and check his e-mail, but in reality to storm along deserted roads like a bat out of hell. The night air was cool. He parked the bike and dismounted, aware that sweat had plastered his clothes to his body, chilling him now that speed no longer boosted the rush of his blood. The ground seemed strange and threatening under his feet, as though it would tilt and throw him off. Gingerly he walked to the front door, went inside and shucked his helmet. Making as little noise as possible, he went upstairs, undressed, put on his pyjamas and got into bed.

He stared up at the ceiling. He knew that tonight again, sleep would elude him. He would see the dawn flush the sky when he got up to drag himself to the bathroom to stare at his own aging face in the new light. He shut his eyes. Discipline was all; he had to teach himself anew to stick to the routine. No nonsense. The world started reluctantly to slink away, like a dog relinquishing a forbidden bone.

'Are you awake too?'

His drowsing eyes flew open with a start. 'What?'

'I can't sleep either.'

'Oh.'

'Sorry, did I wake you?'

'No, not really. What's the matter?'

'Nothing.'

They lay side by side in silence, listening to the night.

'Gopal?'

'Yes, dear?'

There was a pause. He was sure she had more to say. He waited patiently.

'I'm . . . I can't stand it any longer.'

'Can't stand what?'

'All this. I don't know. Something.' Her voice broke.

He rolled over and encircled her with an arm. 'Come on, baby, tell me what's troubling you.'

'I . . .' She burst into tears. He hugged her to him wordlessly, appalled. She buried her face in his chest and convulsed with sobs that were like clonic seizures. Desolate, he stared unseeing into the darkness. Soon she would need comforting. What words of comfort could he say to her?

'Oh god, Gopal, I'm sorry, I'm so sorry. I . . . I don't know what's got into me. Wait, I'll just get a tissue . . .' She got up and rummaged clumsily on the dressing table. 'I'm such a silly,' she sniffed, and blew her nose.

'Come back to bed and tell me what's the matter.'

She came back to bed. 'I told you, dear, I haven't the faintest idea. I know I sound batty but it's the truth. I've been depressed for a while now. But I feel a lot better now, really I do.'

'Don't lie.' He gathered her into his arms again; she sighed and flopped against him. 'It's my fault, I haven't been paying you enough attention. I've been so wrapped up in this damn project. And I've been too preoccupied with my own worries as well. I'm so sorry, darling.'

'What's worrying you, dear?'

'Oh, nothing serious. I just did something foolish and it's been eating me, that's all.'

'What did you do?'

'I let on to the Director that I knew about another group's project. He wasn't pleased. But I think the damage is under control.'

She drew pensively on his chest with a finger, circling again and again.

'Gopal, I've been married to you . . . how long is it now?'

'Twelve years. And we knew each other for a year before that.'

'We've known each other for thirteen years, and I can see that whatever it is that's been eating you, it's a lot deeper than a breach of etiquette in the lab. And whatever it is, it's been getting to *me* too. On top of everything else.'

'What do you mean "everything else"?'

'Whatever it is that's been giving me a hard time. Just boredom, really. I'm so bored I could scream.'

For a fleeting, crazy moment he considered telling her just what he'd found out about the other group's research that was destroying his peace of mind. But no, it was classified, and if he told her he'd be endangering them both. He knew Vidura could keep a secret, but it was his place to protect her, wasn't it? How could he lean on her for support when she was so distressed herself? He tossed the thought away; it was an unworthy impulse and he would resist it.

'You miss Anu, don't you? I should have let her stay. What an idiot I am. You were right, dear, I was overreacting. I should have dealt with it with a cool head.'

She moved restlessly against his chest. 'No, Gopal, you weren't. Don't misunderstand me, I'm not criticizing you, but you mustn't fool yourself. You were determined she should go. Anu was too much of a threat to you.'

'Vidura . . .'

'Let me finish. Something's happened to you. It's been happening for a long time now, so long that I can't remember when it started. It came about so quietly, so insidiously that I didn't even notice. But I'm seeing it now, Gopal. You're . . . so closed up. Like a fort. Or like this wretched Centre. I see you about the house and you're like something switched off. I think you only really live when you're in the lab.'

'Live? I push paper all day in my office and arbitrate squabbles among my men, half of whom aren't interested in the work and couldn't care less about anything except their vile status games and their gossip networks. They only work to earn brownie points, not because the outcome matters to them. If

you only knew what a punishment that lab's becoming to me
. . .'

'Then why do you spend nearly all day there? You're off
in the mornings, you're barely home for lunch, and I don't see
you again until eleven at night.'

'I'm . . . it's like I'm racing against time. Every day I think,
today I'll make an extra effort and get all these piffling jobs
off me, these reports and forms and letters, god knows what
else, so that tomorrow I'll have some time to work. Only
"tomorrow" brings a fresh stack of garbage to sort through and
deal with. And again the next day. I'm running to keep still,
and I'm falling behind.'

'But why? What use are all these things?'

'They're part of the job. Look, most people in my position
love that sort of thing. It makes them feel important. They're
in their offices all day, dictating letters to research scholars and
drawing up unreadable reports. They haven't anything better
to do. But I want to get work done, real work. Only I know
I can't chuck the waste paper because it's necessary, even if
it's meaningless. So I'm doing a double shift.'

'Can't you refuse? Or have someone else do it?'

'I really wish I could. But it'd be wrong.'

She rubbed her face on his shoulder, feeling his frustration
in the tenseness of his muscles. 'It's a pity they won't let you
employ me as your secretary. Then I could get through the
paperwork and you could be in the lab.'

He chuckled. 'I'd like to see the Director's face if I proposed
it.'

She sat bolt upright. 'Let's do it, then.'

'No, silly, it's out of the question. Come here.'

'I'm serious. This has gone on long enough. Oh Gopal, why?
Why are we wasting our lives like this? No, forget it, I'm in
a funny mood . . .' He drew her down to him tenderly.

'I know you want to help me,' he whispered into her hair.
'But this isn't the way. It's me who's at fault. I have to organize

my day better. I promise that from tomorrow I'll get back at a decent time for dinner. I've been really unfair to you. I'm sorry, Vidura, darling. I've hurt you, haven't I?'

'Please don't feel guilty, Gopal, I couldn't bear it.'

'No, I should. I've done wrong. I have to make it up to you.' He stroked her shoulders, pressing his fingers into the base of her neck.

'Mmm, that feels good. Lower. Yes. Please.' He let his hands rediscover her, the places she liked to be touched, the little hollows and curves that seemed unchanged in the dark that hid thirteen years of history.

She murmured, 'Gopal, you know something?'

'What?' He ran his hand down her flank, let it nestle in the small of her back. She lay softly under his touch for a time, then went on with a catch in her voice, 'You haven't touched me like this since . . . I can't remember when.'

He wrapped both arms around her and held her close. The touch of her hair against his chin seemed to convulse his throat, tearing away his careful facade of control. Some strange force was fighting its way to his voice box, and he had to shut it down or it would make him break every rule he'd ever made for himself. He wanted desperately to be the comforter, but his own need for succour was betraying him from within. She lay still in his arms, a little frightened by the intensity of his embrace; suddenly worried that he was hurting her, he relaxed his grip and immediately felt bereft. He wanted to run to some sanctuary, to anything except this empty void he carried within himself. There seemed to be only one way he could turn this turmoil into positive energy. He slipped his hands under her nightdress and slid it off her body, fastened his mouth on hers as if it was his only source of oxygen. She returned his kisses with an equal hunger. *Yes, my darling, I too want to escape. Take me.* She twined her arms eagerly around his neck, but she knew, before the thought was blasted away by the pleasure of being entered, that they were going nowhere.

★

Vidura awoke with a peculiar sense of disorientation. Somehow, she didn't know why, she had not expected to wake in the same room she had slept in for over a decade. Gopal was shaving. She could see his back through the bathroom doorway. She felt a rush of tenderness for him but it did not banish the feeling of unease she had woken up with. He finished and went for a shower; she got up and brushed her teeth. When he came out he announced, 'I won't go to the lab today. I'll call in sick.'

'Won't that cause trouble for you?'

'Let it. I've had enough.'

She held her peace.

Downstairs Vidyadhar's speech lay on the table. Gopal picked it up; Vidura had pencilled extensive comments in the margins. Vidura saw him looking at it. 'Did you attend that lecture?'

'Yes, I did. Can't remember much of what he said, though. All his speeches seem to be the same. He always drags in some greybeard sage, stuff out of the *Mahabharata* or the *Ramayana* and some great big spiritual truth that scientists can't get into their prosaic little heads. I would have bunked it if the Director hadn't collared me in the corridor.'

Vidura took the speech from him. 'I managed to hold my nose and read it through. Gopal, you should be worried about this.'

'That's what Anu said. But people like Vidyadhar never come to much. They just talk big. When the Director gets tired of him we'll at last be delivered from his boring old lectures.'

'What about the Signal Red project? Isn't he here for that?'

'Oh, the Director knows that scientifically speaking it's a lot of moonshine. It's just an excuse to have Vidyadhar here. When he's out, it's out too. The only point of learning the manufacturing process is to use that glass, or something like it, in photonic computing, and there are modern methods for making it that are far superior to anything the "ancients" could have had. It's reinventing the wheel, only worse. Vidyadhar will be booted out when the Director sits through his stock homily once too often.'

'I don't think he's going to be booted out,' Vidura said slowly. 'The sort of thing he's advocating . . . people wouldn't say such things in such a setting unless they were absolutely sure they had the backing of the higher-ups. Look, some of what he's saying is downright . . . I shudder to say "evil" but I can't think of any other word. Quite apart from the fact that he's grossly distorting history, he's trying to project a vision of science that's inextricably linked to a culture that you and I would find impossible to live with. How do you feel about "totalitarianism with a human face", Gopal? Does he mean an Auschwitz where they give you a cuddle before they shoot you?'

'Look, if this were a university and he were corrupting history students, it'd make sense to protest. But we're scientists. We're never going to study that stuff, and I think all of us know his scholarly methods are highly suspect. He's just a bit of entertainment; he dispenses Ayurvedic medicine and holds prayer sessions. No one seriously believes that they should remake Indian science in his image. For one thing, it wouldn't work. If we really tried to apply the science of the Vedas, we'd have to kiss our competencies goodbye in a week.'

'But there's more to science than method.'

'Maybe, but he's not it.'

The doorbell rang. Gopal went to the door and peeped through the spyhole. 'Talk of the devil. It's your little friend. Do you want to see him or shall I tell him we're busy?'

'No, let him in.'

'*Jai Shri Ram,*' Vidyadhar said jovially as Vidura came into the sitting room with the paper in her hand. 'Ah, Vidura-ji, I see you have read my speech. I am very sorry I could not come earlier. I have been very busy, very busy. But today also the

Director asked me to see Gopal-ji, and when the lab said he was ill I came here. I hope it is not an inconvenience. How are you, Gopal-ji?'

'Fine,' Gopal said coldly. 'But Vidura is a little under the weather, so please do not tire her.'

'Of course, of course. Gopal-ji, I have come to show you my work on the poems.'

'Can't it wait?'

'No, no. Besides, I talked with the Director and he agrees that it is now time to go to the field and test these insights. He wishes you to go to Songarh and investigate the processes. He will call a meeting soon, but I thought to tell you now so that you can prepare. I have made some inquiries. The only working of the original glass is making jewellery for fashionable ladies,' he sneered delicately. 'Of course, they cannot melt the glass without destroying the colour, but they have developed processes to work around this. According to me . . .'

'Such processes have no scientific significance, Rahil-ji. I don't see why I should waste the Centre's valuable time studying them.'

'Uff-o, you are very foolish, both of you. Here the Centre is saying, go to Songarh, see the place, roam around, enjoy, and you are saying no to the idea.' Vidyadhar winked elaborately. 'Gopal-ji, Director said you could take your wife with you as well. Better to be together, no? And Vidura-ji has been unwell so frequently, certainly she needs a change. What do you think, Vidura-ji?'

'It's up to Dr Chandran, of course.' But Gopal could see the wistfulness in her eyes.

'Okay,' he said abruptly. 'I'll come to that meeting, but you already know what I think about this. I really don't understand what you're trying to prove.'

'Good, good. *Arre* Vidura-ji, I wish you could come to my talks at the Centre. I also give them at the prayer meetings sometimes. Why don't you come and hear next time? I would be most pleased.'

'No, thank you,' Vidura responded politely. 'I'm afraid you would not be pleased at all, because if I came to one of your talks I would say publicly what I think of your ideas, your politics, your agenda and your methods.'

'Why should I not be pleased? I would be delighted, Vidura-ji.'

'You think so? Can you tell me what you mean by "totalitarianism with a human face"?'

'That is easy. It has been seen historically that the hardest thing to achieve when reforming is to get people to leave their old ways and adopt new and better technologies. That is the weakest link in the chain of progress. All the advances of the West that you people so admire—the motorways, the traffic control, the public works, the health-care system—were carried out by authoritarian governments who forced people to vacate land, follow rules, undergo clinical trials. Democracy is an enemy of change, because it is tied to the opinions of the most stupid, least progressive people in that society. For true progress, authority is necessary, but it must be the authority of the father, mixed with love and exercised for the ultimate good of the children, even if it brings pain. Look at what Lee Kuan Yew did for Singapore. The Nazis may have killed people they disapproved of, but they also gave their nation the Autobahns, the Volkswagen. No government before them had had the virility to do so.'

'Are you saying that we must force people to progress?'

'People are creatures of habit. Habits can only be changed by a stern father. That is totalitarian humanism. Its first condition is love, and only the second is force. It is the instrument of social engineering. We have suffered many setbacks through the accidents of history; we have had no time to catch up with the West. We cannot wait for consensus. We must march forward or lose the chance forever.'

'Why do you call the Taj Mahal infamous?'

'Isn't it? The historical records are very clear. Look in their own records to see how they raised their sacred buildings on the ruins of ours.'

'But haven't Hindus destroyed Buddhist temples and monasteries as well? Didn't Shashank burn the Bodhi tree?'

'Lies! Why should we destroy our own treasures? Buddha Deva himself is an incarnation of Vishnu. He is worshipped by the Vaishnavs, don't you know? And the cave monasteries still exist, and the Sanchi stupa.'

'Don't you think it's wrong to tell scientists they should surrender their moral responsibility to someone else?'

'You are referring, I think, to Arjuna and Krishna? Submission to god is a virtue, I think you will admit. All the world's religions say so.'

'But you were equating Krishna with real people: with the rulers of the nation, in fact. Are you seriously saying their voice is the voice of god?'

'For scientists, the nation is god. God must have a spokesman on earth. That was the other task of the Brahmins in old times: besides gathering learning, they were to interpret the moral rule to the ones who act. The state, embodied as Shri Bharat Mata Devi, is the focus of our love and devotion. We must find virtue in humbly serving her.'

'But who tells us what is right, then?'

'Whatever Shri Bharat Mata Devi requires of us is right. Whatever glorifies her and brings a smile to her tender eyes is good. If we defend her honour she will bless us. We are all her children.'

'So I suppose you report personally to Bharat Mata on the Signal Red project? Doe she send you little memos telling you what to do? Or does she communicate by occult radio?'

'Vidura-ji, I see that you are overtired. Please do not get excited. I do not mind, but others will be less tolerant. You are trying to see some sort of slant in my words. Let me assure you there is no slant. I am as democratic a citizen as the next man, but I also happen to love and respect my own religion. Were it not for its vast cultural and spiritual resources, I would be a speck of dust afloat on the ocean of life. If you see communalism in this, it is *you* who are communal; you, not I. If a man were to walk by wearing a cap and beard, would you pull them off him? No? Then why should I be punished for declaring my identity? It is this mollycoddling of the other, this mincing secularism that has destroyed our nation, and only our pride in ourselves can rebuild it again.'

Vidura got to her feet. 'I'm sure you must be very busy, Rahil-ji. I don't think we need prolong this discussion any further. Please do not invite me to any of your talks, I think you and I would both find it awkward if I were to attend, and I don't wish to disappoint you by refusing. Goodbye, Rahil-ji. Thank you for calling on us.'

Vidyadhar had the grace not to argue. He left without a word. She shut the door behind him, leaned on it and closed her eyes. Gopal said, 'That was very courageous of you.'

'Oh? You're not going to read me the Riot Act for displeasing an important personage?'

'Don't be silly. I told you he's a clown. I'd have thrown him out myself if you hadn't done so. It's you who's been saying he's so interesting to talk to.'

'He was at first, but not any more.' She shuddered.

'Let's forget about him. We've got a day to spend together. Come and sit beside me.'

She came and sat on the sofa by him, put her arms round him and buried her face in his neck. 'Talk to me,' she said.

Gopal was immediately at a loss for words.

'What about?'

'Anything. Whatever you think about all day. Let me share your thoughts. And you can share mine, of course.'

'Most of the time I think about work. You don't want to hear about that.'

'Yes, I do.'

'You do?'

'I said I do, didn't I? I'm your wife, remember? If you can't talk about it to me, who can you talk to?'

'Most of it's classified.'

'I don't want the technical stuff, silly. Tell me how it feels.'

'How does it feel to be a hotshot scientist?' he said slowly.

'That's right.' She had forgotten, it seemed. 'Go on, Mr Inarticulate. Spill the beans.'

'It feels . . . it feels rather like being a battery hen, I suppose.'

'A battery hen! My goodness!' She giggled.

'Yes, exactly like that. You're in a small, confined space, you're not uncomfortable, you have everything you need, except you can't move and you have no choice but to lay eggs. You put a lot of effort into your eggs; it's your blood and guts that make them, but you don't know what they're for, or who'll use them, maybe you suspect they're headed for a terrible fate, but you have no power even to know, let alone do anything about it. Sometimes you squawk and flap your wings a bit, but so long as the eggs keep coming and you don't attempt to break your neck pecking holes in them your masters are happy and they feed you whatever you want. And then when you can no longer lay any eggs, at last they'll give you your precious freedom. Then you'll flop out of your little cubbyhole into a world so strange you'll fight your way back into prison or even out of life to escape it and be safe again.'

Gopal stopped suddenly, the meaning of the words that had just left his mouth finally registering on his conscious mind. *God, what have I done? But I can't take them back now, and if I disavow what I've just said she'll know I'm lying. Oh god, why couldn't I keep my damn mouth shut?*

'Go on,' she said, in a flat, level voice.

He fought the pull of confession and lost. 'Sometimes you get to look through the chicken wire at the other battery hens. They seem happy. They compete with each other to lay eggs; they even relish the thought of what might be done with them.

They see what they do as service, and they look down on all the other creatures who've never known the pleasures of a cage. They care only for their craft. They make more and better eggs! But at the end of the day, we're all for the chop, whether we're reluctant layers or not. And we must never, never think of the death toll of our own kind, a toll we have so eagerly racked up and crowed over. Else we would have to see ourselves as proud murderers of our own children.' His voice broke. There was nothing more to say.

'Something's gone terribly wrong, Gopal,' Vidura whispered. 'It's like some sort of horrific death-ray coming out of the sky. Like a contagion. Sitting alone in this house I've felt it around me. Do you feel it too?'

He flinched. She couldn't know what images she was conjuring up in his mind.

'Gopal, promise me we'll go. Somewhere. Anywhere. If not Songarh, then Palghat. Or Mumbai. Anywhere but here, for as long as we can get away. We'll go mad if we stay here another week.'

'I won't get leave now. Not until the project is finished.'

'Then go along with their Signal Red nonsense, and make them let you take me with you to Songarh. Make them allow it. Please.' She was pounding a fist gently on his chest, a gesture so strange to her that he glanced, startled, at her face.

'Okay, baby. I'll make it happen somehow.'

'Thank you, darling, thank you.' The bunched fist fell open on his lap. He held her for a long time, waiting for the pain to subside.

CHAPTER TEN

Dear Vidura,

So sorry to hear you haven't been well in mind or body. I feel a little guilty because of course it was my coming that upset the apple cart in the first place. You were quite right, I should have trusted our long friendship and confided in you. It's a weakness of mine, I know, that I like to go it alone. My sincere apologies for any pain I may have unintentionally caused you. I'm glad, too, to hear that Dr Sheth and his wife are well; I thought it would do you good to see them. I got his e-mail about the tickets, picked them up and went to the show; thanks a lot. Nalini's divine; we all went for a drink afterwards, it was great fun. Mani had us in splits. As for Agniv, he e-mails me sometimes too. Yes, he's confused and lacks most of the necessary tools to unconfuse himself, but there's something basically sound and down to earth about that boy, which makes me hopeful that he'll pull through one way or the other. I do my best to help him, but he just hasn't been trained to deal analytically with all this, and he feels his handicap acutely. I've been sort of distance-tutoring him.

I'm glad you wrote for another reason. While I was there with you I had the opportunity to watch you and Gopal together, and it struck me that things were not quite right with you. I hope you'll excuse an old friend making this observation, but the feeling was so strong I was even afraid it would affect my objective view of Gopal as a scientist. Had I stayed I would have found a way to talk to you about it, but now I have to fall back on dead words on a page. You see, I've studied some defence scientists' families (I grew up in one, after all) and I've seen this happen in a lot of them. Defence science kind of forces a patriarchal model of marriage on people, where Daddy does something vague and important outside the house all day and Mummy potters in the kitchen or goes shopping, blissfully unaware of it all. I couldn't see either you or Gopal being happy in that state, and my visit to you confirmed my feeling. Believe me, Vidura, you mustn't turn away from the questions you can't seem to ask. Give them time and they'll find words to express themselves. Talk to me about it; I'll do my best to be your sounding board.

Love,
Anu

Vidura folded the letter and put it in her handbag using one hand as she held her wind-blown hair off her face with the other.

'Shall I close the window?' Gopal asked. She shook her head and looked out at the landscape speeding by. If she faced the wind its harsh dusty fingers tugged her hair back. The car, with 'Government of India' stencilled neatly on the hood, was making heavy going of the road, but she welcomed the jolts. They told her she was leaving the Centre behind.

The window framed a landscape of low denuded hills, already dry after the brief rains. Branching cacti had colonized the hollows, with a few stubborn trees grasping the hillside with thick gnarled roots. Here and there pale orange boulders jutted out of the ground like dead teeth, the slopes below them littered with flinty rubble from their slow destruction by the wind and sun. Little piles of crudely cut stone had been made beside some of them; at one point she saw a man patiently chipping away at a rock with a chisel hardly bigger than a teaspoon. They passed a valley with a thin, dark, broken line at the bottom: all that was left of a river. Dusty buffaloes nosed among the stones.

This was the second day of the journey; they had stopped overnight in Ujjain. She had been excited about seeing Ujjain; she had half expected to pass the magnificent universities and temples Vidyadhar had told her about, but it was just a prosaic small town, clamourous and commercial. There she had had a disagreement with Gopal; he had wanted her to stay at the government guest house while he went up to the field station, but she was adamant; if he was going to the site in the village of Songarh, so was she. 'I don't care about the amenities,' she had said firmly. 'You and I stay together.'

Gopal looked worried. 'I'll take you to Chittor after I come back.'

'If we go to Chittor, we'll go from Songarh. Gopal, I'll only stay behind if you think my presence there won't be officially allowed.'

'It's not that. But the place is really primitive, and there's nothing to see or do. A derelict haveli sounds romantic, but it's not so wonderful when you have to wash in a couple of mugfuls of water a day and eat the most basic of food.'

'So what? We'll be together.' And at last, reluctantly, he had agreed.

She watched the road. The hills had flattened; no, they had risen into a rolling plateau. Cacti fenced both sides of the road, so coated in dust they appeared like bizarre sculptures. Once in a while they passed strings of women and girls with pots on their heads; the girls in tattered frocks stared boldly at the car, but the women's faces were hidden by their bright saris. Little boys herded cattle in the gullies; she glimpsed them as the car followed the turns of the road. The children's ribs were as sharp against their skins as the animals'. Above them acacias held misty heads over the land, straining the sun's fury through feathery grey-green leaves.

Gopal told her the haveli had probably been built five hundred years ago with the money earned through his art by the master craftsman who had made that cache of beautiful, mysterious deep-red glass in its storeroom. Not much of the original structure remained; the government had renovated parts, and made additions and alterations. The patchwork haveli was all that remained of the sturdy houses that had clustered there; now only the rag-tag village itself was left in what had been the original fortified citadel. Whether it was robbers or poverty or drought that had killed the artisan community, no one knew, and the descendants of the craftsmen had long since scattered.

The glass had been used for luxury items and jewellery for the Mughal court, but the craft had come into existence in the twilight of Mughal greatness and had declined in tandem with it. The men of Songarh had then been famous for their delicate work—no women were taught the skill; it was the preserve of the masters who guarded their knowledge jealously. The village still clung to vague memories of having served emperors, but the skills and processes had long since been lost, along with most of the topsoil; in the arid uplands of Songarh even grazing for goats was hard to come by. Songarh had kept only the silent, enigmatic blobs of glass.

The evening before they had set out, Vidura had taken from her jewellery box the small medallion of gold filigree embedded in Signal Red glass that Gopal had brought for her from his first visit, made by an artisan in Pratapgarh from a sample Gopal had cut out of that stock. She had sat at her dressing table while Gopal packed the suitcases for both of them, and looked at it for a long time. The filigree was intricately worked; it seemed to float just below the surface of the glass, and the glass itself shimmered. Gopal had told her that was because the glass was heated for a long time at just above softening point so the almost pure gold filigree sheet could sink into it, a task that required immense skill and patience. It was in her cosmetics case now, a lucky talisman to oversee their quest.

The wind was beginning to burn her face; she shut the window. Gopal was looking at his notes. Thinking of the medallion, she asked, 'If you can reconstruct the process, will the villagers be able to make their handicrafts again?'

'It depends; it may be possible to use the process in a modern glass factory. There's still a market for decorative handmade glass.'

'Isn't that a little unfair? After all it is their secret.'

'Maybe. But manufacturing needs capital. And even if you manage to make it under controlled conditions, there are still problems with commercial working.' He rummaged through his mess of papers and held up a dog-eared transmission electron photomicrograph for her to look at. 'See? This is a picture of a really thin wafer of Signal Red glass, a few atoms thick, made by passing electrons through it. These round things are the tiny grains of cadmium sulphoselenide. They're twenty times smaller than the wavelength of visible light. See how regular they are? They're suspended in the glass as a colloid; like milk. The grain pattern scatters everything shorter than red, just like a sunset. It's a very delicate arrangement; you know how milk curdles if you drop acid in it? This is even more unstable than that. Heat it just a little bit and the grains grow and lose their colour; heat it some more and the selenium evaporates, leaving cadmium sulphide, which is yellow: it's used in cadmium yellow paint. So you get golden-yellow glass; then with more heating the cadmium sulphide starts to break up as well and finally you get a dirty colourless sort of thing. Which means that you can't work this glass; you can only cut it cold, or heat it very gently as the jewellers do. So the mystery is: how on earth did the original makers know how to control the striking?'

'Striking?'

'That's what you call the making of glass, when you heat the ingredients to develop a particular colour or quality. The themselves aren't very rare; lots of plants contain ~~selenium~~, and cadmium yellow has been used as a dye for centuries in spite of being highly toxic. Of course, that doesn't answer how they isolated the selenium and got it to absorb in the matrix. It's a long, slow process, making glass. They'd dig a pit in the ground and line it with coal and wood. On top of that would go the pot containing the raw materials: pure sand, soda, cadmium yellow. Then they'd cover the whole thing with earth and bake it slowly for days. My guess is they packed selenium-rich plant material around the pot and channelled the vapours in. We tried it; the result was pretty pathetic. We don't know how tightly it was sealed, whether it was primarily a reducing or an oxidizing atmosphere, what form the selenium was in, nothing.'

'Would you say they had a limited stock of something— perhaps the plants—and they invested it all in one go in the glass? Would that explain why there's a hoard?'

'They might have had a limited supply, but I think the reason why this glass was stored is quite simple. No blown artifacts can be made of it. You can only cut, polish, engrave it; you can't even use it for enamelling. Nothing involving heat is possible. So apart from faux jewels for sword hilts and jewellery and small hollowed-out bowls and boxes, it wasn't much good. The beautiful colour is its own worst enemy. They couldn't use it, but they couldn't bear to throw it away.'

'Yes,' said Vidura, thinking of her medallion.

'I half suspect they invented the jewellery technique out of sheer desperation. Of course, the technique can use any glass and works better, actually, on the ordinary kind than on Signal Red. But Songarh was known for the technique on red glass. That's why it was famous. Most places today where the work is done face an acute shortage of glass; they work mostly on imported stuff, very expensive.'

'So Songarh is sitting on a treasure trove?'

'Not quite. The glass belongs to the government now; to the

Centre, to be precise. Back in the old times when they needed it for red signal lenses, it used to be a closely guarded resource. And now?' He shrugged. 'It's just a curiosity, something to play around with. It's only because the Director has some idea of using colloidal glass for photonic computing that I'm here.'

'Yes, you said. What's photonic computing?'

'You know that silicon circuits are almost at the limit of miniaturization. If we make chip transistors any smaller they'll leak and dissolve in electronic crosstalk. But photons don't interfere with each other like electrons do; they're much more orderly and well-behaved. Circuitry for photons, when we come up with it, will probably be really, really small. So the next big thing is light, or so the Director thinks. People have been experimenting with quantum dots of cadmium sulphoselenide instead of my nano-tubes in video displays. They got good colour-programmable results when they got it right, but the process is very difficult to direct. That's why we're interested to know how these tiny grains were produced, what sort of control they had. Personally I have my doubts about the whole thing. If we ever do use glass in computers it won't be out of some seventeenth-century hoard.'

The sun settled into its westward decline. The earth and rock over which their road twisted now seemed darker, though the sky was still bright. Some time later they came out onto flat land with strange humped hillocks here and there, standing proud of the dusty earth and already wreathed in darkness while the level ground lay in its russet glow. Under the uncertain light the landscape seemed to shift and tremble, like a new planet just cooled from a lump of primordial matter.

They stopped. Startled, Vidura looked out of the window. 'Where are we?'

'We're here.'

She looked around. A low squat building stood to their left; the tricks of the sun's dazzlement had hidden it from her. It had a narrow veranda of stone slabs, onto which windows opened, now showing dim lights. Part of the tiled roof looked new and raw.

'There's the haveli.'

She heard the raucous cough of a generator starting up. The lights brightened, then a long gloom fell through one window—a man's etiolated shadow-head, blowing out a lamp.

'But the village?'

'It's to the north. You were so busy admiring the sunset you missed it.'

The door opened and two men bustled out, greeting them with folded hands and the automatic obsequiousness of government servants to their bosses, holding the car doors open for them. The driver and his helper were unloading their suitcases and taking them inside. Vidura and Gopal got down and the driver parked the car in a new shed which also housed a Jeep. Somewhat nervously, Vidura followed Gopal into the house.

'Memsaab!' The caretaker tried to pull his tall, disorganized body into a respectful slouch and remove the faded hand towel from his shoulder. 'I hope you will be comfortable. The generator has just come on. I have cooked for you chapattis and . . .' Gopal brusquely asked if water was available. It was, in buckets in the bathroom, the man said. He showed them to their quarters, flicking on the lights and apologizing about the roar of the generator next door. A bearer brought them quilts, for the night chill was beginning to strike through the windows, although the walls, made of chunks of rough-hewn rock mortared together, still retained their heat. Promising dinner in half an hour, the caretaker retired.

Standing in the middle of the room, looking delightedly at the rough walls, she hardly cared that the room contained only two rickety camp beds and a rack for clothes. There was a new lean-to bathroom built onto the bedroom, made of brick with bright blue plastic pipes and a tin roof that she suspected became a heat trap in the daytime. Vidura and Gopal bathed together to save water, giggling like children.

At dinner, Vidura learned that the village was a rundown warren of houses some way off the road. It had once, in prosperous times now not even a memory, been fortified. Now the people were poor; the men were mostly away, working in the cities, while the women stayed behind and looked after the meagre crops and herds. The caretaker made a face. 'Very village people,' he said, as though that explained everything about them. 'Very hopeless. Their fortune is bad.'

Gopal used the tight-beam encrypted comlink with the Centre to inform them of their safe arrival. As he signed off he recalled that Mani Sheth had designed this system: here it was, still doing its job, while its creator was as good as destroyed. The thought gnawed at him. Trying to push it away, he went back to their room and ordered mugs of hot steaming tea for the two of them. It was suddenly quite chilly, and Vidura was glad, even after the heat of the day, to sleep under a quilt. Chastely, like brother and sister, they said goodnight to each other and curled up in their respective beds.

★

The block was vaguely cylindrical and dark, even directly under the light as it was now; its surface was slightly rough. When she ran her fingers over it, she could feel the marks of chisels. There was barely a hint of colour, the red seen more in the mind than the eye. 'It's unpolished,' Gopal said. 'If you polish it and put it out in the sun, you can see a sort of red light deep inside.' He showed her a chipped-off piece the size of his fist, the cut surface deep crimson and glowing in the light, like the living flesh of some mythical stone beast. 'They make very pretty paperweights. Look, these are some pieces I had milled by the artisans in Pratapgarh. See this one?' he said as he showed her a small piece, flat on one side, curved on the other like a drop of blood. The light from the bench seemed to make a tiny star inside it. 'They processed this using the technique for making faux jewels. Pretty, isn't it? They'd put these on animal harness, or shoes, or sword belts. They were used instead of real jewels for hard-wearing things that were meant to be showy but not expensive.'

'I see.'

'Would you like one as a memento? They're not much use to me. I've put the samples I want aside.'

'Oh, Gopal, I'd love to have that one. Could I, please?'

'Sure.' He wrapped the little jewel in a scrap of cloth and put it in a matchbox. 'Want any more?'

She shook her head, and ran a finger over the rough surface of the block. 'Are these chisel marks original?'

'You mean made by the original makers? Yes. When it comes out of the mould, it's covered with a crust of waste material. All of that has to be knocked off, and then the glass is polished to remove all the impurities. They only did half the job on most of the blocks. Probably waiting for an order to come in before spending more effort on them.' He smiled. 'Now you've seen all there is to see at Songarh.'

'Well, I thought I'd visit the village . . .'

'Whatever for?'

'Just to see. I've never seen a real Indian village before.'

'You'll be disappointed. Like the caretaker said, it's almost deserted. Only a handful of the poorest are left. People from nearby areas say it's accursed. The darwan will tell you all sorts of colourful stories about the place.'

'Well, that's all the more reason to see it. You always tell me I'm out of touch with the real India. Maybe I should try and educate myself.'

'Okay,' he said, a trifle reluctantly. He looked at his watch. 'But be careful: the Rajasthan sun is not to be trifled with. It's three o'clock now; go at four, the heat will be—well, bearable. And take the darwan with you, and be sure to come back before dark. The darwan only speaks Hindi, I'm afraid. The villagers probably speak the local language, but he can interpret for you. Don't talk to them if you can help it; they won't give you a moment's peace if they think they can get something out of you. And don't accept any food or water, though I daresay they won't spare any. You wouldn't believe the stuff they eat. In fact, get the cook to give you a thermosful of cool water.'

'Oh, don't worry. I'll manage.'

★

Dust lay upon the road in thin drifts as Vidura and the darwan walked down the drive from the haveli. The wind puffed it into little whirls by the roadside ever so often; the driven dust climbed into the air like smoke. But there was nothing insubstantial about the air's touch; it was laden with hot particles that became grit between her teeth and burned in her throat. She rubbed her face and felt the grit there too; she took her hand away and looked in amazement at the tiny bright particles shining in her pores. Beyond her fingers was the emptiness of the sky.

She tried to walk while disturbing as little of the road's dust as possible, her gaze fixed on the edge of the high wide emptiness filled only with the sun's brute fire. The horizon was a knife-edge, the dull earth baked, only the seeming movement of the road under her feet told her she moved.

'Memsaab, this village is a bad place,' the darwan was saying. He had been chattering non-stop; she let him, realizing that he probably had few people to talk to as a rule. 'Nothing like my village at home. There we work, we till the soil, plant crops when the rains come, roam with our animals after the harvest. Life is hard but rewarding, if you work. But these people don't work.'

'Why not?'

He shrugged. 'They are a sickly lot. Very lazy. God's curse is on that village. Memsaab, people say that *before*, in the days of Ram rajya, a *sati* from the next village escaped from her husband's pyre and took shelter there. Her brothers-in-law asked the people of Songarh to give her up, but they didn't. From that day, all the women of the village were cursed to become widows, whether they were daughters or daughters-in-law. So no one will marry the sons and daughters of Songarh. Those who have escaped hide their origin. But still the curse finds them out.'

'And this happened a long time ago?'

'In the days of Ram rajya.'

'And they have been cursed from then?'

'Yes, yes.'

'But in Mughal times I've heard they were very prosperous . . .'

'Maybe, but look at them now, memsaab.' He frowned. 'You cannot cheat a curse. Even if man doesn't know, god keeps track.'

'Why do people still live in the village?'

He shrugged. 'Where will they go? Some of them marry each other. And the women, they don't let their lack of husbands stop them having children.' He sniggered.

They passed a broken-down wall. She bent to examine it. It had been cobbled together from the unlikeliest materials, rubble, stones, what looked like a few properly dressed stone blocks of great antiquity and the thing which had caught her eye, a fragment of what looked like granite but from one of whose edges a spark had flashed. It was a hunk of glass, rough on five sides like rock, while the sixth, newly fractured side showed deep red with a white starburst of cracks running from the spot where the blow had fallen. She rubbed it, resisting the temptation to prise it out of the wall. She looked ahead. The village was close now, hazy in the heat.

As they entered the huddle of huts she was suddenly struck by the silence. The huts were squat, mud-daubed structures, hardly high enough to stand up in, and roofed with a few tiles eked out with dead branches, thin sheaves of straw tied down against the wind. There was no life: no animals or people anywhere to be seen. Between tumbledown walls and beds webbed with fraying strings the dust eddied, blowing orange glittery plumes into the slanting afternoon light. A few strands of straw fluttered occasionally in the wind, scraps of rags holding the feeble joints of beds flapped. All else was still. No birds called, no insects buzzed. The rough daub of the hut walls showed here and there their stone foundation or flaked away from the bare ribs of sticks. The doorways were yawning holes, lacking even the pretence of a door because these people clearly had nothing that was worthy of being stolen. Against one or two doorways was a string bed that blocked the entrance. As she watched, a tile skittered off one roof and thudded into the dust. Then, once again, the silence pressed upon her ears like a blanket in the hands of a languid assassin.

'Where are they?' she whispered, unwilling to break the hush. She peered into a doorway, seeing only an uneven dusty earth floor, an earthen bowl, a rag. A small footprint was visible by the door, once made in the wet mud, now dried hard as iron. She backed away. 'Where are the people?'

The darwan shrugged. 'Who knows where they go?' He peered at the nearest hut, took a deep breath and yelled, 'Putlibai!' Vidura jumped.

Nothing happened. He was looking impatiently at the door blocked by an upended string bed. But now she got the feeling that what she was hearing was the sound of people keeping still. Had she caught a faint rustle on the very edge of her hearing? She took a few hesitant steps towards the hut, and her foot hit something. She picked it up. It was a stick wrapped in a rag, she thought, and then she saw the crude slashes at one end: eyes, nose, mouth.

'Putlibaaaai!'

'Stop that!' she said sharply. The stick was light in her hands, dried out by who knew how many summers; its surface was polished with handling. A necklace had been rudely carved around what was supposed to be its neck, and a child had lovingly folded a dirty scrap of canvas around it in a makeshift sari, then left it in fright in the middle of the road. She approached the nearest door, the sound of her footsteps loud in her own ears. As her shadow fell on the doorway she thought she heard a faint gasp. She peered through the meagre weave of the string bed, trying to penetrate the darkness with her dazzled eyes. Something seemed to move inside. 'Hello? *Koi hai*?' Taking care to remain in the light, fully visible to anyone inside, she extended her hand with the doll in it. 'Is this yours?'

A slight sound from inside like the whisper of a footstep; there was definitely someone there. She stood motionless, bent from the waist, the doll across her palm as though she were offering food to a wild animal. Behind her the darwan muttered. 'Memsaab, let us go. They will not come. We are wasting time . . .' And then a face appeared, blurred by the intervening string mesh.

'Mine,' said a rasping voice. Vidura stared. The child stared back, one eye focussed on her while the other wandered crazily. The girl sniffled, drew a hand over her nose, pressed her face against the bed to see better and coughed explosively. Somewhere behind her a baby began to wail. The girl's coughing shook the string bed and Vidura stepped forward and caught it as it started to fall. Now she could see the girl clearly. Her one normal orb stared back dark and proud like a hawk's eye, defying the rest of her ravaged face; its fierce gaze was fixed on the doll. Cautiously Vidura raised her hand. The girl snatched at the stick, but her clawed fingers caught Vidura's hand as well.

'Hey!' The darwan sprang forward and hit the child in the face. 'Monkey! Devil-child! I'll give you such a thrashing . . .'

'Stop it! You mustn't hit children! Don't you know that? Stop it!' Horrified, she yanked the child up and out of range; the darwan stared at them, bemused at the sight of the little ragamuffin in Vidura's arms. Then he dropped his hand and shouted, moustache quivering. 'Thief! You were going to take memsaab's watch! Memsaab, please put the dirty creature down. What will sir say? Memsaab, you must not be kind to them, they will . . .'

'I'll be the judge of that,' she said coldly. 'Don't touch her. I'm putting her down.' She took the girl under the shoulders to set her down, then found to her astonishment that she was surrounded by bleating, jostling goats.

She turned and looked into a face that was hardly more than a skull, the skin like dark crinkled cellophane over bones like knives. The face contorted with fear and fury. 'Baby!' the woman cried in the same rasping voice as the child's. Vidura impulsively thrust the child into her arms. 'I'm sorry,' she said in her halting Hindi, but the woman just stared blankly at her and dumped the girl on the ground as if she were a sack. The darwan began waving his arms and shouting so rapidly that all Vidura could make out was the woman's name. Under the barrage of the darwan's insults, Putlibai fled into her hut, dragging the girl after her.

Without a word or a glance at the ranting darwan, Vidura ducked under the eaves and followed.

'What do you want?'

Vidura regarded her. Stooped under the low roof, Putlibai was breathing hard, but there was no trace of the alarm or hurt that Vidura had expected and had come to assuage. The woman looked at Vidura with a level gaze, taking in her pastel pink crêpe de Chine salwar kameez, the string of pearls at her throat. 'This is my house,' she growled. 'Get out.' The dark parchment of her face was stretched so tight it made her discoloured teeth stick out like a rat's snout. She bared them now, eyes narrowed in fury.

'I came to say I am saddened by what just happened. The man hit your daughter. Had I known he would do that, I would have prevented it.'

Putlibai's face twisted with bitterness. Vidura couldn't tell whether her words had been understood. She hoped her tone carried the message.

'What do you think of yourself?' Putlibai rasped. 'I've lived in the city; I've seen women like you. You come around the houses of people like me trying to earn virtue by licking our shit. One of you even made me send Baby to school. Much good it did her! Her only reward was that now she can understand the insults that lout flings at us.' The girl, Baby, clung to Putlibai's skirt, her one eye fixed solemnly on Vidura's face. 'Go away, big lady from the city. You don't belong here. Go before our dirt stains your dress.' Baby looked hungrily at the pink silk. Putlibai turned, sat down on the bare earth floor and gave suck to the squalling baby as though as far as she was concerned Vidura had vaporized. Three other children had been crouching in a corner, regarding Vidura as if she were a ghost. Now with a chorus of squeals they charged their mother and fought for her other nipple. Vidura saw that among them a little girl had a deformed arm and a boy had an ulcer on his back. He pulled his sister's hair and made her shriek, then fastened his mouth on his mother's breast. Baby smacked them indiscriminately, but still they fed upon Putlibai as she slumped in weariness against the crumbling wall. Sickened and grieved, Vidura turned and walked out into the sunshine.

CHAPTER ELEVEN

'One two is two, two twos are four, three twos are six . . .'

Many days had passed. Late autumn had brought no relief from the heat; the days were unchanging, only a little shorter as a concession to the earth's tilt. In the hot stillness of noon Vidura watched Baby's face as she arranged stones in pairs on the floor, her small dusty hands moving busily in the dappled light filtered through the broken roof. Already the tightness of famine was around her young face, squeezing away her childhood. Every so often a cough racked her, but when she spoke a spark lit her good eye and her harsh voice danced with questions. Vidura sometimes had a hard time answering them satisfactorily.

The stones had been Baby's idea. At school in Mumbai she had heard kids reciting their multiplication tables: 'Teach me the number song, ma-ji,' she had pleaded. Baby wanted to know where the road went, how cars moved without bullocks to pull them, and why there was water under the earth here where it never fell from the sky like it did in Mumbai. She knew there was water underground: her mother had to walk many miles every morning to fetch it from a deep hole in the middle of fields of cracking mud; when the children were old enough to be left alone, Baby would go with her. Vidura tried to explain about aquifers and water tables, scratching pictures in the dirt with sticks, groping for the words. Vidura asked: did she want to live where there was rain, and trees, and birds?

Baby made a face. 'There are only bad people in such places. It is bad to leave home. Home is safe. Here I and Juggu and Ruby and Billu and Chhotu are safe.'

That first evening, now weeks into the past, Vidura had bribed the darwan handsomely to forget his hurt feelings and give a favourable report of their trip to the village. Then she had returned the following day and found Putlibai lying on the floor of her hut with a fever. She had sponged the woman's forehead with water from her thermos and spoken to her gently. 'I want to learn your language. Will you teach me? And I want to teach your children. You say you were betrayed by women like me. Now let me make amends.' Putlibai had been too exhausted to argue. 'You're crazy,' she had whispered. 'What can I, an unlettered moron, teach you?' But Baby had taken Vidura's hand and said, 'I will teach you.' And she had looked up into Vidura's face with a kind of gleeful wonder.

Only then had Vidura told Gopal. He had been sceptical, but she had insisted he allow her to visit the village. 'I can help there,' she had said earnestly. 'Why should I waste my time sitting here? It won't disturb your work in any way. And if you only saw what it's like! Even the little I can do is something.' At last he had given in, but the darwan still accompanied her, much to the man's dismay—he would much rather be playing cards with his cronies than sitting by Putlibai's hut with a flask in one hand and an umbrella in the other. But at heart he was a good-natured fellow, and as long as Vidura kept the tips coming he was game.

Vidura gently prodded Baby to tell her what they ate (precious little), where they got it, how often they did without. Baby proudly showed her the small stock of coarse grain she had to make bitter flour from; there was a ramshackle shed in the centre of the village where every month a truck would come with sacks of grain, but Putlibai's sister-in-law and other powerful people in the village took most of it for themselves and would dole it out as they chose to the rest of the village.

In the morning after seeing her mother off, Baby would grind a handful of the grain between two stones, make a paste of it with a little water, dry it on a weak little pile of embers and feed her siblings. She would save a scrap for her mother's breakfast the next day. Sometimes the children would still whine; then she would make syrup from a morsel of dirty loaf sugar and rub a little on each of their mouths. That would keep them busy sucking their lips and fingers for a while. And if all else failed, she would go to her aunts and beg for a little opium to keep the baby quiet. Sometimes she got it, sometimes not, but she always got a bagful of insults whether they sent her away empty-handed or not. 'Why do they hate your mother?' Vidura asked, and Baby shrugged. 'We are not strong,' she said, as if that explained everything.

Vidura was beginning to understand them. That was her first goal; what her second would be, she had no idea beyond a pressing desperation, a feeling that seeped out of the walls of that hut like smoke. *I have to help them now*, she thought, *then decide about the long-term. These people can't wait. Day by day they're sinking into hell. Gopal will call me a fool; let him. It's so wrong that they should live like this. Even more than the poverty, it's the hopelessness that's killing them. They struggle for survival, and yet they seem to survive only to suffer.*

'Why don't you feed the children on the goats' milk?' Vidura had asked Putlibai once, and been told that a mug of milk was gone in a second but its worth in coarse grain lasted two days. Putlibai had looked her full in the face for the first time that day, in weary surprise that anyone would even think of asking. That look told Vidura much more than her bald explanation. And she had noted how the goats seemed to treat the hut as though it belonged to them, butting the children out of the corners as they pleased, so that Putlibai had to kick and curse them when they got too aggressive. Then, once they were comfortable, they would lie around chewing their cud lazily and watch Putlibai feed her children with milk worth even less than theirs.

Now it was afternoon; the sun's heat was dimming. Putlibai was away with her goats; Vidura was alone with the children. Baby had finished her chores and fed her brothers and sisters. Vidura kept them occupied so they could be fed as late as possible; they would be less hungry when Putlibai arrived and wouldn't mob her.

Vidura wasn't yet confident of bringing them food herself; she didn't want Putlibai to think she was offering charity. 'I want to be your friend,' she had said in the beginning, and Putlibai had snorted weakly with laughter. 'How can a big lady like you be my friend?'

'Why not?'

Pultibai had shrugged. Such things did not happen, that was all she knew. Then she had turned back to the drudgery of her life, stealing a glance now and then at her daughter in Vidura's company. Vidura felt that gaze boring into her whenever Putlibai was around; the gaze of a mother trying to shield her children with whatever small strength she had left, torn between fear of this powerful person who was so close to them, and her own despair.

'Four twos are . . . ten . . .'

'No, eight. Look,' Vidura sorted eight stones into groups of two. 'One, two, three, four. Eight.'

'Eight.'

Vidura added two more. 'Ten.'

'Ten.' Baby put down two more. 'Twelve.'

'Good! You're very clever, Baby.'

Baby beamed. 'Do you like my doll? Her name is Motibai. She likes to play kho-kho, but there are no friends for her to play with, and her mother makes her work all day. See? She's crying.'

'I have a present for you.' Vidura pulled her handkerchief out of her bag. 'You can make her a nice dress with this.' Then

she took out a needle and thread and showed Baby how to pleat
the handkerchief into a skirt. Baby stroked the white cotton with
awe, fingering the delicate embroidered flowers. 'Now she's a
queen!'

Little Chhotu snatched at the bright white shape and Baby
wailed as her doll was tugged out of her grasp. Vidura picked
the child up and hummed to him, snapping her fingers in time.
He gurgled. While Chhotu was distracted she slipped the doll
out of his fist and gave it back to Baby. Then she jiggled the
little one and sang *Bye Baby Bunting* for him. The other
children listened, wide-eyed. They didn't understand the words,
so she got them to make up their own song to go with the tune.
Giggling, they made one up about a naughty child who wanted
to fly and fell out of a tree. Halfway through the song she heard
the bleating of goats. Putlibai was standing outside, listening.

They finished the song. Putlibai's bent shape darkened the
hut's doorway, turned sideways as she chivvied her goats
inside. 'Still here?' She came inside and sat down. 'Why are
you teaching my brats to sing? They'll only become lazy good-
for-nothings. Not that they'll do any differently otherwise.'

'They'll be happier for it.'

Putlibai grunted. She hauled Chhotu onto her lap and stuck
her nipple in his mouth. 'Songs never filled anyone's stomach.'
But the rancour of the first day was gone; instead, she seemed
uneasy as though she knew she was doing wrong by having
Vidura there and expected to be punished for it. Vidura
desperately wanted to reassure her, but she had no idea how.
She concentrated on keeping the other children busy. Putlibai
stared impassively at the baby's puckered face as he laboured
to extract what milk there was from her body.

'Why have you no children of your own?' she asked
presently. 'Is that why you want mine?'

'I won't take them away from you, Putlibai. Haven't you
realized that by now?'

'Then why?'

'I want to help.'

Putlibai spat. Her head remained turned away.

'All right,' said Vidura. 'Would you accept it if I said I was lonely?'

'We are your playthings, no?'

Vidura shook her head. 'If you are my playthings, then I am equally yours. You can hurl as many insults as you like at me, vent your anger, question me, accuse me. You can see me as the symbol of all the rich, uncaring people you've hated, except that I can listen to your story and feel sorrow with you. I have nothing to give you but that.'

Putlibai's face came round again reluctantly. Bravely Vidura held her gaze, willing some spark in the dying afternoon light to show her clear sincerity to Putlibai's tired eyes. Putlibai's frown held fast for a long moment, then slowly her papery cheeks relaxed into a smile. It was a genuine smile; it transformed her face and knocked years off her age. Vidura realized with a shock that Putlibai was in fact quite young.

'Very well. If you really must.'

Vidura smiled as well. 'You think I'm crazy, don't you?'

Putlibai shrugged, as if to say there were many things in the world she did not understand and Vidura's motivation was only one of them.

'Why are you so angry, Putlibai? What has life done to you?'

Her face twisted again. 'What has it not done to me?'

'Do you want to tell me?'

'No.' But after a long while, when the baby had tired of tugging at her breast and fallen into a weary sleep, she said, 'I used to live in the city. My man and I, we went there together. He was an artist: after all we of Songarh have followed art for many ages. Once we were kings among artisans: that is why we have been cursed by the jealous gods, they cannot bear to see good fortune.' She coughed, spat again, but this time her eyes returned to Vidura's face. 'He went to the city to work as a sign painter. For a while we were happy; we thought we had beaten the curse. We had six children; we lived in a hut with an electric line from next door and a table fan. Then he lost his job. Now they don't want sign painters, everything is done with big big machines. He drank. One day he didn't come home. I waited many days. I found work in a house of big people, but one day, when I was not there, some men came. They found Baby; she was only six. They did what men do. They said, we'll come back for your mother and do it to her too; she'll make good money for us. Then I fled with my children. My eldest son died on the way here. And now I live in my father's old house, or what's left of it. My husband's people threw me out.'

Vidura was silent. Baby was unconcernedly playing with her doll. Putlibai leaned against the wall, her eyes closed. 'When we came here, we thought we had escaped; we felt fortunate. But we soon found that the curse hadn't finished with us. There was no grazing; strangers had fenced off our old forage lands. The big babus came and said it was now state property. There was only one place we could go, the death forest, over there.' She pointed with her chin to the west. 'It is a bad place; people go there and strange things happen to them. When I came back, so many people had already gone missing; others would find them, much later, half rotted away in the forest. After a while the deaths were less common, but people would come back and feel sick. Every time they went there, the curse took away a little of their life. The children especially, for they went the farthest with the goats. That is why I go myself, now, and Baby here looks after the house. You see my younger daughter's arm? She scratched herself once on a thorn in the death forest; her whole arm turned black. My second son, too, look at his back; he fell asleep there once, and now his back won't heal. And that one,' she pointed to the third, 'he had a fever, and now he does not speak. The doctor people come sometimes from the city and give us jabs, but they say there is no cure. It is the curse. There is no medicine for god's wrath.'

'When do the doctors come?'

'Every few months. We all line up and they put machines on us and poke us with needles. Then they give us medicines, but the medicines never work. We tell them not to waste their time, but they keep coming back. And now they won't let anyone leave the village. They say it will get worse if people leave, they say we must remain for we are marked. It is our fate.'

Vidura frowned. 'That can't be right. Are they government doctors?'

Putlibai shrugged. 'They come in a big white car and stay at the haveli, where you are.'

Vidura made a mental note to ask Gopal about that. Curse, indeed. Since when did doctors make it their business to spread superstition?

Suddenly Putlibai's eyes filled with tears. 'You know, I haven't been able to talk like this since my sister died. If you only knew the sorrow we bear in this village. It is beyond the strength of flesh and blood. I know I will die soon. Just a handful of years here have sucked away all my strength. But what will happen to my children?' she coughed weakly, wiping her mouth with the back of her hand. 'Baby too is ill, and she can't do everything. When I am gone they will all blow away on the wind.'

Wordlessly Vidura put her hand on Putlibai's.

Outside, there was a sudden babble of voices. She heard the darwan arguing loudly with someone. Vidura understood only half of it. Then a strident woman's voice called, 'Putlibai! Putlibai? Where is she, the bitch? Come out, you whore's child! What do you think you're playing at, fucking around with some big lady from the city, you bag of dirt? Come and face us and we'll humble your arrogance, you slut!'

'Memsaab is inside!' the darwan's outraged voice rang out.

Putlibai crumpled up in fear, but Vidura laid a hand on her shoulder, then stepped around her and out into the light. 'Are you looking for me?'

The ragtag band of people gaped at her. They were mostly scarecrow women, with a few scrawny men holding sticks in the background and looking nervous. They had not expected to see her, and confusion transfixed them for a moment. Then the woman who had shouted said, 'Who are you?'

'My name is Vidura Chandran. I am staying at the haveli. I have come to visit my friend.'

Another woman elbowed the first and said unctuously, 'Memsaab, we are sorry. We were looking for Putlibai. Is she here? We want to talk to her.'

'If what I heard you say just now is what you want to tell her, you'd better talk to me first.'

They stared at her, baffled. Her face was open, kind, interested, untouched by fear. She seemed to be waiting to hear them, genuinely wanting to know what they thought. But they had come on a tide of emotion; they had no words, only insults. Villager looked at villager, trying to recapture the charge of hatred and envy that had just energized them. Vidura looked on politely. In her teens she had faced down gangs in Brixton; she prayed that she still remembered how to do it.

'What's your name?' she asked the first woman who had shouted; the woman shrank away. 'Where is your house? If you don't mind, I would like to visit you too. I would like to be friends with everyone in this village. I happened to meet Putlibai the other day, so I came to visit her. Now I have met you. Will you take me to your houses?'

The darwan wrung his hands. 'Memsaab!' he hissed.

The other women looked at each other. Their shouted taunts now seemed as deadly as tinsel spears: they stopped thinking of themselves as a crowd and edged away from each other. They had come to punish Putlibai for her presumption but now they didn't know what to make of the situation; the ones in front milled around, while those who had hung back joined their men on the edges of the crowd and fled. Not wanting to be left behind, the ringleaders beat a hasty retreat, throwing black looks over their shoulders as they went. Soon Vidura and the darwan were alone.

Putlibai poked her head out of the hut. 'They ran away!' Her face was grey with wonder and ebbing fear.

'Do you know them?'

'The one who was shouting, she's my sister-in-law. The rest are her friends. They're jealous.'

'I'd like to visit them. Oh, not today,' she added, seeing Putlibai's look of alarm. 'Some other time. If they come again, tell them I said so.'

'Can we go now, memsaab?' The darwan ran shaky hands over his brow.

'Now? It's early yet. In a little while.' And she disappeared back into the hut before the darwan could object. 'Why is he so nervous?'

'He's afraid something will happen to you, and then his job will be gone.'

'Nothing will happen to ma-ji,' Baby said stoutly.

'Baby, you haven't practised your letters. Come and sit down.' Vidura opened her notebook, one of Gopal's old ones with 'Centre for Advanced Research and Development' over the top of the page. Soon they were tracing the Hindi alphabet together. Vidura's grasp of written Hindi was poor, so she had got Gopal to write the alphabet out on a piece of paper to which they both referred. Baby was tickled by the fact that Vidura knew only slightly more than her. Soon she was playing the role of teacher, making Vidura trace the letters and correcting her work. The other children watched, or played with scraps of paper. Vidura had tried to get them to join in, but they only tore the pages listlessly. 'My aunt is a very bad woman,' Baby said. 'She threw Mai out, and all of us, on to the street. We came here to my dada's place. It was deserted, and the roof had completely fallen in. Mai fixed it; she was stronger then.'

Vidura looked at Putlibai. She was slumped against the wall

again, her eyes closed. Vidura couldn't tell whether she was listening or not.

'Now she is sick,' Baby went on in a low voice. 'When she wakes up at dawn her joints are so sore she can't move. I have to rub her until she can get up and fetch water. If I don't she just lies there, moaning.'

'You do a very good job, Baby.'

Baby beamed. 'You're so nice!' she burst out. 'Promise you won't go away!'

'Go away?'

'Go home to the big city. Darwan-ji said you would go. I fought with him,' she finished loyally.

Vidura looked at Baby's smiling face. 'I . . . if I have to go away, I'll come back, Baby. Really I will. I'll find some proper doctors to make you well. I'll . . .'

'Promises,' said Putlibai in a voice like lead. 'Your husband won't let you. Is he happy that you're coming here?'

'No, but he won't stop me . . .'

'Do you think I am a fool? I too have been married. He will make you behave as your kind should. Women are never free.'

'I'll prove to you that you're wrong.' Vidura got up. 'Even if I can't stay, I'll get help for you. I have friends; I know people who can change things. You won't have to live like this much longer. I'll . . .'

'Do it, then talk if you like.' Putlibai turned her face to the wall.

★

'Memsaab, this is not good you are doing.'

They were walking back. Dusk was falling, the same red light she remembered from the first sunset she had seen here.

'Memsaab, those women are very bad. They will do bad things if you keep going there. They are jealous of Putlibai. They may hurt her or her children.'

'I will visit them too. Then they'll have no reason to be jealous.'

The darwan shook his head sadly. 'They don't want you there.'

'But why?'

He looked baffled. How was he to explain the obvious? He had heard this woman had come from *abroad*, no wonder she didn't know the most basic things. Perhaps they didn't have poor people in *abroad*.

'Big people and little people don't mix.'

She shrugged. They had reached the haveli. The darwan went round the back; she continued on into the dining room. Gopal was there, nursing a cup of coffee, a spread of papers on the table in front of him. He looked up as she walked in.

'Why are you scratching your head?' he asked sharply. 'Good god, woman, don't tell me you've got lice.'

She realized she had been scratching unconsciously for some time. 'Oh is that what it is? I thought it was dandruff.'

'And I don't even have any medication.' Gopal scowled. 'We'll have to go into town to get some. I was thinking of making a trip to Chittorgarh anyway. You'd like to see the fort, wouldn't you?'

'Oh yes. And I want some vitamin supplements for the children.'

He folded his papers away grimly. 'I need to talk to you about that. Vidura, just why are you going down to that village? What's in it for you?'

'I'm making friends with the women there.'

'Really? You sit in that hut with those children and teach them. You spend hours in their company. Does this make sense to you? And what about their feelings? They think the darwan is some big babu; to them, you're like a creature from outer space.'

'You're talking just like them. If they think that of me, well, shouldn't I try to prove them wrong? And women are never totally alien to each other. We both love the children, Putlibai and I. Her world is so different, so much harsher. And here I am, living in the same country, and I don't even know what hardship is. I wanted to reach out to them, to . . . well, to convince them that I'm human too. And that there's some hope, that they shouldn't give up . . .'

'And then what? Are you going to invite them round for dinner?'

'Gopal, that's not the point.'

'Yes it is. You're being inconsistent.'

'Not really. They have their dignity, Gopal. I've never offered Putlibai anything. She'd throw it in my face.'

'So you just go there and offer them loving-kindness? What will happen when we have to go back home? Have you thought about that, or did you just follow your heart and plunge in?'

She was silent, then said slowly, 'Baby . . . one of the children . . . asked me the same thing today. I . . . I don't know what to say, to you, to myself. I told her . . . I'd try to arrange for help. But I have no idea how to do that. I . . . I was just so moved that I had to step forward, there was no way I could have walked past.'

Gopal patted her arm. 'That's my soft-hearted Viddy.'

'Oh Gopal, could I stay? Just until I could set up an organization to help them? I could come every once in a while and check on it. Please, Gopal.'

Gopal raised his eyebrows. 'That village belongs to the Centre, Vidura, you'd have to get permission from the Director, which quite frankly I can't see him giving.'

'The *Centre* owns that village?'

'Well, the land it's on. There's a buffer zone around this field station owned by us, so that no one can come and construct anything here. That would be a security risk. The village was there from beforehand, but we don't give permission for new construction, not that anyone's remotely about to build anything.'

'I see. And what about local administration, panchayats, all that sort of thing?'

He looked at her in surprise. 'You've been doing some thinking, I see. Well, the population hereabouts is so sparse that the local government hardly bothers with it. I think the village sends a representative to the panchayat, but the people hereabouts rather shun the Songarhis because they think they're cursed. They certainly look it.'

'Gopal, one of the women there told me that government doctors visit the village every few months. They stay here in the haveli. Do you know anything about that?'

'She must be mistaken. No authority can use this station except the Centre, and sending doctors to a place like this would be incredible efficiency for the village-level administration around here. No, they're probably quacks out to make a quick buck. Plenty of sick people for them to prey on.'

'Why are they so sick, do you think?'

'Malnutrition, poverty, bad drinking water, lots of insect vectors, poor hygiene, animals in the same buildings as humans. Oh, and opium. Need any more causes? Speaking of insect vectors, you need lice medicine fast. Let me ask the darwan if he has any.'

'No, don't; it's too embarrassing.'

'Well, madam, you'll have to keep your distance tonight, then. Are you game for a trip to Chittorgarh tomorrow? We'll start really early, at first light.'

'That sounds great.'

'We'll check in to a hotel there so we can freshen up, and you can rid yourself of creepy-crawlies. Wear a headscarf next time you go to visit your little friends.'

'I can't do that. They'll think I don't trust them.'

Gopal's face assumed the long-suffering look she dreaded. Before he could speak, she burst out, 'You think I'm a big silly, don't you? You think I'm amusing myself, playing the charity lady and slumming, and pretending I'm learning about life? Well, I've got news for you, mister. Those people are more genuine by far than your horrible, scheming, lying, nasty friends at the Centre. They may be poor and dirty and illiterate, but they'd never stab anyone . . .' Suddenly the room swam around her; her hands came up and clutched the edge of the table almost by reflex. She stared at the tabletop as though its scarred formica surface was the only real thing around. Her hands didn't seem to belong to her, they felt heavy and numb, deadweights. 'What's the matter?' Gopal's voice seemed to come from a long way away. He made her sit. A glass of water, held in his hand, appeared before her. She looked at it for a moment in dumb incomprehension. 'It's all right,' she mumbled, taking the glass with trembling hands. 'Just a bit dizzy.'

'Probably sunstroke.' But he looked a bit worried. 'I think you should go to bed early today. Then see how you feel tomorrow. If you like, we can postpone our trip. Or you can stay in bed and I'll go into town and get your medicine. Or we can send the driver, though I'm sure he's been nicking diesel. Feeling better now?'

'Yes.'

'You're all keyed up. Relax, Viddy, this is supposed to be a holiday.' He grinned his boyish grin. 'But to be on the safe side, I think we'd better get you checked out in Chittorgarh. You might have caught the odd something in that village. Nothing serious, I'm sure, but you don't have the antibodies.' He grinned again. 'British pathogens are far more civilized.'

'I've lived in this country for more than ten years now, Gopal.'

'Living in the Centre is like being in a self-contained space station. No wonder you're gobsmacked by real life. Poor Vidura, it's my fault for trying to make things easy for you. I should have . . .'

'Don't say it's your fault. It's always your fault. Why can't we take a holiday together, drat it?'

'But we are, at least when I'm not working.'

'No, no, you always ask me, "are you disappointed?" or "are you happy?" as though it's your job to make me happy and save me from disappointment. We don't take holidays together, you *give* me holidays. And you hover anxiously to see how I like it, and whether you need to do anything more to make it an unforgettable experience. Like a stupid tour guide. It really, really pisses me off.'

'Language, Vidura dear. No, don't get excited, I see what you mean. I can see why that annoys you. If I do it again tomorrow, just hit me with your handbag.'

She grinned, then laughed. 'I'm sorry,' she murmured, taking his hand. 'I don't know what's come over me, I'm all edgy and nervous. I guess it's seeing those children day after day, the way they live. It's . . . quite hard to take.'

'So I imagine. And I don't blame you for being fed up with the Centre; I'm pretty cheesed off with it as well. Only I can run away into my work. You can't, can you, Vidura darling? You've got nowhere to go.'

'I run away into the TV.'

'That's no escape. No, we need to think seriously about this. You know, your idea about an organization might be a good one, if we can get the necessary permission. It will keep you occupied, and I'm sure the Centre won't mind if you confine yourself to social work. They're a bit shirty about things like that, as you know, but we might bring them round. I mean, the Director's wife does all that charity work for the temple. Why should they object to your little venture?'

Vidura looked doubtful. 'I don't know. I thought of it on impulse, but how would I fund it? I'd need a school and a hospital at the very least, which means I'd have to pay staff, buy supplies, not to mention put up the buildings. Where would the money come from? And in the beginning there'd be a pile of organizational work to do, which I couldn't entrust to managers. It would be a huge task. Do you really think they'd give me permission?'

'Don't come down to reality with a bump, dear. Dream a bit more, we might find a way. And even if we don't, at least you'll have tried.'

'I suppose so.'

Satisfied, Gopal went back to his papers.

CHAPTER TWELVE

'Look, Vidura! Up there. Isn't it huge?'

It was only when she was right under the walls that Vidura realized the hill they were approaching was in fact the fort. Against the blinding sky great ramparts ran, rows and rows of thick embrasures with arrow slits winking with light. They had come through the crowded, sprawling town with its blue whitewashed houses and rows and rows of hotels and jewellers and souvenir shops. On the way she had asked their driver to take her to the most expert jeweller in Chittor, and there she had given the store owner the little round piece of Signal Red glass. 'I want it set like this,' she said, drawing a neat diagram on the back of a spoiled cash memo. 'How long will it take?' The man had said proudly, 'Three hours: my workmen are the best in Chittor. I do much work for foreigners.' She nodded. 'Three hours, then.' They settled the price. Gopal looked at her quizzically, but said nothing.

The car began to crawl up the ancient stone approach that zigzagged through a series of massive gates set in the stonework. The way seemed endless, as though they were climbing a road made for giants, even when they passed the junction of the village that nestled in the lap of the fort's great bulk with steep stone paths rising from it to the summit. And then they were there, at the final gate. Gopal leaned out of the car with some money in his fingers; they were waved through.

'Are we taking the car inside?'

'Yes dear, it's a huge place and I don't want you to tire yourself out.' Alongside them groups of children ran, clad in their garish best, laughing and calling to each other. The white Ambassador with 'Government of India' on the hood inched past. They stopped at the first ruin.

'This is said to be Padmini's winter palace,' Gopal said. 'Come on, I'll show it to you.'

They climbed the short ramp to the narrow door, surprisingly mean and unpretentious. Gopal pointed to a huge round structure facing it, like a gigantic rolling board. 'This is actually the back door of the fort. That thing down there is where they used to crush the building material for repairs and maintenance. They'd have a huge stone roller pulled by horses or bullocks. It was just under the balconies so the queen could supervise the whole thing. They were working queens, those Rajputs. We remember them for their beauty, but they were also as warlike as their husbands; they practically managed the place while he was away on campaign. Not decorative flowers by any means.'

They squeezed past an old dog drowsing in the doorway and came out into a courtyard of dressed stone, surrounded by the plinths of rooms and half-tumbledown walls. Gopal pointed to a delicate balcony that was still preserved.

'That was for sun worship. The Rajputs believed they were descended from the sun, so every morning and evening they had to salute it. Every Rajput palace has a place set aside for this. These were the stables. And that over there is the belvedere from which the king addressed his people.' She crossed the courtyard and looked down. 'They sat there in the plain to listen to him.'

'Could they even see him, so far away?'

Gopal shrugged. 'They'd see a lot of flashing gold, silk, colours, hear lots of royal noise. Kings in those days didn't have a lot to say to the people. It was enough to be seen to be ruling. The rest happened behind closed doors. Come over here, let me show you the real attraction of the place.'

She looked out at the other ruins scattered on the plateau, but Gopal was already striding down a narrow stone corridor, now roofless and ruined. 'See this hole with the steps going down?' he asked as she caught up with him. 'This used to be the underground passageway that took the queens and their attendants to the bathing ghat; the royal women were in purdah, of course, so no one was allowed to see them. They'd leave the palace through this tunnel and go to the *suraj kund*. I'll show you where the passage comes out. It widens out underground, and the ASI has found fragments of ash, bone and ornaments that suggest the queens must have burned themselves there. That must have been the last sack of Chittor, when Akbar invaded from the rear, that's the way we came up, in 1567. They must have been totally taken by surprise and didn't have time to go to the regular *sati sthal*, which is a platform near the Tower of Victory where the queens would sacrifice themselves when the fort was in danger of defeat. So they made do with the passage. Although I suspect they died of suffocation, really.'

She stared at the rectangular pit, like the entrance to someone's cellar, gruesome in its ordinariness. 'You can't go in now, the ASI has sealed it,' Gopal chattered on. 'Previously they allowed visitors and people almost tore the place apart, looking for souvenirs. So now this is as far as you can go.'

'It's horrible.'

'Yes, isn't it? But the rules were different in those days. There was no Geneva Convention, you know. Women got the worst of an invasion. And if they were dishonoured, the pure bloodline would be jeopardized, so they thought it best . . .'

'Gopal, don't tell me you approve of it?'

He shrugged. 'I don't, of course. But the times bring forth the necessary customs. Not that I know much about it; history isn't my line. But it seems to me fallacious to try and judge them by our standards. They did what was right for them.' He glanced at her. 'You don't agree, I take it.'

'I . . . I can't be so cold-blooded about it.'

'Okay, let me tell you a happy story.' He took her arm. 'See that palace over there? It's called Panna Dhai's palace. Panna Dhai was a nursemaid who saved the scion of Chittor during the last sack of the fort. She smuggled Prince Uday Singh out of the fort in a basket of old clothes. Uday Singh grew up to found Udaipur, which became the new capital of Mewar, and Panna Dhai sacrificed her own son by dressing him as the prince and presenting him to the invaders . . .'

'You call that a nice story?'

'Well, it shows that women weren't all helpless. They played politics along with the men, and sometimes more successfully. Immolating yourself is the ultimate political action, isn't it? In the olden days travellers used to take a sage or two along, so that if they were attacked the sage would threaten to kill himself and heap his death-curse on the heads of the robbers. It was a powerful threat. By killing themselves, the Rajput women were proving that they were better than the invaders, made of sterner stuff. It was a mind game. They figured their time was done anyway, so why not die nobly? It was worth it if they could deliver a psychological knockout punch to the enemy.'

'But it didn't work, did it? This place was sacked three times, and then the Rajput women started marrying the emperor anyway.'

'Yes, but didn't it come to pass that marrying a Rajput princess became the ultimate proof of emperorhood? Nearly all the Mughal emperors after Akbar had Rajput mothers and grandmothers. And didn't those princesses wield enormous power behind the throne? No one would have respected them like that if their sisters who died for the cause hadn't built up the legend.'

'So according to you it was all a good thing?'

'No, but I'm trying to show you they weren't victims.'

'And the children? The young girls?'

'Vidura,' he put his hand on her arm, 'you're getting upset. I'm sorry, I know I'm an insensitive git. You're right, it was horrible. Never mind. We won't go to see the *sati sthal* if it bothers you. Come on. Let's go back to the car.'

Back in the car, they inched forward through the crowd, which was mostly country people from their dress and language with a few bemused foreigners clutching guidebooks. There were large family parties in unnecessary sweaters talking loudly about what they'd had for dinner the night before. Gopal pointed out the Tower of Victory, with its bulbous head rising above the plateau. 'See the water tanks? They were all rain-fed. There are no springs on the plateau, and no agricultural land. The fort was impregnable, but it could only hold out as long as it had stores of food and water, which was about six months. Once it had surrounded Chittor the besieging army could leisurely gather the Rajputs' crops from the field under their very noses and leave them to starve. Given a sufficiently determined besieger, Chittor was doomed to fall every time.'

'Where are we going now?'

'Are you sure you don't want to see the other end of the tunnel and the *suraj kund*?'

'Only if there aren't any horrid stories to them.'

'Hmm, it'll probably be very crowded, and the stairs are wickedly slippery with the water from people bathing. No, forget it. Let's go to Padmini's summer palace instead. That's a more cheerful place, very pretty.'

The car crossed the worst of the crowds and picked up speed on the comparatively emptier road beyond. Isolated columns rose out of the dusty bushes; here a foundation, there a tank with crumbling stone steps going down each of the four sides. All were dry. Far away there were ramparts, and below them, down on the plain, the blue shapes of closely-packed houses to be glimpsed through breaks in the walls. They stopped at a long, low whitewashed building. 'Here we are.' He helped her out of the car. 'You look a little tired. Are you okay?'

'I'm fine, Gopal. Do we have to pay here as well?'

'No, just show them your ticket.'

There were people here too, nearly all country folk out for the day, the men in western clothes, the women mobile bundles of bright jewel-coloured cloth, invisible from head to toe. There was a group of reed-thin boys, all teenage smirks in tight shiny trousers, with twisted scarves tied round their heads. They had one camera between the twelve of them. They followed women with their eyes and grinned behind their hands.

There was really no building; only walls around a courtyard and, to the right, ruins. On either side of the stone path, beds of roses nodded in bright jewel colours. 'Probably wouldn't have been there in Padmini's time,' Gopal said, pointing. 'Roses came with the Mughals.' Vidura bent to sniff them.

Behind them voices whispered. 'Ever seen one like that?'

'Bigger than Lali's!'

'Look at it! Round like a pumpkin!'

'Raju, hey, take a picture!'

The flash went off behind her. She straightened sharply from the rose she was inspecting and looked around. Gopal frowned and took her arm. 'Come on, I'll show you Padmini's little hideaway on the lake.'

They came through another courtyard, and another, to a little whitewashed cell with prosaic wire mesh on its three windows. Through the central window they saw a white building standing in a few feet of muddy water, utterly featureless but for a small portico with steps leading to the water. That was all there was to see. She turned, and noticed a huge mirror above the door they had come in. Gopal grinned. 'Stand here.' He positioned her in the middle of the room. 'Look in the mirror. What do you see through the window?'

'The steps of the little white house leading to the water.'

'Now turn around and look through the window. Can you still see the steps?'

'No.'

'Remember the story of Padmini? Alauddin Khilji, the emperor of Delhi, saw her picture and became infatuated with her. He laid siege to Chittor just because of her. Then when the people of the fort were in dire straits he told the king, her husband Ratan Sen, that he'd lift the siege and go away if he could only get one glimpse of Padmini. But of course she was in strict purdah, so what was poor Ratan Sen to do? He brought Alauddin up here, and said, look only in the mirror, you'll see her face reflected in the water. So the emperor did, but he broke his promise and turned round to look, when of course he couldn't see anything. And he was so enraged that he sacked Chittor anyway.'

Some women entered the little room, tugging on their rose-coloured veils with swift hands at the sight of a strange man, instantly becoming non-people. And there outside the door were the boys from the garden. Their gazes flitted indifferently over the bright bundles of the women to rest on Vidura again.

'You're standing in the very spot where Alauddin fell for the Rajput queen.'

He looked at her expectantly. She felt moved to say something.

'How . . . how pointless. Pointless and tragic. Why . . . why should one human being do that to another, and to one that he . . . he *loved*, in a sense? Why, Gopal?'

'Vidura . . .'

And then a great weariness came over her. 'Let's go. I've had enough. My feet hurt.'

'Oh dear. Would you like to rest a bit before we set off again?'

'No, Gopal.' She tried not to sound impatient. The boys were making no effort to get out of the way as she took a step towards the door. They stood silently shoulder to shoulder, as though they had paid their price and wouldn't budge till the show was over. Then Gopal pushed forward, and his frown scattered them. She was free. Holding on to Gopal's arm and hunching her shoulders she came out into the sun. She clung close to Gopal as they went back to the car, almost pushing him out of the gate in her hurry to get away. He said nothing, but as the car made its way back down the hill and through the traffic-clogged streets to the hotel she could feel his gaze on her. She saw herself suddenly like a person she didn't know, reflected in his puzzled eyes.

★

'Here's your tea.' Gopal pushed the cup towards her. 'Are you sure you don't want anything more?'

'Yes. It's the heat; it takes away your appetite.'

Gopal looked at her carefully. 'You look . . . well, not ill, but sort of . . . stretched, as though you're . . . I don't know . . . excited or . . . Vidura, are you taking any medication?'

Vidura gave him a look. 'What sort of question is that?'

'No, it's just the way you've been acting, not like your usual self at all. I don't mind admitting it's making me nervous. Please, Vidura, tell me what's going on.'

'Nothing's going on.' Vidura sipped her tea, trying to sound calm.

'Don't be annoyed. I'm only trying to help.'

'I'm not annoyed, Gopal. There's nothing wrong with me and I haven't been taking happy pills, if that's what you're worried about.'

'Please Vidura, don't be angry.' He put his hand on hers. 'I'm just really, really anxious about you.'

She sighed. 'I know what you mean . . . I've been sort of surprised at myself as well. I've been doing things and thinking thoughts I never would have done and thought before, reacting in strange ways, feeling . . . I don't know . . . different about everything. You say it's not like me at all, and maybe you're right; god knows you've known me long enough. Only . . . Gopal, what *is* "like me"? I mean really me, deep down inside?'

'Eh?'

'The way I've been at the Centre, with you . . . the way I've been for years . . . I don't know, sometimes I'm heartily sick of who I am. Or what I've become.'

'What have you become?' Gopal asked a little nervously.

Vidura shrugged, and put the cup down. 'A caricature of myself.'

'What on earth are you talking about?'

'I wish I knew, Gopal. I've been trying to find words to express it, but . . . it's like trying to stick a pin in water. It's not that I'm unhappy: don't get me wrong. There's nowhere else I want to be but with you. But . . . Gopal, when we were young, in Cambridge, did you dream about what our life together would be like?'

'Er . . . maybe.'

'Is this what you thought it would be like?'

Gopal looked around the hotel dining room, with its tarnished mirror work and dusty puppets presiding over plush polyester chairs and wrought iron tables, the whole shrouded in the gloom of sun film peeling off the windows, trying ineffectually to tame the light. 'Can't say I did.'

'No, silly, I don't mean *this*, I mean everything. All of it.' She moved her hands as though trying to gather into them a wide heavy tapestry.

'Um . . . I didn't have a very clear idea . . . I mean, of course we'd be together, we'd have a home . . . maybe a kid or two.'

'Yes,' said Vidura heavily.

Gopal reached across and took her hand. 'Viddy,' he said softly. 'That's what draws you to those children, isn't it? Look, what say we adopt a child? We've waited long enough. Let's do it before it's too late.'

'Is it too late?'

'I don't think so. Do you? Maybe we should have done it before, when it became clear we weren't having any luck.'

Tears pricked Vidura's eyes. 'It shouldn't matter. You and I should be enough for each other. It's so . . . so Malti Prasad, if you know what I mean. As though people get married only to have kids, and once they've safely done that they can forget about each other and go on with their lives. You know what people say; every time a young couple has a tiff it's all "Oh, it'll be all right when the baby comes", and then when the baby does come, wonder of wonders, the two people have got something to talk about, something to do, they don't spend the evenings getting on each other's nerves any more . . .'

'It won't be like that for us. It doesn't have to be, you know.'

She looked at him with eyes blurred with tears. 'But you're hardly ever home. I'd have to bring her up on my own almost. That's not what I want.'

'That'll change. I'd be delighted to spend more time at home; I've reached the stage in my life where I can if I want. Look, Viddy, we won't be doing it for . . . those reasons. There's no pressure from the family; my parents have given up asking for grandchildren. It'll just be us: you, me and the baby; a family. Why are you so doubtful? We're lonely, both of us. It'll be magic in our lives.'

She blotted her eyes with the paper napkin. 'I hope you're right, Gopal. But it's such a big responsibility, bringing up a child. It's an obligation for years and years. Can we handle it? And will the poor thing be able to take being adopted? You know what the Centre people are like. They won't let their kids play with her, and they'll treat her like . . .'

'They'll just have to educate themselves. People will adjust to things if they have no choice. We'll hold our heads high; they'll have to accept us, in the end. If we apologize for it they'll walk all over us.'

'I wish we could move to the city,' Vidura murmured.

Gopal patted her hand. 'I'll start looking at adoption agencies,' he said. 'As soon as we're back at the Centre. Trust me, Viddy, it's the answer to all our problems. I can see how miserable you are, however much you put a brave face on it, Viddy darling. It's cruel of me to leave you alone all day; I hate it. At least with the baby you'll have company. And I'll come home and play with her every day.'

'That's not . . .' then she opened her hand and let the scrunched-up napkin roll onto the table. 'They'll think I'm cheating.'

'What?'

'Those people at the Centre. As it is they think I'm a fake, I'm not really a wife, as they understand the word. And every time they talk about it . . . us not having kids . . . they nod and purse their lips and look smug. They'll think I've finally bowed to them, that I want to be like them, be validated as a mother like them. And they'll scorn me, because even my motherhood will be a fake. Oh, Gopal . . .'

'Viddy, Viddy, don't think like that. Don't let them defeat you. Viddy, no.' He handed her another paper napkin. 'Well, to make you feel better, Viddy, let me tell you a piece of gossip. I didn't tell you at the time because I know you hate gossip. Remember Minnie Chandravarkar?'

'Raghav Chandravarkar's wife? What about her?'

'She's got a young son, right?'

'Yes, three years old. Why?'

'He isn't hers.'

'What? But . . .'

'She went home pretty early, stayed there throughout the "pregnancy", came back with a baby boy a year later. But the baby was already ten months old. Rumour has it it's Raghav's cousin's son; she had fraternal twins, both boys, "lent" one to her sister-in-law. It was all planned by the family. Birth certificate and everything.' He chuckled. 'Pot calling the kettle black.'

'But I'm not going to go through all that ridiculous pretence. It's so *sick*. I won't hide it, Gopal, I can't, it'll be public knowledge, it has to be. I couldn't lie to them, I'd feel so . . . unclean. And . . . they'll be even more vicious because of their guilty secrets. They will, Gopal. You don't know what they're like.'

'I know well enough,' he said grimly. 'Let them try it, that's all I'll say. I'll give them something to talk about all right. Don't worry, Viddy, I know enough of their secrets to shut them up for good. You won't have to worry.'

Vidura twisted the paper napkin between her fingers, staring at her lap.

'I'll just go and make some phone calls,' Gopal said. 'I won't be long. Order some more tea if you want.' He went out to the reception desk. The clerk there directed him to the office, where a tatty booth housed a dusty telephone. As Gopal laid a hand on the door to the booth someone pushed it open from inside.

'Oh! Hello, Chandran. Having a nice holiday?'

'Prasad! What the hell are you doing here?'

'Same as you; playing truant from work.' Prasad eased his long body out of the booth. He yawned. 'Drove all night down from Delhi. Had to pack my driver off; the man was exhausted. I was just coming to spring myself on you in the dining room. Can I come along with you to the field station? Otherwise I'll have to wait till tomorrow.'

'Certainly. But what are you doing with Signal Red?'

'Field work, just like you.' Prasad winked. 'How's your charming wife?'

'Fine. How did you know we were at this hotel?'

'Called ahead to the station. Talked to the caretaker. He said the darwan was mighty glad memsaab wasn't there to take him walkies. What has the lady been up to, Gopal?'

Gopal felt heat beginning to suffuse his cheeks. 'She's been busy. Why?'

'Just concern for her health. The sun can play nasty tricks on you if you spend too long in it.'

'Vidura's capable of looking after herself.'

'Hmm. What's this I hear about a school?'

'School?'

'Hasn't she set up a school in the village?'

'No, she hasn't, Prasad, if it's any of your business. She just teaches some of the kids there, informally.'

'I hope you realize that village falls within the purview of the Centre's field station.'

'So what?'

'Civilians aren't allowed to operate there,' Prasad said blandly.

Gopal clenched his teeth. 'That's all nonsense. Vidura is not a "civilian" and she isn't "operating" there.'

'Well what is she doing? Organizing a kitty party?'

'My wife will do as she wishes and sees fit,' he growled.

'You're terribly trusting for a married man, Gopal.'

'Are you insinuating that my wife . . .'

'Oh no, no, don't get me wrong, of course not. It's just that you know the rules, and you ought to keep her in line. She can do her charity in Sitarampur, but not in Songarh. It's a protected area, which means, "Keep Off". You know that, Gopal, and I'm sure you've told her once or twice, but it's up to you to make your authority stick. I'm afraid I'll have to report this security breach to the Director. And if you can't even get your own wife to obey you, I'm afraid you're going to be a poor prospect for promotion, and I have it on authority that the Director was thinking of you for a pretty big post. I'm just telling this to you as a friend. Stop snorting.'

'I do not,' Gopal said icily, 'keep Vidura "in line".'

'Well, you should. My wife is quite happy to take my lead; she would never dream of going against my express command.'

'Vidura is not like your wife!' Gopal shouted.

'That's your problem in a nutshell,' Prasad said sympathetically. 'It's not good to have a wife who is so educated; they become dissatisfied. You can't make them happy with jewellery and saris; they want fulfilment and space, whatever that means. I appreciate that it's tough for you, Gopal, but you really must try and get her under control. You're not on a UNICEF junket; this is serious business. So keep her out of that village.' With a look of almost indecent satisfaction on his face, Prasad waved airily and disappeared into the foyer.

CHAPTER THIRTEEN

The red light of sunset had died by the time they arrived at the haveli. Prasad had snored through most of the trip, sprawled on the front seat next to the driver, his long legs scrunched awkwardly into the kneehole under the dash, among the makeshift tools and jerrycans of water. His head lolled on the back of the seat, rolling this way and that with the jerking of the car. Vidura and Gopal sat stiffly at the back, unable to talk to each other. Vidura tried to breathe through the bubble of annoyance that seemed to coat her throat with bitterness. She felt cheated, betrayed, and that feeling left no room for rational thought.

When Gopal had finally returned to the dining room that afternoon, more than twenty minutes had passed. He had barely begun to apologize when Prasad strode in breezily and announced that he had told the driver to be ready to leave in half an hour; it wasn't safe to be out too late on the roads. He had chivvied them off to their room to pack. Gopal hurriedly told her about his meeting with Prasad she had had no chance to question him about it. All she registered was the suppressed anger with which he recounted the conversation, nothing of what caused it.

The thought of Prasad's company had filled her with deep dismay. When they were barely ready Prasad had herded them down to the car and off as though seven devils were after him and then promptly fallen asleep. His manner was that of an

exasperated tour guide with a bevy of pensioners to look after,
yet this was *their* car, wasn't it? *He* was the guest.

It was evening when they arrived at the haveli. Supper was
not a convivial affair. Prasad ate his vegetarian meal at top
speed and disappeared into the other room without even taking
his leave. Vidura was relieved, but she did not speak to Gopal
until they were in their own bedroom.

'All right, Gopal. Tell me what on earth's going on.'

Gopal shrugged helplessly. 'He was the last person in the
world I expected to see in that hotel lobby. But it turns out he's
down here for field work, or as he says. Damned if I know
what that means. He hasn't had anything to do with the project
till now. That I know of, at any rate.'

'Why would the Director put him on Signal Red? He works
in—what was it again?'

'Nano-powders,' Gopal said shortly. 'I can't imagine what
interest he could have down here. There's absolutely nothing
connected with his field.'

'Why were you gone so long at the phone? Was he talking
to you?'

'He buttonholed me before I could make any calls and by
the time I'd got rid of him there was a queue. I was boiling
by then; he really got under my skin. He . . . he wanted to
know about your visits to the village; the caretaker told him
about them. And then he read me the Riot Act about the whole
business.'

'What on earth for?'

'I haven't a clue. First he said he was concerned for your
health, then he said the Director wouldn't like it and he was
going to report me for a security breach. He even accused me
of not "keeping you in line" and compared you unfavourably
to Malti, of all people. Load of impertinent nonsense! He seems
to think it's part of my job description to treat you like a
doormat.'

'Don't they all? I suppose he told you to emulate his

splendid example.'

'No prizes for guessing that one. And it wasn't just what he said, it was the way he said it, as if he was having a good laugh at our expense. All the same, while he's here it'll probably be wise to avoid going to the village. We don't want to give him an excuse to nag the life out of us.'

Vidura bit her lip. 'I see.'

Gopal sighed. 'Do you want tea? It's getting rather chilly already, isn't it?'

'Yes, please.' Gopal called the cook and asked for tea. They went into the bedroom. Vidura watched Gopal sort through a mound of papers. 'We're nearly finished,' he said. 'I should think I can wrap it all up in a couple of days and we can go home.'

'That's good, dear.'

'And the Centre will be Prasad-less for a while, because he'll be stuck here. Whoopee!'

'You don't like him either, do you?'

'He has a brilliant mind but he's an insufferable person, I'm afraid. Odd how those things so often go hand in hand. My guess is the genes are located on the same chromosome.'

'Gopal, did he say anything in particular about . . . me and the village?'

'Apart from what I told you? Not that I recall.'

'Do you know of any . . . dangerous project that was carried out here that might have affected the village?'

'Here? No. The Centre's only taken over this place for three or four years, since the government lost interest in exploiting the glass. Signal Red is the first project that's ever run here.'

The tea arrived. Vidura wrapped her hands around her cup and asked, 'Could there have been a secret project?'

Gopal frowned. 'It's always possible, but unlikely. The place was completely untouched when we set up the field station, as far as I know. Of course, I wouldn't have been told if there had been, but I don't think it's likely.'

'I see.'

'Nevertheless, Prasad wouldn't have talked to me like that if he didn't feel totally secure about giving me hell about that village. Which probably means that messing around in it is really a no-no and the bosses are going to be unhappy if they find out. Although he may just be bluffing; he can't resist having a go at people if he thinks he can get away with it.' Gopal gathered up the papers. 'I'll just go file these. Be right back.'

'Gopal,' she said as he was leaving.

'Yes?'

'Have you ever . . . . Has it ever come to your notice that the authorities have lied to you?'

Gopal frowned. 'No. Why do you ask?'

'Would they lie? I mean, if it were really important?'

'No, they just wouldn't tell you. Information is controlled on a need-to-know basis.'

'I see.'

'Don't worry about it, Vidura darling.' He looked a bit closer at her face. 'What's the matter?'

'Nothing, just . . . I so wanted us to be alone tonight, in Chittor, away from the Centre and its muck, not back here. I wanted . . . wanted to celebrate, with you. A new beginning. And he spoiled it. He spoiled it so thoroughly I . . . I can't see the point of . . . of . . .'

'I know, Viddy, I know. I was looking forward to it as well. I'll make it up to you somehow, don't worry.'

'It's not that. I wanted it to be an occasion, because . . . But I can't give it to you now. Somehow it's not right any more. And yet . . .'

'Not right? Give me what?'

Wordlessly she unclasped her handbag and took out a small box, opened it and handed it to him. 'For you,' she said in a flat voice. 'Because you always give me things, and I felt it was about time I did my share.'

He put the pile of papers down and took the box from her. It was the piece of Signal Red glass, held in four tiny gold claws.

'It's a tiepin,' she said tonelessly. 'Do you like it?'

'It's beautiful. Is this what you had the jeweller make? You designed it yourself? Vidura, you're a genius.' He kissed her tenderly on the cheek. 'You had me wondering: my Viddy doesn't normally hit town and head for jewellery. I should have known.'

'Glad you like it,' she said, but she knew her voice didn't sound like she meant it.

★

The next morning she woke heavy-headed and disoriented, and lay like that for some time before remembering where she was. She rose with a start—it was 10.30 a.m. She bounded out of bed, then almost cried out as a wave of dizziness and nausea threatened to throw her to the floor. She groped for the bathroom door and hung on for long minutes as the ground churned under her feet. Then she stumbled inside and threw up. Great heaves convulsed her body; thin threads of mucous ran down her chin. The heat from the tin roof beat down upon her head, but the water in the bucket was cool on the skin of her face.

Oh god, she thought, holding on to the towel rack. *Perhaps I really am ill.*

She felt curiously heavy and unbalanced, as though perpetually about to fall over. *Have I been drugged?* she wondered. *No, surely not. Who could possibly have drugged me?*

But I certainly feel very strange.

'Memsaab!' exclaimed the cook when she appeared in the dining room. 'Prasad Sir was looking for you!'

'Really?' she said, annoyed all over again. 'I don't want breakfast; just give me some tea.'

The tea tasted like dishwater. She pushed it away half-drunk. What should she do with herself now? She was feeling a little better; in fact, now that the nausea had passed, her head felt preternaturally clear, as though the poison had drained out and the world had swum back into focus. *Must be something I ate,* she thought.

'Good morning.'

Oh no. 'Good morning, Mr Prasad. I trust you slept well?'

'Slept? I've been working since 5 a.m. And now I can't find the damn driver. He's making me late.' In spite of his words he sat down as if he had all the time in the world. 'And how have you been?'

'Fine.'

'In perfect health?' His eyes bored into hers.

'Of course. Why, shouldn't I be?'

'I only hope you continue like that. But let me give you some advice, Mrs Chandran. Stay away from those people. You should have more sense than to spend time in a dirty village.'

'Really? Well, Mr Prasad, I've listened patiently to your advice, and I must say it doesn't impress me. In any case, the fact that the village is dirty reflects badly on the landlord who I'm given to understand is your employer. Surely its condition is a scandal for the Centre?'

'Scandal? We don't use that word about the Centre, which is my employer and your husband's. The Centre has its own policy for the village. As for "scandal", all information about the village is classified and will stay that way. What that means, Mrs Chandran, is that if you breathe a word about it to the press or that friend of yours from Mumbai, you and Chandran will face severe penalties. You should stay out, that's all I'm saying.'

'Why?'

He glared at her, baffled. 'Can't you do as you're told?'

She stood up and faced him. 'You're talking about a village of real, live people who are living in subhuman conditions because you, Mr Prasad, or people like you, can't be bothered to help them. And you know something, Mr Prasad? I had almost decided not to go there again, but your attitude sorely tempts me, I must say.'

'Do you mean you'd go there just to spite me?'

'Haven't you heard of something called politeness?'

'Oh,' he looked amused. 'I'm sorry if I ruffled your feathers. I'm a simple man of science, not even a PhD like your husband; I don't understand your fancy foreign ways. In this country we speak our minds. I'm just advising you for your own good.'

'I'm fed up of being advised for my own good. You're all determined to treat me like a child. And you have no idea, *no idea*, of the real world you say I'm out of touch with. Tell me, Mr Prasad, have you ever been poor? I mean really, really dirt poor with nothing to call your own?'

'No, but then neither have you.'

'I don't think I'm better than the rest of the world because of it.'

'Oh, so you're a liberal as well as a social worker. Will you be applying to the UN? Or to Save the Children?' He was almost laughing now; his eyes glittered with glee at the joke.

'The point I'm trying to make, Mr Prasad . . .'

'Is no doubt an interesting and valid one, but I'm afraid I don't have time for it.' He got up. 'I'm warning you, Mrs Chandran, stay out of that village or you'll come to regret it. And please don't set this up as some sort of personal vendetta between you and me; that really would be childish. Please believe me when I say I have your best interests at heart. I think it was very wrong of the Director to send you here, but then he does not understand your mind as I do. I'm afraid most of us really find it incomprehensible when women like you act in this headstrong fashion.'

'Is anything the matter?' It was Gopal, looking from one to the other with concern. Prasad looked away and laughed. 'No, nothing.'

Gopal took in Vidura's pale, determined face, the dark circles under her eyes, the glint of bone showing under the skin of her forehead. 'I just came to see how you were, Vidura. You look very . . . . Is anything wrong?'

'Ask him.'

Prasad snorted. 'I was merely telling Mrs Chandran she ought not to visit the village. Really, you are making an inordinate fuss over a little thing, Mrs Chandran. You aren't here on a guided tour of Rajasthan; you've come to provide support and comfort to your husband while he works. Can't you occupy your time without getting mixed up in things that don't concern you? If not, then I really think you should return to the Centre. Gopal, I think Mrs Chandran is bored here. What do you think?'

'Vidura can speak for herself.'

'Yes, regrettably. She seems to think there's some dark plot behind my friendly advice. Do forgive me, Chandran, I thought *I'd* speak to her as *you* seemed to be having no success. Sometimes an impartial outside voice does the trick. But I see she's as stubborn as ever.' He put a hand on Gopal's shoulder. 'You have my sympathies.' And with the same ghoulish look of satisfaction he went out. Vidura turned on her heel without a word, went to her room and lay down. 'Just leave me alone,' she murmured to Gopal. 'I'll be okay when I stop being furious.'

Much later, Gopal came to call her for lunch, his face grim. She knew at once that Prasad had spoken to him, but she did not question him about it; how did the answers matter? She was not free; he was not free. They were more locked in than Putlibai in her crumbling mud hut. Now she really felt as if the village was in another world, governed by different rules, warmed by a different sun. No means had yet been invented that could transport her from this world to that. She was exiled, hedged about with barriers. All her lofty hopes had come crashing down.

That is all my friendship is worth, she thought: *the fear of an angry look from a powerful person. Putlibai was right. My kind are owned by others; the plots of our lives are written by other hands. We can only mouth our lines, take our cues. We're puppets. Without the hand of authority to stiffen our backs, we're as limp and powerless as rag dolls.*

She remembered the dusty folk-art puppets that had decorated the hotel's dining room: the men with their ridiculous thread moustaches, the women with their shiny skirts. All alike, all frozen in that same silly half-smile. They had kept her company for twenty minutes while her fate had been decided in another room.

Prasad did not turn up for lunch. Gopal and she ate in silence; she tried to shut her ears to the unbearable sound of food being chewed. Then Gopal went back to work, and she returned to her silent room, lay down again, her hands and feet neatly aligned as if four men would come any moment and lift the bed shoulder-high, carry her out of the door and away from life.

She stared at the rough ceiling, aghast at her own feelings. She would never have believed that such volcanic, incandescent rage was possible inside her own body. Rage like molten lead spilled out of her head and down her throat into the bile-pit of her stomach, it ran like fire along fuses into her nerves and tingled in the soles of her feet. *I must destroy something or die,* she thought, and the fire whirled higher for there was nothing within her reach that she could blast apart with her human bomb of rage.

I'll start with Prasad's face, she thought, *and then I'll ride the wind to the Centre and tear it apart brick by brick, and scatter the people over the four corners of the world so they'll never come together in smug harmony again. I'll pulverize them, I'll turn them to less than dust.*

After a while the feeling faded. She sat up and smiled, bitterly, ironically at herself. She was well-mannered, mild little Vidura again. *Of course I take it back,* she thought. *I always take it back.*

But maybe not this time.

Spots of light reflected from the floor had moved, tracing the arc of the sun's rays narrowing their angle to the earth; this face of the planet was slowly turning to the dark of space again. Out there, beyond the earth's insubstantial skin of air, was unimaginable nothing, so hostile that even death was alien to it. The whole solar system adrift in that void was far, far less than a whirl of mica in the wind.

She got up suddenly, as though the bed had grown red-hot. Without looking to left or right, she crammed her feet into shoes and walked out into the road. She did not stop to check whether the darwan saw her or not; it did not matter. By the time they realized, she would be far away.

She walked. The light was still golden, but it had a hint of red in it; the sunset was bleeding into the dying day. There were new tracks in the road, Jeep tracks. They turned off the road after a little way. Her feet felt the rough unevenness of rock and mud dried hard as rock under her thin soles. This was what the earth would look like when it was dead, when all life had played out its pathetic drama and left the earth less than a grave. Atoms and molecules would resume their brute chemical dance, untroubled by the whirligigs of genes, the cycles of eating and rotting. Dust would no longer gather water within subtle lattices and rear its height above the earth—if it moved, it would only be by the wind's dead strength. There would be no throats left to choke upon its mineral harshness; the only voice that would howl would be the wind's.

She walked on. Far ahead, the shapes of the huts were prematurely dark in the scintillating landscape of afternoon, like the humps of beached turtles left helpless by the receding tide. The sun flashed on the nugget of glass in the wall as she passed it. She did not notice if there were people about; she had just one goal to reach. She came to the hut and entered it without breaking her stride, as if it were her own home. At

first in the dark she could see nothing, then the reddening chinks
in the walls showed her the shapes of children. Three lay there,
huddled together, too exhausted even to whimper. Baby and
Juggu were missing. The stillness of the three little shapes
alarmed her, but her hands told her they were warm and
breathing. As she stroked their scarecrow bodies, a long, low
cry reached her ears.

She crouched at the entrance and listened. It came again,
hoarse, and tailing off into a sob. Yes, it was Baby's voice.
She got up carefully and stood before the hut, turning her head
this way and that. Again.

'Jugggguuuuuu!'

That way. She walked on past the other huts, to the broken-
down wall, clambered over it. In the plain beyond she saw a
small dark figure running towards the sun, her rags flapping
with the wind of her speed. Vidura ran too, following the little
silhouette, but the girl was faster. Falling behind, Vidura called,
'Baby!'

The girl stopped and looked round wildly.

'Baby!'

'Ma-ji!' She dashed to Vidura and threw her arms around
her waist. 'Ma-ji! Mai hasn't come back! Juggu went to look
for her, now he's gone too. What shall I do?'

'Where had Mai gone? Was she with the goats?'

Baby nodded fearfully, her eyes round with unspoken fears.
'The one who was pregnant died yesterday. Mai was up with
her all night. She could barely keep her eyes open in the
morning. I said I'd go, but no, she had to go. And now Juggu
is gone too. I didn't want to leave him with the others and go
myself; he always fights. Come on, we must search!' She tugged
at Vidura's hand, her splayed feet throwing up dust as she tried
to drag Vidura into the agony of her own abandonment.

'Which way did she go?'

Baby pointed. Far ahead there was a dark mound of rock
and scrub on the bright land. 'She went to the death forest, like

every day. Oh, quickly, before the light goes, ma-ji, we must find her. Chhotu is starving. He will die! We must look for Mai and Juggu and the goats!' Baby rushed ahead.

Vidura took the small torch out of her purse and held it ready in her hand. Then she followed.

They stumbled over the shifting gravel-and-sand dunes for some ten minutes. From time to time Vidura had to slow to a walk; Baby ran on ahead, calling, crying. As they climbed the scree-ridden slope Vidura saw it was a low broken rise fringing a hollow, covered with a mangy coat of bushes and thorns about the height of a man, with a few taller shrubs here and there. It did not seem to extend very far, though it was difficult to tell in the uncertain light. Baby stood on a big rock at the top of the slope and called, 'Maiiiii! Maiiiii! Jugguuuu!'

Vidura looked down at the darkening basin, then she pushed a little way into the undergrowth, the small beam of her torch pointing the way. She too called, 'Putlibai! Putlibai!' her own voice thin and reedy between Baby's rasping shrill shouts. The scrub played tricks with the waning light; shadows multiplied each bush. Baby crept up close and held her hand.

'We have to leave before it's dark,' Vidura whispered. 'Otherwise we'll be lost too.' Baby clutched her arm and breathed noisily.

There was no sound: all was deathly silent. Vidura looked up at the sky between the thorn branches. 'We have to go, Baby. We'll look for them in the morning. It's no use. Come, the others will be wondering where we are. I can try and find some milk for Chhotu for tonight.'

Baby nodded.

Vidura turned to go back the way they had come. They had only been there a minute, a straight retreat should get them out. She looked down at Baby's small head. Would a search party tomorrow be too late? But they had tried, now, here; Baby would not grieve that the search had been given up too easily. Then she realized that in Baby's world grief was currency only for the living; you saved it up for yourself, because those who were dead didn't need it. What Baby was looking for was news that would tell her whether to open her little store of grief for the children who were left. She tucked the girl's hand more securely under her elbow. 'I'm sure nothing's happened to them. We'll find them in the morning.'

They had only been there a few minutes, but the sun was leaving them now. Above her head she could see light in the sky, but her feet were invisible as if she floated in black water. It seemed harder to move her hands and feet against that viscid tide, dark as blood or slime. She pushed on. Her torch picked out a few branches and stems in blinding detail, throwing the rest into darkness. Shapes of disembodied light seemed to jump out at them. She wrapped her dupatta round her forearm and brushed away the thorns from her face, trying to shield Baby with her body. Her feet stumbled and rocked on the loose stones underfoot. She looked again at the sky and led Baby on.

A branch snapped somewhere ahead, sounding like a pistol shot.

Vidura felt something jump in her throat. She pressed a hand to her mouth, trying to keep the torch steady with the other. The bitter taste of the morning was spreading again upon her tongue, making it difficult to breathe. She forced her feet forward, the padded forearm before her face; she could feel the thorns tearing their fill from it. Baby clung to her arm and whimpered; Vidura tried to see what she was looking at, but there was only darkness. 'Come on.'

She started forward again, trying to sidestep the thorns. Her carefully mapped bearings were in danger of dissolving. How had she walked in so easily? Now the bushes forced her to follow a winding path; trying to make headway, she pressed against the branches where they seemed weakest. Hollows yawned beneath her feet; she could hardly see where she was stepping. Every so often Baby's feet slipped and her weight dragged at Vidura's arm. Vidura paused to get her balance and steady her own head. The sky was blood-red now. That strange, dark shape far ahead must be the rock at the head of the slope.

A puff of wind clattered the thorns together, an evil merry little sound. Heat rose from the earth like warmth from a new corpse. The darkness was congealing, thickening around her limbs; she could feel it rising above her head. She fought the feeling: *This is just a forest. There is a child with me; I must be brave for her.* A deep throb of pain had begun in the small of her back, radiating down her legs so that each step seemed to stab the soles of her feet. The shape of the rock seemed to have moved away. The stars; why were there no stars? Something like a cloud seemed to be gusting against the sky. There was a strange smell, like a room that hadn't been opened for years.

And then the thorns moved back and showed her a clearing over which the beam of her torch shot like a harpoon line leaping for the whale's heart. Light glittered on slick black skin and shiny metal and then, as the torch jerked up in her hands, someone shouted her name and two huge chitinous eyes blazed out of a black man-shape and into her face.

PART III

GOPAL

CHAPTER FOURTEEN

'You've been very lucky,' the doctor said, putting the sheaf of test results down on his desk and looking up at Gopal. The clean white room they were in was in the Centre's own clinical facility that was attached to the Bioscience department. A week ago on the night of Putlibai's disappearance Vidura had been airlifted back to the Centre by helicopter, thanks to Prasad's connections. Dr Golwalkar had been flown in from Delhi to attend her. She was in isolation on the second floor; all visitors had been expressly forbidden. 'In fact, I'm amazed at your luck.'

Gopal rubbed his temples. 'I suppose I should take your word for it.'

'No, really. When I saw the list of tests Mr Prasad gave us to do I have to say I didn't give two paise for your wife's chances, but so far she's clean. Like I said, only tremendous luck could have brought her through, and in her condition!'

'Her condition?'

'You're even luckier than you think. She's pregnant.'

'What!'

'Five months gone at the very least.'

'But . . .'

'Look, just because you didn't suspect doesn't mean it's impossible.' The doctor's eyes twinkled. 'Your wife should have realized, but she told me it never crossed her mind. I had to give her a tranquillizer after I told her.'

'My god! Is she all right?'

'She's fine. About the baby, well, it's too soon to tell. But all signs so far are normal. We will of course keep her under the closest observation and make sure that the baby develops normally. All the nasties on this list have short incubation times; they'd be worthless for R&D otherwise. Antibody concentrations don't indicate a high exposure. Since your wife hasn't shown any symptoms so far, I think we can be cautiously optimistic.' The doctor held out a hand. 'Congratulations!'

Like a man in a dream Gopal took his hand. 'Can I see her?'

'She's sleeping now. Try tomorrow; we don't want to excite her too much, you understand. She is of course rather over-age to be a primigravida, but her hormone levels are within acceptable limits, so I don't think there'll be a problem. The history of dysmenorrhoea needs to be investigated, but I suspect the pregnancy itself will clear that up. We'll run more tests to make sure.'

'And there's no long-term damage from her ordeal?'

'Physically, as far as we have determined, no. Mentally, I'm not so sure. She was raving about a monster whenever she came to in the first few days; that's gone now. From her description it seems she saw the researchers in protective gear. In bad light and in her state it's not surprising that she couldn't process what she saw. Humour her if she tells you stories of aliens or monsters. After a while the memories will fade. How much of the truth you tell her is up to you, but I would recommend that you keep it to the absolute minimum. Quite apart from security, we don't want to alarm her unnecessarily. And we have to think of the child, obviously.'

'Of course.'

'As far as possible, prevaricate if she wants to know the fate of the woman and her children. Let's make the psychological burden as light as possible.'

'Yes, I see.'

'I'll recommend that she stays here for another three weeks.

Then, if all's well, you can take her home.'

'I can't thank you enough.'

The doctor twinkled again. 'See you tomorrow.'

★

'Hey, Agniv, come and see this!'

Namrata peered excitedly at her computer screen. Sachdeva, standing over her, waved to Agniv, who left his machine to see what they were looking at. On the screen, orange puffballs exploded one by one on a bright green background, seeding, growing, expanding, dying, seeding again, dancing gracefully like fireworks.

'What it is?' he asked.

'My new simulation,' Namrata said proudly. 'Sachie helped me with the code. It works better now!'

'What it simulates?'

'Epidemics. This is insect vector data. The one with airborne data gets over too fast.' Namrata waved a sheaf of printouts. 'Sachie showed me how to optimize the parameters while setting up the database. He's too good!'

Sachdeva beamed. 'We took virulence to be 50 per cent, that's half of exposed population get infected,' he said. 'That's a conservative estimate. If you set it higher it just flashes by.'

'Means less people fall sick?'

'No, more die. The really deadly ones can hardly be seen— zip and they're gone. This one has high Mb and low Mt.'

'High morbidity, low mortality,' Namrata translated. 'So beautiful, no? It'll look too good in my PowerPoint,' she beamed. 'It works for plants and animals also. Using it I can find how long it takes to defoliate medium-sized forest area with deployment of different agents.'

Agniv watched the orange explosions flower, grow and die, throwing out little bomblets all the while that seeded new starbursts, blooming and fading. Namrata restarted the

this substitution

programme. He watched the dance of death begin all over again.

'This is how god looks at people?' he asked.

Namrata looked annoyed. 'How should I know?' She shut the programme down and copied it onto a CD. 'Thanks, Sachie. I owe you one *papri chaat* at Lalu's canteen.'

'Come on, Agniv, let's go now for tea-shee. Save and exit, ok?'

'But I have to . . .'

'Agniv *yaar*, Gopu-ji Sir isn't in office today also. Have fun till your free time is there.' Sachdeva leaned over Agniv and hit 'save'. 'Come, let's call Shweta and Rahul and go into town.'

Outside, the winter cold bit through their thin shawls and sweaters; Agniv wrapped his muffler round his head and chin. He didn't really want to go into town, but it would be too much trouble to struggle out of it. He followed Namrata and Sachdeva out of the lab.

'Hey Rahul, Shweta, *chalo chai ho jaye*. Namrata's buying us *chaat*.'

'No *yaar*, I can't buy for everyone, just for you only.'

'Whooo, Sachie! Special treatment, *yaar*! What's the deal? *Kuch baat hai kya?*'

'What nonsense,' Namrata sniffed. 'I only took his help for my project, *bas*.'

'Ya, Namrata, you borrow my books again and see! *Chaat* for Sachie only! What *yaar*, we're not your friends or what?'

'What, I bought you *chaat* last week only. And you took my *Ek Do Teen* CD on Monday.'

'Okay, don't fight guys, since Namrata's buying me *chaat*, I'll buy for you all, on one condition.'

'What?'

'You guys treat me to a picture, that's all.'

'Hawww! So money-minded you all are.'

'Okay, I'm there, Sachie. Want to see *Pyar Hai Na?*'

They unlocked their bikes and headed out of the lab complex. From the top of the steep road going down to the gate the sharp wind of their passing blew their words away. They hurtled through the chain of soft orange streetlight glows, flashing by with alternate gloom and light. Agniv's black depression lifted a little. These days he found it hard to concentrate on what he was doing. So many questions battered at his mind.

'Light. Put on your cycle light.'

The security guard at the gate was pointing to the front of his bike. He got down and set the dynamo cog against the back wheel rim, his fingers stiff in the cold. Then he pedalled hard to catch up with the others.

It had been so easy, once upon a time. His seniors had told him such tales, of how they had spent harsh months of despair grappling with what looked like impossible problems, of stormy scenes with supervisors, dwindling grants, SOS calls home. He had listened politely while hugging a kind of scorn to himself. *He* could do better than that. All it took was dedication, the determination not to be defeated, never to look back, always to say, *One more try and I'll crack this*. That was all it took, the willingness to give yourself totally to the work.

And here he was.

It wasn't the experiments. Nothing had changed. He had in fact collected some promising results that could be followed up. But the serene space of thought and inquiry was now a wasteland of doubts and questions.

'Agniv! Hurry up, we had to wait for you! Move, *yaar*.'

The evening was hazy and smelled of smoke. Tiny dead leaves fluttered lazily from the trees in a whispering yellow cascade as they entered the outskirts of the town. Here, under a great bare tree, was the shabby stall with 'Lalu Tee and Snaks' written over the door. The cold had driven the street dogs into the coal store where they lay curled on the sacks.

Steam rose in great clouds from the stove. The benches were empty; not many people were about. 'You want *chaat* or *masala dosa*?' Agniv mumbled something. 'Rahul? Shweta? Namrata? Okay.' Sachdeva took a deep breath. '*Bhaiyya! Teen chaat aur do masala dosa. Aur panch chai.*'

They sat on the rough benches on either side of a faded Formica table. The man who stood on the other side of the windowed partition was wearing a T-shirt over his usual grimy singlet today. The heat from the coal fire made the area pleasantly warm; the tables had been moved closer to the shop. In summer when it was stiflingly hot to sit here they would take their lassi and snacks to a little platform under the tea stall's overarching tree.

'It's eight o'clock,' said Rahul. 'We'll sit till eight-thirty, then go for night show.'

Namrata looked a little worried. 'Will it be okay to return back so late?'

'*Arre*, what will happen, *yaar*? We are here, *na*?'

'You? What will you do if some goons attack us? They'll give one blow of their mouth—*phoo!*—and you'll fly away.'

Rahul looked downcast. 'But I play badminton every day,' he said plaintively.

'What good does that do? Anyway, I play better than you.'

'Hah! I'll beat you any day.'

'Bet?' Namrata grinned smugly. She was in fact a head taller than Rahul, which gave her a great advantage in net games.

'Okay, bet. One ice cream, Okay?'

'Oho, too smart you are. Here we are shivering with cold and he wants to bet ice cream.'

'Agniv's very quiet. *Arre*, Agniv, *kuch bolo.*'

'Oh, leave him alone, he's sad because his supervisor's back. Now he'll have to work hard for his seminar, no, Agniv?'

'What did you expect, Agniv's sir and his Mrs will stay there forever? They finished their work and came back.' Rahul winked.

'Ho, Agniv, is your Gopuji Sir going to give us sweets? After so late he's having good news.'

'Yes, Agniv, treat, treat!'

'What for treat?' Agniv suddenly exploded. 'You don't really care, no? All you want is your treat!'

'What're you saying, Agniv? Of course we care. Hey, what's the problem? Hey, come on, *yaar*.' Rahul grabbed his shoulder and shook it.

'*Arre*, why so worried? Your sir's so distracted about Mrs Gopu-ji he won't notice anything. Haven't you seen how he was rushing around, every day three times to Bioscience? Till the time his Mrs is having issue you can make up. Too much time is there. Don't think for it.'

'You are not understanding!' Agniv burst out, getting to his feet. 'Always you are laughing at me!'

'Okay, Agniv, cool it. Sit. Don't fuss. Okay? It's all right, *yaar*.'

Agniv stood and blinked at Sachdeva. Then he slowly sat down, raking his gaze, one by one, over each of their faces. They sat uncomfortably, waiting for the food to arrive and break the tension. They could tell Agniv was still wound up like a spring, and they knew what that meant. Namrata began murmuring a film song, looking desperately at the others and willing them to join in.

'What're you staring at, *yaar*?' Sachdeva mumbled. 'Has my face turned black or what?'

'Why you came to join Centre, Sachie?'

'What sort of a question is that? I got selected, I came. So?'

'Why you applied?'

'Are you crazy? Why did *you* apply?'

'I wanted to learn science,' said Agniv, each word meticulously positioned like atoms on a silicon wafer.

'Ya, so?' said Namrata. 'That's what everybody wants.'

'Nah,' said Sachdeva. 'What learn science! You came to get a good qualification and job status in life. And a fat pay packet when you join for work. Nice wife, car and flat with AC when you get married. That's right, guys?'

'Speak for yourself,' Namrata said tartly. 'Shweta and I can get all that for ourselves, no Shweta? We don't have to depend on our parents for dowries.'

'All that learning science is for the interview boards.'

'Rahul? Why you came here?'

'Because I couldn't get into a big place. And I didn't want to rot in some regional engineering college. Everyone wants to work for government. Once you're in, you're made for life. *Bas*. No worries, no hassles. All problems solved.'

'Shweta?'

'Oh, I didn't get microbiology.'

'Namrata?'

Namrata licked her lips. 'I wanted to serve my motherland,' she said.

Agniv shook his head in wonder. 'You were not wanting job?'

'Oh, I want job as well. But I also want to serve my motherland.'

'Well, if you put it like that,' Sachdeva said uncomfortably, 'I also want to serve my motherland. But hey, you can't do any good by rotting in some small town. And we all want to be big people in the world. Otherwise why did our parents get us educated?'

'If we can get good place in life, then India also gains, no?' Rahul added.

'And the work we do is for nation's good,' Shweta said firmly.

'Yes. We have not gone off to work in America or Germany or any abroad place. We're all here serving our nation. Even as research scholars everything we do is for nation's good. We work on defence projects with our supervisors; what is better for the nation than that?'

'Yes, and we have heritage also. Haven't you heard

Rahil-ji's talks?'

'Yes, we have not left our roots like those abroad-wallahs. We are sons of the soil. We work for national security.'

'You all are so sick,' Agniv growled suddenly.

They stared at him, shocked.

'What are you talking about, *yaar*? And what for you insult us, hey?'

'Yeah, apologize!

'What sick-vick!'

'Have you thought . . .' His voice broke. He tried again, trying to rise above their indignant clamour. 'Have you ever thought *why* . . . I mean deep down really, truly what for we are working? Have you ever thought?'

'What's there to think?'

Agniv goggled at him. 'We are killing people!' he shouted. 'We are learning to kill people! That is what we are learning to do over here! They are all killers!' He jumped to his feet. 'Even your Rajguru-ji! Even Prasad Sir. Even Dr Gopal-ji!'

'Hawww!' Shweta covered her mouth with her hand. Over her bunched-up cheeks her round eyes goggled at everyone. Sachdeva got up slowly as Agniv stood there, trembling, the muffler like an untidy bandage round his jaw and temples.

'Agniv, you are like this because you have been without a guide for so long. Don't you think we haven't noticed? You are not being able to work and so you're mad at everyone all the time. So what if you're having problems with work? We've all had them. We're your friends, Agniv. We'll help you. Can't you trust us?'

Tears rose in Agniv's red eyes. 'I cannot trust even Gopu-ji Sir.'

'Don't talk like that, Agniv, do one thing. Go and see the doctor tomorrow morning. No, I'll take you. You need a rest, you've been working too hard, no guys? I'll ask Dr Gopu-ji to give you off.'

'No!'

'All this talk is because you . . . Agniv! Wait!'

Sachdeva clutched at Agniv's shoulder as he rose from the bench but he tore himself away, ran to his bike and pedalled furiously off into the darkness.

Sachdeva turned to the others. They avoided his eyes and handed round the plates. 'I'll go check on him tomorrow,' Sachdeva said vaguely, sitting down and wrapping his hands gratefully around a hot cup of tea.

'What did he mean, Sachie?' Namrata asked nervously.

Sachdeva shrugged. 'Who knows what Agniv means? Does anyone want his *chaat*?'

★

'What we really need,' said Rajguru, 'is a war. Don't you agree, Chandran?'

'Isn't life difficult enough?'

'Precisely my point. I'm having a hell of a time getting these guidance systems tested. Either we should have a war or get our people into Chakravyuh, which would amount to the same thing. Which would you prefer, Basu?'

Pradyumna Basu chewed his pen. They were sitting in Gopal's office, having their daily briefing, but Rajguru was in a chatty mood and had come in with a page from the *New York Times*, where some American defence analyst had been holding forth on the power balance in South Asia. Rajguru had waved the article around indignantly and insisted on reading bits of it aloud. 'They can't tell the difference between a military dictatorship and a democratic country!' After that the discussion had become rather heated; Gopal had tried once or twice to derail it and failed.

Basu said, 'Chakravyuh? What makes you think it exists?'

'Oh, it exists all right. Else why are there all these rumours? And if it doesn't then it ought to. The country needs it. We need it. You know what I'm talking about, Basu, so answer my question.'

'Hmm. The Chakravyuh master project (assuming of course that it indeed runs) would perhaps provide us with better control of testing conditions. But a war—well, it's the ultimate test, isn't it? And if we had a real war we wouldn't need to go through all the security hassles we'd have to face to get into Chakravyuh. That place will be securer than a black hole; no one who joins the project will ever come out again. Also, how do we know the project will work smoothly once it's finally set up? If, that is, they succeed in passing the bill. Suppose they cut your funds after six months? If that happens you can't work, and you can't quit either.'

Rajguru smiled mysteriously. 'Quit? Don't be silly. Funds won't be a problem in Chakravyuh, there'll be no fear of anything like that occurring. I happen to know that the set-up phase is almost in the final stages now. They have bought and installed the best equipment from around the world, under top secret conditions. No one, not even the CIA, has any idea what it'll be used for, so clever was the smokescreen operation. Sometimes it was sourced in bits from three different countries, I hear. You cannot imagine. And all this will be the playground for the best minds in Indian science. I wonder who's likely to be tapped from here. I hear they'll be on the lookout for people soon. Watch out for defence conferences. Isn't one coming up in Pune?'

'Well, Prasad's team is a natural choice. The rest of us will have to fight for places.'

'Yes, but what an opportunity! Fast-track military development, the Director called it. No interference from anyone, not even the Army. Security tight as a drum. State-of-the-art facilities, anything you like, no risk of security leaks, no questions, as close to total freedom as you can envisage. We'll never have to worry about sanctions again.'

Basu said, 'But unless there's a war it'll be difficult for the government to justify that kind of spending.'

'Ah, but there's the beauty of it!' Rajguru rubbed his hands. 'You've seen the bill; it gives the authorities carte blanche to decide how best to use the funds. Once it's through Parliament nothing further need come to the public eye! The work of Chakravyuh will be so top secret even other members of the team won't know. Only the coordinator will have all the details of who's doing what, and no one will know who he is. And the project will have its own special commando detachment to help test the products. The generals will only see our stuff when it's issued to the troops. By then it'll be too late for anyone to object. If we're clever enough about it, the media won't get a whiff of controversy even when it's used in the field. And once we have the weapons, international opinion can go hang.'

'Yes, but will the bill be passed? You know there are all those busybodies who'll yell about transparency and what have you.'

'Don't worry about them.' Rajguru waved the paper. 'You might not have heard, but I have it on good authority that the country will face a severe defence crisis in the next few weeks. The panic it will generate will be enough to pass the bill. No one will argue with the need to defend the borders. And with terror strikes reaching as far as Calcutta, I shouldn't think even you, Basu, can deny that the time has come.'

'I wouldn't dream of it,' Basu said mildly.

Gopal coughed discreetly. 'Can we come back to business, gentlemen?'

'Chandran, what chance do you think we have of getting in?'

'None, if you keep talking about it, even here in my office. Don't you know what "secret" means? All these rumours you're happily retailing have been put about to give people the wrong idea. Probably there isn't even any such project. And if there is, you ought to have the sense not to discuss it.'

'Oh,' said Rajguru, crushed. 'All right. Sorry.' He began crackling the pages of the *New York Times*.

'Gentlemen? Please report on progress so far. Basu, you first.'

One by one around the circle, they described the work completed and the work to be done, discussed ways and means of making progress, short-term goals and needs. When all was over and the men were shuffling their papers, Rajguru said, 'Oh, by the way, Chandran, congratulations.'

'What for?'

'Your issue, of course. Do pass on my felicitations to Mrs Chandran. When can we expect sweets? My wife was asking.'

'Yes, yes,' the others chorused, beaming. 'Hearty congratulations.'

'How did you all know? I haven't told anyone yet . . .'

'Oh ho ho, do you think we live with our heads buried in the ground?' Rajguru winked. 'When good things happen to our friends, should we not utilize our networks to find out, eh? Not all rumours turn out to be false.'

'Yes, Chandran, sweets!'

'All right,' said Gopal, 'next week.'

He watched them leave.

★

Dear Anu,

Well, you'd never believe me if I told you everything that's happened to me over the last few months. First, let me tell you the big news: I'm a mother! Yes! I can't comprehend it even now, with my baby daughter lying here asleep next to me, nice and snug under her blanket. It's a miracle; I wake every morning and have to remember it anew. Nearly all my life I've been reconciled to not being able to control the vagaries of my body, I've learned not to want what I can't have, and now . . .! I don't know what to do with myself, and that's a fact.

Motherhood is amazing. I thought I was prepared for it

and I'm not, I'm not. It's so big and solemn and frightening and joyous. I can't get over her tininess; she's such a small, perfect, tiny human being. Her eyes are so beautiful! I never thought breastfeeding could be such an experience, like being god. Feeding another creature from your own body; what a wonder! She doesn't even drink water; all her sustenance comes from me, and will do so for the next three months at least. Watching someone feeding a baby just isn't the same; when it's you, it fills the universe.

I've named her Vatsala. We have a nurse to take care of the nappies and things, but mostly she does my share of the housework while I spend all my time with little Vatsala. I suspect the housekeeping is going to pot but I don't care. Gopal does what he can, but he's really busy. There's some sort of competition on between all the teams at the Centre, with some big prize in the offing. Gopal isn't very excited about it but his team members are dead keen to be in on this, so he has to work extra hard. Poor fellow! I can see he'd rather stay home with me and the baby, but he's helpless. I thought I'd regret not having him around to watch her do her amazing little things, but I'll let you in on a secret: I'm actually glad I can have her all to myself!

It's funny; when we were in Rajasthan we sat down and planned to adopt a child as soon as we got back. And all the while Vatsala was swimming about upside down inside me, smiling to herself! I felt really foolish when I realized that. I mean, how can a woman miss the fact that she's *pregnant*? I did feel odd, not my usual self, and I did some incredibly foolish and emotional things, but those aren't the usual indications, are they? I just thought my period was late, it usually is, and I sort of lost track of things. And I didn't really have morning sickness or anything like that, except once. But the doctor said it's not unusual for older women like me who think they're barren to carry a child to term and not realize what's happening. One woman who came to him actually thought she was having a premature menopause! Makes you wonder, doesn't it?

You really must come down and see her some time. She's such a darling. Having her around is nothing like what I thought it would be. I was so scared when they told me, I thought, I'm not ready for this, I can't be responsible for another human being. And then I thought, well, if I'm not ready now, when will I be? Perhaps Mother Nature knows best. And you'd be amazed how it's changed the attitude of the women around here. Now they're all smiling faces, dropping in to coochie-coo and give me lots of advice. It's funny but I don't resent their busybodying any more; it's like I've bought my membership to the club. Now we talk about feeding and colic and nappy rash and immunizations. And I love it! I should have nagged Gopal into doing this years ago.

I hate to sound like an aunty, but you really should consider it for yourself. Making another person inside yourself and then seeing her in the light of day, caring for her; what can compare with it? Find yourself a good man and go for it is what I say. If you need any help, you know where to find me. So I hope to see a nice red card drop in the post some day!

Love,
Vidura

CHAPTER FIFTEEN

'Today we have a guest speaker: Dr (Mrs) N. Meenakshi Sundaram of the Parampara Evam Sanskriti Kendra. She is going to speak on Hindu thought and society in the modern world. Dr Meenakshi Sundaram, please.' Rahil Vidyadhar handed the microphone to the woman in a silk sari sitting to his right. Gopal heard someone behind him give a groan. 'That windbag was bad enough,' a voice whispered, 'now he's brought a friend.'

'*Jai Shri Ram*. Can everybody hear me?'

There was a chorus of yesses and one no.

'Respected Director, scientists, students, colleagues and my dear friends. You are all aware that Hindu civilization has many glories. As a devout Hindu, my heart swells with pride when I think of the achievements of my culture in times past. Indian art is a storehouse of treasure, Indian philosophy a subtle and beautiful garden, Indian literature a magical galaxy of worlds, Indian science the mother of mastery. Because I believe that all of us in this room share that pride, I have come here today to celebrate it with you. I also want to put before you some of the difficulties that Hinduism is facing today, and make some suggestions as to what can be done about them.

'I was brought up in an orthodox Hindu family, as most of you were. As a child, I worshipped our family god and followed all rituals with full discipline. However, my father was unusual among orthodox men in believing absolutely that his daughters should be educated, and he scrimped and saved to send my sisters and me to school.

'As I grew, I learned that there were people who could not participate in our rituals, even though they were supposed to be Hindus like us. This saddened and shamed me. Over time I learned more about this practice. For instance, my maternal uncle campaigned in our village to have a missionary school closed. He said they were converting poor low-caste people to Christianity. But if these people were Hindus, and that must be so if we call their choice of faith "conversion", then their customs of contractual marriage, gender equality, wine-drinking and beef-eating are Hindu practices, and should be available to all Hindus as part of our religion. If they are not, then these people cannot be called Hindus and we have no . . .'

'Excuse me, Dr Sundaram, but you are straying from the point. Please confine your remarks to the subject of your talk.'

She turned wide kohl-rimmed eyes to him. 'But that is what I am doing, Dr Vidyadhar-ji. These questions are very important and every Hindu must confront them if we are to heal our society. Please do not misunderstand me; I am as devoted to the Hindu faith as you are. Every day I rise at dawn to chant the name of Krishna five hundred times. I am speaking of these issues because I want every Hindu to have the right to taste the nectar of truth—why every Hindu, I want every human being to have knowledge of it. Do you not agree that this has been our strength, historically? That we have no church and no scripture, but instead many traditions, many ways of living? In the present age, when barriers between groups and individuals are rising higher and higher, we have a duty to teach the world how to be tolerant.

'You may ask: if we tolerate everything, wherein lies our identity as Hindus? And furthermore, if other traditions do not want to join with us, if they persist in maintaining their own exclusive identity, then what do we do? These are valid questions, and I do not think a definitive answer can be given to them, because that would be to set up dogmas and orthodoxies. So I can only give you the answer that I have found, and leave you to find your own.

'Firstly, in the Hinduism which I have chosen to follow, there is no institutionalized inequality, no division of human beings according to what they do or whom they worship or which part of god is said to have given rise to them. Secondly, my Hinduism believes in symbolizing abstract forces in the persons of gods and goddesses, because this is a uniquely human way of viewing the world. As a limited human being, I can have only a conceptual understanding of pure abstract love, but I can imagine an ideal pair of lovers in the form of Krishna and Radha and I can *feel* what devotion is from contemplating their story. My Hinduism moreover delights in the abstract thought of the Upanishads and loves to contemplate the wonderful non-dualities of *advaita*. Thirdly, my Hinduism does not turn away from festivities, but acknowledges that festivals are for people, not people for festivals. Fourthly, my Hinduism will not follow any social practice that causes pain, distress or humiliation, or asks for unjust sacrifice. Fifthly, my Hinduism believes that women and men are capable of the highest and most fulfilling enlightenment, that there is a rule of righteousness that is part of the fabric of life and must govern our actions, and that there is a sum of evil and good that we carry and add to throughout our lives to the end. Finally, my Hinduism recognizes no special privileges, no automatic salvation and no hatred. That is my Hinduism.

'As for the boundaries set by others, I recognize that others have the right to be different from me. This does not give me the right to hurt or harm them, nor they to harm me. They are irrelevant to my belief system: I share the secular space of the state with them, and we are bound alike by the law, but in questions of belief we will go amicably our own ways.

'You can see clearly where I differ from what you all know as "Hinduism". For some of you, this difference is more serious and unacceptable than for others. Before I began this talk, I asked myself if I should risk angering you by mentioning the things that my Hinduism is *not*. But I have come here to be honest with you, so I must take the risk.

'My Hinduism is not a religion of kings and priests and princes, and it does not exist to give some men an excuse for ruling over the rest of us. It belongs to everyone who chooses to call themselves Hindu, and anyone who calls himself Hindu must be treated in matters of the spirit as *no different* from anyone else. No one person is born closer to god than another person is. That means I believe that anyone can be a priest, anyone can worship god, anyone . . .'

'But Dr Sundaram,' Rahil Vidyadhar's brow was creased in irritation. 'How can you allow anyone to be a priest if they have not studied the scriptures? This is absurd.'

'Everyone should be free to study the scriptures, and also to worship without scriptures if they so choose. Gods belong to those who believe in them, not just to those who have memorized . . .'

'Worship is one thing,' said Vidyadhar sternly, 'but priesthood is another. I have often said that our education system should train young men properly for a priestly vocation. In my own centre I have advocated courses in traditional learning. There is at present no degree-giving recognized body, and there is too much unemployment among upper-caste youth now with all this reservation politics. It is not good for society. I am campaigning to have the duties of priests and astrologers recognized as essential services. I think now we can take questions from the floor.'

'But I had not finished.'

'No matter: you have already given a most provocative talk. I am sure many wish to comment on your, ah, solutions to our problems. May I exercise the chairperson's privilege, and begin?'

She nodded mutely.

'Dr Sundaram, I must say that your formulations strike me as rather naïve. You seem not to have read the Purusha Sukta of the Rig Veda. This is, you will admit, one of the most ancient and fundamental texts of Hinduism. In it, the basis of *varnadharma* is laid out plainly for even the most obtuse person to see. The four varnas are associated with the head, the arm, the stomach and the feet of god: that is thought, action, production and service. You may ask, since you think of yourself as a modern person, whether this is not,' he sneered delicately, 'out of date? But there is a rational basis for it. Division of labour is the basis of modern production, as your Marx has shown. Hinduism divided the labour of society between the four *varnas*, so that we could be the most efficient society of our time. Even today, we have scholars like yourself dealing with words, while others deal with other things. Do you make stone idols in your spare time, Dr Sundaram?' There was a titter of laughter.

'As a matter of fact . . .'

'Well, that's all we seem—yes, Dr Batra?'

Dr Batra got to his feet. 'I would like to ask madam how she can think that our enemies will be satisfied with such passive non-violence. It is a reality of the modern world that non-violence is seen as nothing but weakness. If we take her seriously, she is advocating that the government shut this centre down.'

'May I answer?' she asked diffidently. Vidyadhar nodded. 'No, I was not saying that. A state must have the means to defend itself. But to target others because they persist in believing differently is not defence, it is tyranny.'

'But those who believe differently will sooner or later act against us. We have to pre-empt them with overwhelming force. *They* do not tolerate us as you say we should tolerate them.'

'There is no such thing as pre-emptive justice.'

'That is a foolish belief. You are saying we should wait for others to hurt us before we hurt them. That is nonsense. No state behaves like that in the real world.'

'On the contrary, many states do. But they are not the neo-imperialist states that certain people in this country wish to emulate, hence in their view of the situation they do not count. You are implicitly comparing our country with the big bullies of world politics. Why should we behave like them?'

'Madam, I am sorry to say you are speaking total nonsense. Our neighbours are the worst bullies, as you call them. We must fight them, or allow them to destroy us.'

Rahil Vidyadhar pointed to the back of the hall. 'Yes, Dr Nayar?'

'I would like to know from madam why she has not mentioned among Hinduism's good things the *Bhagavad Gita*, and why she has nothing to say about the *Ramayana*, which even foreigners recognize as our greatest epic.'

'I do not endorse the beliefs implicit in either of these texts.'

'How can you be called a Hindu then, madam? Every Hindu believes in the *Gita*. Why, it has helped thousands in their hour of need. As Vidyadhar-ji said in an earlier talk, it even helped Oppenheimer after he realized the true nature of the Manhattan Project. How can you dismiss it so casually?'

'Because it does not really examine the ethical basis of action, but appeals to fate and duty and the will of god. I cannot accept that a pragmatist argument designed to get a reluctant prince to kill his brothers should be the basis of my everyday life.'

'Bah! Then you have understood nothing of the *Gita*. Go back to your village school and study it again.' There was more laughter. Rahil-ji chuckled audibly into the mike. 'Yes, indeed. If there are no more questions, we will stop here. Thank you very much for your lecture, Dr Sundaram.' There were a few polite handclaps, quickly stifled.

'I have a question.' Gopal's voice cut across the shuffle of people gathering their things and getting up. Vidyadhar had already turned away, but Dr Sundaram switched the mike back on and said, 'Yes?'

'Dr Chandran, the lecture is over . . .'

He ignored Vidyadhar's red face. 'Dr Sundaram, did you expect a better response from this audience?'

The thick eyeliner made her eyes seem sunken. He realized she was in fact close to tears. 'Yes, I did,' she said at last.

'Why?'

'Because you are scientists. I had hoped that your training in rational thought would make you eager to consider these questions objectively.'

'Thank you, doctor. That's all I wanted to hear from you.'

★

'Sir, may I come in, sir?'

'Agniv! Yes, do come in. Take a seat. I've been meaning to talk to you.'

Agniv sat down and clutched his file, 'Sir, why, sir?'

'I've just been terribly busy and couldn't find the time. Well, tell me how things have been going.'

'Sir I have been running that series of tests you asked me to carry out. The results are there. But they are . . . not completed.'

'Why? Was there a problem?'

'No, sir . . . I could not finish, sir.'

'Again? Didn't you find the time?'

'Not like that, sir. Sir . . .' Agniv swallowed. 'I have . . . not been able to concentrate, sir. For many days, sir.'

'What's on your mind, Agniv? What's preventing you from settling down?'

'Nothing, sir. I am only . . .' Agniv's fingers worked convulsively on the edge of the file.

Gopal looked at his troubled face. 'Is there something you need to tell me? You can speak freely with me, you know that.

Are you having a hard time at the hostel? Is there trouble at home? Come on, Agniv, you know you can trust me.'

'Yes, sir,' said Agniv wretchedly, 'but can you trust me, sir?'

'Of course I trust you, Agniv.' Gopal paused, uneasily aware that he was getting nowhere. 'Agniv, you can tell me. I've been noticing you're distracted and you haven't got your mind on the job, but I've been so busy at home . . . Agniv, please believe me when I tell you that anything you say about your problem, whatever it is, will not go beyond these walls. I will talk to no one and take no action without asking you. But please don't suffer on your own. I'm here to help you.'

Agniv hung his head. 'I do not know what is wrong in me, sir.'

Gopal permitted himself a small sigh. He would have to do a lot of digging here, he could see. Luckily he had nothing else scheduled for the evening.

'Okay, Agniv, let's try to work this out. You tell me you can't concentrate. I know for a fact that you have great powers of applying your mind. Therefore something in particular is distracting you. Is this so?'

Agniv nodded mutely.

'Tell me, when you are at work, do thoughts pop up in your head and distract you?'

An eager look suddenly animated his face. 'Yes, sir.'

'What sort of thoughts? Is it to do with money? Home?'

'No, sir, it is work.'

'Has anyone been causing problems while I was away?'

'No, sir . . .' Agniv looked despondent again.

'Look, Agniv, you have to help me here. You have to open up a bit. Tell me how you feel about these doubts.'

'Afraid, sir.'

'Why?'

'I ask myself, what I am doing . . . and why I am doing. Why I am here? I am asking all time, asking asking.'

Oh dear, Gopal thought. 'In what sense do you mean that?

Is it being at the Centre you're not sure about?'

'No! Please don't send me away, sir!'

'I won't do anything you don't want me to, Agniv,' Gopal said gently. 'But it's evident you're not happy and we have to find the reason and do something about it, because it's affecting your work. If there are doubts they must be doubts of something. Look, everyone has doubts at some point or the other. Do you think I don't have doubts? It's natural. But we find our way through them and go on working. It's nothing to get so upset over.'

'Really, sir? You too have doubts?'

'Of course. It goes with the job. But that doesn't mean I'll chuck my work and go and do something else. Sometimes there's discouragement, apathy, a lack of energy. And then it passes. Research is a tough job. We can't feel positive about it all the time. Sometimes what this feeling means is, we've been pushing ourselves too hard, our minds have got stale. Then we take a break, rest, enjoy ourselves and suddenly our minds are full of ideas again. That's how it works. You didn't go home last holiday, did you?'

'No, sir.'

'I'm sure that's all it is. You mustn't allow it to overwhelm you. Science is important but it isn't everything in life. Sometimes it's exhilarating and sometimes it leaves you down in the dumps. Then you need to pick yourself up and find the strength to go on.'

Agniv was silent, looking down at his hands. Gopal said quietly, 'That's not it at all, is it?'

'No, sir.'

'You'd better tell me.'

'I am not having words, sir. I have tried, for many many days. I sent many, many e-mails to Anuprabha Aunty-ji. But even she couldn't find for me words. So now I am trying alone.'

'You e-mailed Anuprabha Shastri?'

'Yes, sir. She is so nice lady. I told her my troubles. But

I think only I can solve my problem. She only said same thing.'

'I see. What did you tell her?'

Agniv folded and unfolded the corner of his file. 'I am coming from very poor background,' he said softly. 'My parents worked too much to teach me reading–writing. When I got into Centre they invited whole village. It was *chulha nibhar*: no one lit their oven for that day. All, all came and ate with us, like it was a marriage in our family. They told my father, such big-big *mithai*, so many items, why you are spending so much? He said, everyone brings daughter-in-law to house. But how many can send their sons to become doctor of science? When time comes my son will pay for his own wedding.'

'Were you disappointed when you came here?' Gopal asked gently.

'No . . . maybe a little, sir. I had thought people would be talking of new things all time, but they talk of small things, their families, their worries, not science at all. Just like in village. But, sir, when I had seen you and talked for the first time, I knew I had come to a good place. I had wanted to be like you, sir . . .' There were tears in Agniv's eyes.

'You will be like me, Agniv. You are very, very intelligent and capable. You're one of the best students I've ever taught.'

'Thank you, sir.' Agniv pulled a handkerchief out of his pocket and rubbed his eyes. 'I am sorry, sir.'

'Don't put too much pressure on yourself, Agniv. I know the hopes of your whole village are riding on you. That can make it difficult sometimes. You mustn't think about the cost of failure. Just keep going, tell yourself you can do it. So much successful research comes from a positive attitude.'

'But, sir, I cannot keep positive attitude because I think about death, sir.'

'You're not going to die, Agniv.'

'Not me, sir. People.'

'People?'

'We make weapons, sir. Weapons kill people. We make weapons for killing people better and better, more and more. This I cannot forget. I lie awake at night and think of people crying, cursing me. So much pain, so much pain I am causing by being here, sir.' He twisted the handkerchief as though he wanted to rip it to shreds. 'How to work with this in my head, sir?'

'What made you think of that?'

Agniv was silent for a moment. Then he said, 'Is it not obvious?'

Gopal shook his head. He stopped and tried to speak, then he shook his head again.

'You are angry with me, sir.' Agniv's eyes filled with tears again.

'No, no, Agniv, I'm trying to find the words to reassure you.' Gopal came round the desk and took the chair next to Agniv. 'Agniv, look at me. I'm going to tell you a story.'

'A story, sir?'

'Yes, about me when I was like you. When I began research here at the Centre I was only a few years older than you. I remember when I went for my first field test. We were testing body armour. Before we went to the field we tested it many, many times on dummies. I was absolutely confident there was no problem with it. So we issued some prototypes to soldiers. I still remember the name of the first volunteer. Kartar Singh, his name was. Well, we instructed him to walk towards us from a point we'd marked and we would fire guns at him. He was grinning from ear to ear as he went out on the range; he didn't seem to feel any fear at all. And with the first shot he fell flat on the ground.'

Agniv stared at him with a ghastly question in his eyes.

'No, he wasn't shot. He had just been taken off guard by the strength of the impact and slipped. He got up in a moment and laughed and laughed. There wasn't a scratch on him. But I'll never forget his face in the sights as he went down and that awful moment when he lay still. Just then even he didn't know if he was alive or dead. That brought it home to me, what these things are I'm making. And I thought, when Kartar Singh's out there for real, my inventions are going to keep him safe.'

'But the gun . . .'

'Yes, I know, Agniv. War is both offence and defence. I know it's not enough to say we protect people. We also threaten them; we can't escape that knowledge. And the armour our soldiers wear means they will live to kill others, not just escape death themselves. That is true. But think of this: war has always been part of civilization. Sometimes, when all else fails, you have to fight. There have been wars for good as well as evil. So long as we believe our country will never go to war for an evil cause, we can give ourselves entirely to this battle. We have to have faith. At the end of the day, if we believe that our lives are good, our society is based on the good, then we must defend ourselves to the best of our ability. And that's what makes it right to kill. That, and nothing else.'

Agniv smiled. His squarish face lit up with relief and gratitude. 'Sir, thank you, sir. I feel much more better, sir.'

'Much better, you mean. I'm glad. Don't hesitate to talk to me if you need anything, Agniv. I'm here for you.'

'Yes, sir. Thank you, sir. I will remember your words, sir. Good night, sir.'

Agniv went out.

Gopal sat looking at the closed door for a long time after he left. He felt a pang of guilt over the fact that Agniv had suffered his doubts in patient silence while he had been away, and had then wrestled with them over these long months before finally getting up the courage to voice them. And he had been too busy and too worried to notice Agniv's agony; it was only now, with Vidura safely delivered of the child and wrapped up in the daily routine of her little life that he had been able to look up and see.

It was late; almost eleven. Time he went home. He began

to close the windows, shut down the computer. The night air was chilly; he hugged his anorak about him. Strangely, the cycle shed was empty. He stared at it, frowning; where had he left the bike? Oh yes, he had been late back from lunch and had parked it next to the seminar hall to save time. Oh, well. He quite enjoyed walking in the cold though; the air was dry, but it still reminded him of the long walks he used to take in Cambridge. Vidura would come with him sometimes, and they would chat together of the future, and of little things.

To reach the seminar hall shed he had to go through the corridor next to the Director's suite of offices. To his surprise a light was on in one of the rooms overlooking the corridor; the curtains were tightly drawn, letting through only an indistinct glow. Who could be working so late? This was the administrative wing; there were no labs here. But as he crossed the lighted space he heard his own name spoken in anger.

He stopped. Someone was having an argument inside, and it involved him. He knew he shouldn't stand there and listen, but curiosity overcame him. He crept closer. Now he could recognize the voices: it was Vidyadhar and the Director. The window was closed, but the glazed ventilator above it was open and sound carried clearly in the still air.

'. . . impeccable credentials!' Vidyadhar was saying. 'How was I to know she would be such a disaster?'

'She came with your warm recommendation, Rahil-ji. That means it was your business to know.' The Director sounded surly.

'Well, at least I prevented her from giving her entire speech. And you needn't worry, most of the men condemned it roundly. And rightly so.'

'But you couldn't prevent Chandran asking a question, could you?'

'Does it matter? It was an innocuous question. And now that his wife has a child he seems to have become easier to manage.'

The Director grunted. 'Good it's a girl; they'll try again.'

'Yes, and it will keep her out of mischief as well.'

'Indeed! It was a great mistake to send her with her husband. It is thanks to Prasad's good thinking that the whole business didn't end in calamity. I was most shocked when I saw how bad Chandran was at handling his own family.'

'He may be a good scientist, but both of them are tainted by the West. We will have to watch them carefully, especially now.'

'Yes, we cannot afford any more such security breaches. I will have to have a word with Chandran before I send him to Pune.'

'We have to be absolutely sure, now that we know the timetable. The bill will be tabled as soon as Operation Dhritarashtra is on track. With luck we should see the results within days and that should push the bill through without trouble.'

'But I am still doubtful about Gaya as a target. It will anger the Japanese.'

'Precisely, Director-ji. They were among those who slapped sanctions on us after the last tests. We and they will be co-victims of this dastardly strike. It will open their eyes. Remember the effect the Bamiyan Buddhas had on world opinion just before the First Afghan Cleansing? Those Westerners would do anything for a stone Buddha.'

'I am still dubious. Firstly there is the question whether Dhritarashtra will activate at all. Secondly, the question is, will they hit the agreed target or something else? Suppose they hit a real site?'

'If they are so foolish as to do that, India will rise like a nest of snakes in fury. When the world sees the point of origin of the Dhritarashtra strike, India's position will be vindicated. Each of our neighbours will stand exposed and naked, while Mother India, demure as Draupadi, will be clothed in the truth.'

'Very poetic, Rahil-ji, but I am a practical man. Can our moles really infiltrate their defence systems and trigger this strike? If so, why has it not been tried before?'

'The time has never yet been ripe, Director-ji. And infiltrators so far have tried to gather information. That is harder; information leaks speak for themselves and such intelligence is by nature perishable. But this mole is not there to learn but to *do*. He is a sleeper in the highest ranks. He even has the sympathy of many hardliners. They think such action would further their interests, which shows how short-sighted they must be. We are not looking to win a battle here; we will win the war. Some losses are inevitable in such an enterprise. But we will solve our problem once and for all.'

'And you will no doubt set up your Ayurveda centre within Chakravyuh?'

'Yes, only Chakravyuh can make it possible. Dr Sheth is too tough a case, but in future we will need to monitor our men carefully and nip any trouble in the bud. My datura derivatives are almost ready for testing.'

The Director grunted. 'They may well be, but we cannot manufacture disaffected elements for you to try your experiments on.'

'But the drugs are mild! They alter moods very gently. Those on medication won't even suspect.'

'Nevertheless, the long-term implications are unknown, as well as the effect on performance. I won't have you destroying my scientists' brains with your potions; I'd rather have them normal though dissatisfied.'

'But with Chakravyuh I will get all the facilities I need for my work.'

'Hmph. Let us hope then that they set it up as soon as possible.'

There was a scraping of chairs. Gopal stepped quickly back to the shadows, then made his way silently and rapidly to the car shed. There was only his bike and the Director's car there. They would hear him start the engine. No matter. He started up and headed for home. At the gates of the lab complex a white Ambassador passed him. He watched its red tail lights disappear into the misty spring night.

CHAPTER SIXTEEN

'Is this all you've done? You've barely sorted out the layout and half the material is missing. Where's the copy? Do you really think all this is going to fit on one poster? People won't be able to read it.'

Sachdeva hung his head. 'Yes, sir.'

'Why are you in such a mess? Can't you do a thing without Agniv here? I have to attend a meeting today about the Pune conference. The Director will want to know our state of readiness. What will I tell him?'

'We have selected the photographs, sir. They will be on this layout like this, sir. See, sir, this is one I took with Agniv before he left . . .' Sachdeva nervously fumbled with the prints.

'What did I tell you, Sachdeva? We can't use these.'

'Sir? But these are our best . . .'

'Exactly. They're our most accurate and most revealing photographs. And look at how you've explained them at length in the text! No wonder it's too long. Anyone with knowledge of the state of the art can take one look at this and immediately see where we are in the development of this technology. If we use these not only will others steal our process, we'll probably lose our jobs. Do you think the authorities don't keep an eye on what we say and show at these events? You really must appreciate this if you want to work in defence.'

'Sorry, sir.'

'Those photographs were for the record only. They shouldn't

even be out of the file. In fact, give them to me; I'll put them in the safe in my office. Where are the lower-resolution ones you and Agniv took?'

'Sir, I don't know. I will look in Agniv's desk.'

'You do that. Now I don't want any more excuses. I've told you in detail what to put on those posters. Do it.'

Sachdeva scurried away. Gopal went back to his office, locked the photographs away and sank down in his chair, head in hands. Agniv had gone. A week after he had talked over his doubts with Gopal, now some months ago, he had called from the railway station. 'My mother is ill,' Gopal had heard his faint voice shout above the din of soda-bottle-wallahs and snack-sellers banging their iron skillets. 'I have to go home today only, sir. I will see you when I return back. I am sorry.' Gopal had tried to reassure him that it was okay, but the line was bad and Agniv's money had run out.

There had been no word from him since. Gopal was deeply worried. Agniv had only just begun to regain his balance after his dark period of doubt. It would not take a lot to send him over the edge again. He knew Agniv's sense of duty; since he had failed to make any sort of contact with the Centre the situation was truly serious. God alone knew how long he would have to wait for news.

He was stranded, blinded. Without Agniv he could do nothing but sit and chafe furiously at the piles of paper that landed every day on his desk—every sight of the peon entering his office now made him writhe. But there was nothing he could do. Agniv's village was in rural Jharkhand far away from any urban centre and had no electricity and only one phone, which never worked. He had tried the number incessantly in the beginning, only to admit defeat at last. No one at the Centre came from that area and their extensive kin-networks could not help him.

When he had asked the students about Agniv's state of mind when he had left, they had been embarrassed and evasive. Only

Sachdeva had volunteered the information that 'he had been in a very strange mood.' Gopal hadn't pressed him. Clearly they had noticed Agniv's crisis, but with the usual freemasonry of students had kept it from the authorities. There was no point in making an issue of it.

Gopal sat up straight suddenly. Yes, there was one person who knew. He scrabbled in his diary for the number.

'Ambedkar Institute. May I help you?'

'Could you connect me to Dr Anuprabha Shastri please? Thank you.'

He listened to inanely cheery music as the extension rang.

'Hello? Dr Shastri.'

'Anu, it's Gopal Chandran. Could I ask you a few questions, please? It's important.'

There was a short pause. 'Is this about Agniv?'

Gopal's patience snapped. 'You're damn right it's about Agniv! What have you been saying to him? Do you know he's done a runner on me? What's your role in this?'

'Calm down, Gopal. I don't have any "role" in this, if you must put it like that. Agniv's been talking to me as a friend. He's been very confused about himself and his work. And now his mother has died and his father's suffered a stroke. Didn't you know?'

His anger evaporated. He slumped in his chair and clasped his temples with his free hand, letting his neck go limp. 'No, I didn't,' he mumbled. 'If you know more about my own student than I do, I must be doing something wrong. I'm sorry, Anu. I didn't mean to shout, I'm just worried stiff. Agniv called me from the station as he was leaving to tell me his mother was ill. I haven't heard from him since. It's been three months. When did he call you?'

'A week ago. Look, Gopal, please don't read more into this than you should. The elder brothers are quarrelling about the land and property. They don't want to go on paying Agniv's fees; they want him to come back and help them on the land, such as it is. And he's scared of talking to you because he didn't take your permission before he left and because you might insist he return immediately. He says if he leaves now they'll cut him out of the arrangement; he has to stay until everything is settled.'

Gopal clutched the phone with both hands. 'I'll arrange a scholarship for him. For god's sake, if he calls you again tell him money's no problem.'

'It's a bit more complicated than that. Did he . . . talk to you about his doubts at any time?'

'Yes, he did, once or twice. But I got the feeling they had been resolved.'

'I certainly hope so. But I think he was having trouble adjusting to his new place in the scientific elite.'

'So you told him he was a farmer's son and should stay that way?'

'Quite the opposite. I told him he wouldn't be happy if he denied his intellect to please his family and friends.'

'Well, I suppose I should be grateful for that at least.'

'Yes, you should.'

Gopal sighed. 'Why do we always fight?'

'Personally, I'd change that pronoun.'

'You mean it's me who's the problem. But you provoke me as well.'

'I don't mean to. I guess it's just because we're standing on opposite sides of the fence.'

'You mean you don't approve of what I do.'

'It would be useless to lie: no.'

'Look, can we bury our differences on this? I think we agree that it would be a disaster for Agniv if he elected to remain in his village. I need your help, Anu. Somehow he's nervous about talking to me; I can't get him to open up. You can. Can you try and bring him back to me? I'd go down there myself, but it's so hard to get away from the Centre and I haven't a clue how to get to his village.'

'Of course I'll help you, Gopal. I care about Agniv's future as well. But there's no reason why he shouldn't talk to you if you listen sincerely. Don't try to close him down; he really needs an impartial hearing from you. Some of the things he said to me I can see would be quite shocking to you. Don't react emotionally to them; let him have his say.'

'Well, thanks for the free advice. I do know how to listen to my students, you know.'

He heard her sigh, but she only said after a pause, 'Okay, Gopal. If Agniv calls again I'll tell him about the scholarship. And I'll use whatever persuasive powers I have to get him to go back to the Centre.'

'Thanks, Anu, I really appreciate it.'

He hung up and massaged his temples. His fears were now confirmed and there was nothing he could do. A great wave of helplessness washed over him. *What did I do wrong?* he asked himself again and again. *Was I not convincing enough when I justified our work to him? Did I really react emotionally, did I make him think I had a closed mind, that I didn't want to listen?*

Do I believe enough in what I said to be convincing?

He stared at the question in the throbbing darkness of closed eyes. With the heels of his hands pressed into his eye-sockets he could cease for a moment to be Gopal Chandran, head of Nano-Tech (Glass), and reach down into a deeper level of himself. *What do I believe?* he asked. *If my belief is sufficient for me, why am I paralysed whenever I try to work? Why should the loss of Agniv matter so much to me? Why do I feel betrayed?*

A shudder of revulsion spread through his body. The memory of that night when he had talked in vain to Agniv brought back also the memory of the overheard conversation, standing in the chill mist outside a lighted window. He had tried to thrust it out of his mind, dismiss it. He had almost succeeded; then there had been that strange incident in

Naigaon, a tiny village near Gaya. Five houses had been flattened by what the press had originally reported as a crashed surveillance aircraft, but CNN had said that a missile had been tracked in Indian airspace seconds before the incident. The defence ministry had denied the rumour, but it had gone on building until suddenly the government did an about-face and said, yes, it had been a missile, albeit unarmed; they had even displayed pieces of it on the news. Some of the wreckage was in fact in the Centre, being analysed right now.

What was he to believe? There had been no nuclear strike, clearly; the damage was minimal. He had rung up friends in Aerospace to ask if the damage pattern was commensurate with an unarmed missile strike; they said yes. So the plan, if it was a plan, had gone awry. Or sanity had prevailed at the last minute. Yet, in a way the rumours were whipping up more hysteria than a real strike would have caused. People were becoming polarized: either you believed war had unofficially been declared and something must be done, or you didn't. Some newspapers were even warning that further strikes were to be expected and detailing the woeful inadequacy of India's war machine. There had been a lot of hand-wringing over the lack of indigenous options and the difficulty of buying from abroad. Hadn't that been one of the objectives: to stimulate defence spending and get people to agree to the bill?

Strangely, there had been hardly any outcry and precious little comment on the bill and its uneventful passage. The guardians of democracy had slept on. Maybe they were right to do so: maybe democracy really was safe and its death was only the stuff of a madman's dream, not worth fearing in the light of day. Surely the leaders must know the country would fall apart under anything else, however they might dream of kings and gods and ancient empires? At the most they might try to co-opt democracy, not destroy it. And no one with any real power would play with such muck.

I hope.

What would I do, he asked himself deliberately, *if I had evidence that my bosses and superiors were no longer to be trusted? What would I do if I thought that their goal was really to do evil? Would I leave, like Agniv? Would I quietly fade away, like Dr Sheth? Or would I pursue the research goals set me for the sheer pleasure of excellence and damn the rest, like Prasad? Where do I fall in this?*

I've always known that to be in this business you have to be a little hard-hearted. For the good of society there have to be executioners as well as paediatricians. I've always prided myself on having the moral courage to do this job without letting it warp me, without taking the pleasure in death and destruction that some of them take, designing weapon systems like kids on a spree. But I've never asked myself what my moral courage feeds on and what will happen if it starves.

Suppose I'm now suspended by a thread, not knowing when it will snap and plunge me into evil? Suppose I were to come to see myself as having blood on my hands? How could I look Vidura in the face, knowing I was a killer? What sort of dreams would stalk my sleep at night?

He sat in the screen glow inside his windowless office, tossing questions into the abyss of himself.

★

'Gentlemen, tea will be served now, and then we will begin the discussion.'

Secret meetings always meant better biscuits. Suryavanshi greedily took three.

'Is this without sugar?' Prasad asked.

'Yes, yes, Prasad, now you must look after your health. You are very important person!'

Prasad smiled condescendingly. 'So are you, Batra.'

'Yes, we are, all of us. Very important.' Batra winked. 'Just wait till after Pune, you'll see.'

'The last thing I want,' said Gopal with a studiedly casual air, 'is to be an important person. It invariably leads to paperwork.'

'Well, in that case you shouldn't be such a good scientist,' Prasad said. 'Being the best has its responsibilities.'

'Maybe, but I find the responsibilities tend to gobble up the science.'

'Oh, there'll be no danger of that in future.' Prasad sipped his tea smugly.

The peon went out with the tray. The Director shuffled his papers. People put down cups and endeavoured to look alert; the air-conditioning was acting up and the May heat was making everybody wilt. Gopal mopped surreptitiously at his brow.

'Gentlemen, I have called you here for a very urgent and top secret meeting,' the Director began pompously. 'You have all been invited to the Defence Systems and Materials Conference in Pune. I have been specifically requested to ensure that each of you attends that conference; you have each been particularly named in the memo that arrived yesterday from the ministry. You will be going there to present before an august audience the best work of the Centre, and as our representatives you will interact there with some of the most exalted authorities in defence today. As you know the Defence-Oriented Research Act has been passed. In any case it is only a formality; the defence set-up has already undergone a drastic overhaul, thanks to the foresight of certain people. I hear the new facilities are almost complete and funds are ready. They are now looking for the relevant personnel. There will be special scrutiny of the work of the Centre in this regard. You understand, therefore, the importance of the Pune conference?'

They all nodded solemnly.

'You are the elite of this Centre and your work is already integral to the defence effort even here. You will showcase your cutting-edge, state-of-the-art achievements, taking of course the necessary precautions not to disclose the scientific kernel of them: you know of course that even though this is a "closed" conference restricted only to defence labs we must still be careful with information and control it on a need-to-know basis. We expect you to give a creditable account of yourself. The authorities have expressly requested me to require you all to be present on all the days of the conference, and especially to attend your poster displays in person at all possible times. Any questions?'

Gopal raised a hand. 'Sir, I have a doubt about the Defence-Oriented Research Act and its implementation in the Chakravyuh programme.'

The Director gave him a cold look. 'The bill has been passed. What's there to doubt?'

'Sir, I've heard my colleagues discussing it in the department and they seem to think that absolutely anything can be a subject of research within the new system. I am worried about the moral implications.'

Prasad nudged him furiously and looked pointedly down. He saw on Prasad's scratch pad the inch-high capitals, 'SHUT UP.'

The Director's eyes bored into him. 'What moral implications?'

'I mean . . .' He grimaced. Prasad had kicked his ankle; he should have been careful to sit somewhere else. 'Isn't it an important safeguard that here in the Centre to some extent at least we're accountable, even if only to the Army? The Indian Army is still largely a body of principled men and I know there are some weapons they just won't use, even if we make them. Surely we have a duty . . .'

'Dr Chandran, you are not naïve. I do not need to tell you that the nature of warfare has changed. This is the age of technology. We are living in a world governed by strategic nuclear weapons, pulse bombs, neuro bombs, biolock bombs that can seek you out at your daughter's wedding and just kill you. I can name at least seven major countries that possess such weapons, and at least two are our neighbours. Our armies have to fight in the world of today. The question is irrelevant.'

'Are you saying India ought to be one of those countries?'

'Exactly, Dr Chandran. Recent events should have convinced you, or are you so much unaware of current affairs? Don't you know the country is facing the greatest test ever? Gentlemen, the meeting is adjourned. Kindly stay back, Dr Chandran, I wish to talk to you.'

The room emptied out. Prasad turned on Gopal. 'What the hell were you playing at?'

'I could ask you the same thing. Since when is it a crime to ask questions?'

'Since you joined defence, friend. Look, don't you realize you're being offered the opportunity of a lifetime? You seriously want to rot here forever and take the rest of us with you? Don't look a gift horse in the mouth, Chandran. Or in any other orifice.' And Prasad disappeared down the corridor.

'The Director will see you now.'

It was the Director's secretary, standing patiently by his elbow. 'Can't it wait?' Gopal asked irritably. 'I need to think about this.'

'The Director wishes to see you. If it is inconvenient, perhaps you will explain to him yourself?' The man looked hunted. Gopal sighed. 'All right.'

The Director was at his desk. The chill from the air-conditioner hit Gopal in the face like a blast from a morgue.

'Sir, I know you wish to talk to me but I would like a few days to think it over and . . .'

'What is there to think? I want to see you leaving next week for Pune with the others. I do not want to hear these doubts. There is no point wishing for the world to be otherwise than it is.'

'I thought my questions were about things that every intelligent person . . .'

'Chandran, Chandran, the world order is now the rule of

might. Only if we are strong will people listen to us when we argue the right of this, the wrong of that. That is the plain reality.'

'Sir, I'm afraid I'm not convinced . . .'

'Tell me, Chandran, how is your child?'

'My child? What has she got to do with this?'

'Vatsala, she's called, yes? A delightful name. I trust she is developing normally?'

'Yes, there haven't been any problems so far . . .'

'Then, Dr Chandran, explain why you are so unmindful of the situation. Do you not remember how by your irresponsible actions you and your wife both endangered the life of your child? I have to tell you that we nearly demoted your security status after that incident. It was only the intercession of your colleague Prasad, who took all the blame on himself, that saved you. I was not going to tell you this but your inability to understand the situation makes it necessary. After such an incident I would have thought you would jump at the chance to get back in the good books of the Centre. Yet, you are causing more problems and sowing doubt and dissent among the researchers. This is not good. If you persist in this indiscipline I am afraid I will have to report you to Delhi and they will take a very serious view of the matter.'

Gopal's heart sank. 'Are you telling me I don't have a choice, sir?'

The Director's jowls shook as he said vehemently, 'That is exactly what I am telling you. Either attend this conference and remake your reputation, or go and sit idle like Dr Sheth.'

Gopal opened his mouth to say that Dr Sheth wasn't idle and had done wonders with the gardens, but thought better of it. There was a time for factual accuracy and this was not it. 'I understand, sir.'

'Well? What is your choice?'

He was silent. He looked down at the thick blue carpet on the floor, dented with the myriad dimples of vanished chair legs. What he really wanted was more time, time to sort out the tangled mess in his mind, time to face the actuality of having lost Agniv, time to look into the magpie-bright eyes of his child and ask her silently what he should do. But when he had had all the time in the world, he had only thought about rushing blindly into the future. And here it was.

Slowly, without looking at the Director, he took out his wallet, extracted a coin, balanced it on the thumb of his right hand. He tensed the muscles of his wrist, seeing the hollow appear between the tendons of his thumb. His thumb nail dug into the underside of his index fingertip, then flicked free. The little droplet of silvery metal whirled up, up, turning dark against the neon light, then silvery again as it fell and was captured by his outstretched palms.

He opened his hands and started at the little metal circle.

'Well?' The Director's impatience was evident in the tone of his voice.

'Heads. I go.'

'Humph!' The Director pressed the bell under his desk. 'Very well, Chandran, I expect to hear a favourable report of you.'

★

'Wonderful! Wonderful! This is great. Have some more brandy, Chandran, it's all yours. What happened next?'

'And then, we went down to Parker's Piece after the race, and there were all these rugger buggers from Magdalen or somewhere. And one of them said, "Have you been down the mine?" and my mate Roddy punched him in the lug.'

'Ha ha! And you weren't even in mining engineering.'

'No no, it's a racist comment. It means, why are you so black? And do you know I didn't even know it? Roddy told me afterwards. But in half a minute of course we were in a right brawl. The police came and took us away. We were bound over to keep the peace.'

'They tied you up?'

'No, we paid a fine and promised not to do it again.'

'Bearer! More brandy please. Napoleon.'

'I'd like some Cointreau, please. I haven't had it in years.'

'Of course! Bearer! Ask for anything, anything. You are very important person!'

'The first time I had Cointreau was when I met my wife, at the King's College May Week Ball. I'll never forget how she stood there, dressed all in white chiffon. She looked like a princess.'

'Ho ho! Did you do ball dance there?'

'No one dances at balls any more. At least not that sort of dance.'

'So what happened next?'

'It was hot in the bar, so we went for a walk. We talked about life, about everything that mattered to us, about work, family, happiness. I knew that day itself that she would be my wife.'

'So romantic, no? Just like in movies. Here we do not get opportunity. Although young people these days . . .'

'Bearer! More brandy!'

'So Dr Chandran, you miss your wife very much?'

'More than I can say.'

'In so few nights you have such sorrow for her? Come, come, you must be more strong. And if you cannot be, well, we have ways of easing your pain.' He winked.

'Thank you, Mr Saigal, it is very kind of you to be so concerned about me.'

'Everything is possible here, is what I am saying. We know you will soon embark upon a new *sadhana*, a great pursuit of knowledge and wisdom in the interests of the nation. We do not expect you to be a *sanyasi* all the time. Have fun while you can!'

'Amazing.'

'You will be amazed,' he winked again. 'That I promise

you.'

Mr Saigal strode off under the glitter of several crores worth of crystal and indirect lighting. The others crowded around again. 'Are all hostels really coed in UK? Girls and boys are living together?'

His gaze was swimming now. The air had a chemical taste, or was that his tongue? Faces seemed to balloon and collapse around him. Some small point inside said quietly, *You're drunk, Gopal Chandran, drunk as a lord. Yes I know*, said the rest of him, narrowly avoiding falling over a chair. *What fun, ha ha!*

Heck, I only had three neat brandies and a Cointreau. Let's have another. Here's to Vatsala! May she grow strong and tall and never, ever become like her dad.

Oh shit, I feel sick. It's all these people. Make you sick. There's too many of them, far too many, too loud, too big, too brash. Gosh, look at the way they've done up this conference room, it's like a bordello. Who could listen to seminars in this place? And this is supposed to be the swankiest hotel in the city. No wonder I didn't understand a word of what they said in the orientation. Disorientation! That's the way to go.

Whoops!

He sat down heavily on a sofa and burped. A little Cointreau slopped out the glass onto his tie; he brushed ineffectually at it, scraping his hand on the Signal Red tiepin. The small point inside him cringed with shame. *Oh shut up*, he said crossly to it. *I've lived like a monk since I came to this godforsaken country. Aren't I due a little fun? Damn it, I can't remember when I last got this rat-arsed. Must have been in Cambridge. Never felt sick then, even after eight pints of beer. No, I tell a lie, I sicked up the next morning. Bit of a delayed reaction there. The scout was livid.*

Jesus, I need to go to bed. No, I need to pee. Then I need to go to bed. Where the hell is my room?

'Hey Saigal, what's my moon number . . . room mumber
. . . you know, where I sleep? I've fog . . . fog rotten . . . er.'

'You are not staying for cabaret?'

'I'm a cabaret all to myself, Saigal! I'm so pissed . . . Jus'
lemme go.'

'The desk has your room key. Sandhwa will fetch it for you
and take you to your room. Anything you would like?'

'Yeah, a cuddly teddy bear or, failing that, my wife.'

'We'll do our best. Good night.'

Sandhwa returned in a while and took his arm tactfully. He
barely came up to Gopal's shoulder. Gopal looked down at him
and burst out laughing. Sandhwa smiled without amusement.
They made their slow and stately way down the corridor, into
the lift and out again to the room. Sandhwa piloted him
expertly through the doorway and let him collapse on the bed,
then left.

Gopal got up again. *Who did they think he was, some
undergraduate who got legless on three little brandies?* He
drank half the carafe of water, went to the bathroom and was
gloriously sick. When his head stopped spinning he drank the
other half, peed for what seemed like fifteen minutes and lay
down again.

Hah! Amateurs, the lot of them.

He stared up at the pink ceiling with its white mouldings
along the angles with the wall. *It's like being inside a birthday
cake,* he thought, annoyed. *Of course this isn't the swankiest
hotel in Pune, they just said that to impress us hicks from the
sticks. If it is, where are the foreigners? Nobody but a load
of functionaries and government bootlickers. For them, this is
the high life.*

*Well, they've certainly spent a bomb of money on it, I'll
hand them that. And that brandy tasted genuine. Of course,
after the first two you can't tell the difference.*

Suddenly he was overwhelmed by a savage loneliness that
seemed to tear open his chest and breathe freezing air upon

his naked heart. He got up and went out to the tiny veranda. There were two chairs there, chattily positioned as though two invisible people were having a conversation. 'Sorry to interrupt,' he mumbled, and sank down in one. Ghosts. A hotel room was always peopled by ghosts. Real people faded into phantoms in this soulless, homeless luxury; denizens of the unreal acquired faces, peering out of ornate mirrors, walking their inverted selves over the gleaming bathroom floors. *Any more of this and I'll go mad. I've explained my stupid piddling research till I've frothed at the mouth. People here seem to make a career out of asking idiotic questions. If this is what it's like at the top, I want to go home.*

I want to go home.

The city sparkled below his balcony railing. He leaned his head toward his chest and dreamed.

CHAPTER SEVENTEEN

The huge black thing in front of his eyes was a car tyre; he could see that now in the faint light that seeped through the air. It was only a few inches away from his nose; he could feel gravel in the wounds on his cheek as sharp points of pain. Far in the distance he sensed great beams of light sweeping the night sky. Something sticky was drying on his forehead and along his nose. All he had now in the place of the last few minutes was the dull mental aftermath of violent destruction, but his body felt numb. He tried to move his hands and feet. Cords of some sort restrained him. He could smell petrol, sump drainings, hot metal cooling.

The tyre loomed above him, the faint light picking out the sipes, the bits of gravel lodged in the right hand grooves, the wisps of grass caught in squashed droplets of tar, the worn places. Fascinated, he studied its material reality, its living history of hard use. It seemed to soar into the sky, the perspective of his worm's-eye view making of it a monolith, curving invitingly like a great weather-beaten black breast. His nostrils filled with its brute mineral smell. He felt an idiotic kinship with it, a sympathy for its hard knocks, an intuition of how it must feel to bear the weight of the indifferent vehicle, shielding passengers from the roughness of the road, itself the lowliest part of the structure, discarded and scrapped at the slightest malfunction. Passive, driven from above, commanded and moved by an unquestionable force . . . His consciousness began to spiral inwards; with difficulty he gathered his scattered thoughts and tried to grasp rationality again.

He shifted his gaze, hoping to make out what manner of vehicle he lay under. There were patches of rust in the undercarriage showing through peeling red lead primer, its struts vaulted against the dull sky like some profane temple of gearbox and differential, suspension and transmission, the secret workings of things bared for the privileged few. An Ambassador car, probably; not well maintained. He tried to think.

What was he doing here? Who had tied his hands? Why had he been left in the road behind this rusty vehicle? What did his captors plan to do with him? Had he lost at last? *No! I am a valued person, they would not leave me here like a forgotten sack of rubbish.* They needed him; he knew they needed him. At the very least they would question him. He could make excuses, bargain for his life. It would not end like this.

There was no sound, except of crickets and mosquitoes. No voices, no crunch of footsteps. He strained to look under the car's dark bulk and see what lay ahead. Persistently he felt there were beams of light scanning the air, though he could see nothing, only feel a faint sizzle of photons hitting suspended dust, a fugitive scintillation. Was that suggestion of lines against the sky a perimeter fence? Some sort of camp? A secret base, a control centre? Something no one knew about?

A sound. The tyre shuddered. Then, with a crunching, hiccupping roar, it withdrew into the night.

There was darkness all around. He couldn't say where the beams of light had gone. He twisted his bound fingers, wincing at the pain. There was a hole in his memory; he couldn't remember how he had got here, couldn't reconstruct the chain of events that had come to this. He lay back, breathed deeply. *They've gone*, he told himself. *Get a grip*.

Shutting out all thought, using the powers of concentration

he had developed over so many years of single-minded work, he curled his fingers and picked at his bonds. They had wound cheap jute string many times round his joined wrists and there was a bit of play in the loop; he could work it down to the centre of his palm from his wrist. Breathing shallowly, he dug his nails into the string, untwisting the fibres, then separating them.

That's right. He could feel the strands parting. They weren't going to win. Against all odds, he was going to escape. He felt a sudden jolt of fierce joy. It didn't matter where he would go next, how he would leave this godforsaken road, let alone the country. They had been cheated at last, their power denied, those whom he had believed all his life were the arbiters of his fate. *I am free.* His slavery had been an illusion, a laughable dream. There were places he could go, people who would help. He could disappear into the crowd, become an ordinary, unremarkable person; he would only stand out if he tried to be himself. *I am not I.* He would kill his old self and create another in its place, a self with no history, no guilt.

Half the strands gone. He worked at them with the concentration that brooked no interruption. Which is why at first he failed to hear the noise. An approaching, rattling hum, returning the way it had gone. Only when it reached ear-splitting levels did he look up.

A dark blind bulk roaring, only faint sidelights lit. Dead centre of his field of vision was the tyre again, no longer a wrinkled shape of pathos but a blur of avenging speed. As he lay on the rough tar the black shape that had watched over him roared along the road towards his face, filling, then annihilating his world.

★

He awoke with a start. Something had touched his face. No, there was a roof over his head. He was on the veranda of his hotel room. A woman was standing over him.

'Viddy . . .?'

'Good evening. I have been sent to entertain you.' The voice was soft, silken, chiming in professionally well-modulated tones.

'But I thought the cabaret was . . . downstairs . . .'

She brought a cool damp cloth and sponged his face. A few moments later he moved her hand away and stood up shakily.

'Who are you?'

'Didn't you ask for me? If there has been some mistake . . .'

'I didn't. . .'

'There has been a mistake,' she said softly, folding the cloth. 'Good night.' He watched her walk to the door. She was tall; she wore a shimmering gown of some black material that clung to her curves, the weave had subtle spangles in it speaking of taste and wealth. A mature and stunningly beautiful woman. It occurred to him that he hadn't got a good look at her face.

'Wait! Wait . . . do I know you? Did I meet you downstairs and forget about it? Look, I'm awfully sorry . . . if there has been a misunderstanding the fault is all mine.'

She turned. She had wide, upturned dark eyes set over high cheekbones; her hair framed her face and was piled high on her head, adding to her height. He had never seen her before. This was not a face he would lightly forget.

'No, I . . . I'm sorry, I . . . don't know you.'

She paused, her hand on the doorknob. Then she smiled, turned the knob to the locked position and came and sat down.

'You're lonely,' she said.

'How . . . how can you tell?'

'It's my job to tell. I take pride in doing my job . . . competently.'

'Job?'

She turned full face to him at his tone, then suddenly her eyes sparkled with amusement. 'You still haven't worked it out,' she said indulgently. 'I'm a prostitute.'

The word seemed to form in the air like a little black cloud. He sat transfixed. She went on, 'I was called in tonight to entertain you, since your friends determined that you wished for . . . company.'

'I'm sorry, but . . .'

She smiled. 'You look like a decent person,' she said in the same soft tones. 'May I ask you to allow me to sit here for a while? Just a little deception. And when they ask you how the night went, just say "fine". Otherwise I won't be paid.'

He sat still, shocked into silence by the beauty of her face, the wide sculpted mouth that seemed too perfect to be flesh, until she spoke. Her dark eyes danced with kind amusement. She opened a packet of cigarettes and offered him one. 'No, thanks, I . . .' he bit the rest of the sentence off and reached for one. She lit it for him, then for herself. They sat on the balcony and looked out over the naked city.

Then he said softly, 'May I ask you a question?'

She shot him a keen glance, the smear of light in her pupil sparking with the movement. 'You may, but I should warn you. You can do with my body what you like, but don't try to enter my mind. I might be more than you can handle.'

'What makes you think I want to invade your privacy . . . that way?'

Again that gold sparking glance. 'I can see you sitting there and thinking, she's so beautiful, she could be in films or on the ramp. What's she doing in this hell-hole?'

'You read minds as well?'

'No, just faces. I've had a lot of practice.'

He was silent, digesting this. She said softly, 'Do you really want to know?'

He nodded.

'Why?'

'I don't know. A morbid curiosity? A desire not to be alone in misfortune? A feeling of camaraderie? I really don't know.'

'Hmm.' She took a long slow drag on the cigarette and let

the smoke flow out. 'You're shocked at who I am. On the other hand you show no surprise at my understanding words like "camaraderie".'

'I can see you're an educated woman.'

'You see further than most. Although I suppose they too understand at some level; it makes it more exciting for them.'

'Them?'

'My clients.'

He was silent again, unable to bear the reality of the thought.

'You know them,' she said softly, 'you've sat in meetings with them on countless occasions. But you'll never see the side of them I see. I have access to their deepest fantasies. I act out for them their most depraved hankerings. There is a man at your Centre who loves to take me from behind, in the anus. As he violates me, he beats me and shouts the name of his boss, heaps filth upon him, furiously pounds the degradation into him. He fantasizes that he is tearing the flesh of his boss's wife, his child, his dog. He once had to pay me five lakhs when he tore my rectum. I am for him not much more than a lump of bifurcated meat that can move and scream. They pay. Or their bosses pay. I give them something they value beyond money.'

Silence spun out. She blew a cloud of smoke into the space between the stars and went on.

'I understand, you see. I understand that it's hard to be a man. The world constantly threatens and attacks your identity; minute by minute you fear its loss. What men get from me is a world of unconditional masculinity. There are no doubts, no questions, no standards to meet, no duties to perform. They can let their true selves free. And for me, there is the wherewithal to live as I choose, free of the claims of men. You look shocked? Tell me, am I any different from the anxious mothers scanning matrimonials, selling their daughters' bodies to the highest bidder. Selling? It's they who pay. At least I get the money. I'm the best, and for me it's a sellers' market.'

'How . . . how could you be brought to this?'

Her smile suddenly twisted. 'You want to hear about the beginning? Remember, I warned you. You can stick your cock into any part of me you choose, play out any obscene fantasy you wish in my flesh, but beware of looking into my mind. That takes different kind of balls.'

He said nothing. After a while she began to speak again, in a flat, expressionless voice.

'I was born in a small town north of Delhi. My father was a shopkeeper. I went to college in Delhi, but didn't complete my degree. Boys kept following me home; my parents decided I was too much of a liability and married me off at the age of nineteen to a man working for a small company. My husband never saw me till our wedding night; he fell in love with my photograph. They were so impressed, they refused a dowry. But on our first night together, as I lay in the pose on the bed that his mother had arranged me in for him, he couldn't bring himself to make love to me. Instead he cut my finger and smeared the sheets with blood.

'In the fifth year of my marriage my husband took a job in a larger company, in Mumbai. We moved. His boss there was a modern type, believed in office parties, that sort of thing. With much reluctance I, the small-town girl, went to one of these swathed in my wedding sari, the only evening wear I had. He saw me. He asked my husband to arrange for him to meet me. They struck a deal. One evening the boss came to our tiny two-room flat in a slum area. My husband introduced us. I made tea for them, took away the cups. Then my husband moved aside the centre table and pinned me down on the floor while his boss fucked me. My husband got a pay raise, then a promotion. He wanted a partnership. When I cried he would shout at me, "Your beauty is the only dowry your skinflint father gave me. I'm going to wring every last paisa out of it." This happened every day for a month; I was forbidden to leave the flat, locked in by day and night. Sometimes I screamed but nobody came. They put it about that I was mentally disturbed. My husband got another promotion. Then one day his boss brought a friend. I ran into the kitchen and tried to set myself alight.

'My husband had taken the precaution of locking away the kerosene. There was only the stove with half a cupful in it. I splashed it on my legs and lit it, but it went out. The pain was indescribable. That did not stop the men; they found it piquant to take me as I writhed and moaned in pain. After they left I pretended to have convulsions. My husband tried to ignore me but after a while became worried that I might die on him. He made me dress and took me to the hospital. On the way there I opened the cab door and flung myself out.

'After some days of wandering on the streets I was picked up by the police and put in a remand home. My husband filed for divorce on grounds of insanity and won. A women's organization taught me to sew and gave me some capital to set up a business for myself. I did so. In those days I really thought I was beginning a new life.

'Sewing was hard. I worked long hours, going round to houses to get orders, working late into the night. My health started to deteriorate. Then one of the more well-off women said, why are you breaking your back over this work, when you could be minting money? Take to modelling, I'll give you some numbers. She paid for a series of skin grafts by one of the best surgeons to fix my legs in return for some favours. So once again I began a new life.

'Do you know what modelling is? It's like a drug. You wear clothes worth lakhs that don't belong to you. You masquerade in the skins of the rich and famous, you live their lives, vicariously. You lick the rind so much that after a while you long for the fruit. But at the end of the day you return to your one-room hovel and your plastic bucket and soap in a tin. It is more than human dreams can bear.

'I am not so selfless. I believe life is to be seized, to be wrung dry. I see all this luxury and I want to own it, to squeeze it in my hands and caress it with my tongue. Well, you can't own anything without money. So I slipped, without much fuss, into this life. It's a good life. With the proceeds of one big assignment I can visit my favourite spa, drink famous wines, wear a millionaire's ransom round my neck. I can do what I like. The price is small; a few hours of pain, maybe, a loss of some fictitious thing called dignity. A pandering to some man's view of himself, an acting-out of some furtive puerile fantasy. My clients lose their dignity too; it's safe with me. Discretion is part of my stock-in-trade. I have a surgeon friend who patches me up for a consideration whenever things get rough. I have scar tissue all through my genitals and anus. It doesn't bother me, and my clients never notice. But each time my surgeon friend shakes his head and says, next time there won't be enough meat left to stitch together.' She shrugged. 'It'll last long enough. And the same goes for the world's favourite bogeyman, AIDS. I'm not worried; if it comes to me I'm only giving back to them what they saw fit to give me in the first place. I don't intend to hang around long enough to see the symptoms. I have better things to do with my life than grow old.'

She lit another cigarette. So did he. A wind sprang up and caught the little heap of mingled ash in the tray, whirled it into a tiny dust tornado, then left it scattered on the polished floor. A dying butt tumbled away in a shower of embers.

'Ashes and sparks.' She finished her cigarette and stubbed it out. 'And you? What yawning hollowness were you attempting to fill with my pitiful story?'

He took a long time answering. 'You're right,' he whispered. 'It's all hollow, everything I've done, the tunnel of nothing that's brought me here, sucked me into this room like a vacuum. Everything, all my achievements, all my pride. This is where it's brought me.'

'To a hired room with a hired whore? Come, don't be so

hard on yourself. You're an important man. I don't come cheap; the bosses don't do this for everybody.'

'Must you make a joke of it? Are you so hardened that nothing is sacred? Or are you just putting on an act for my benefit?'

'Hardened? Call it professional detachment. If I allowed myself to feel, I would not survive.'

'So you're still human.'

Her lips quirked with amusement. 'Not yet a deity, no.'

'Listen—' He stopped. 'I don't know your name.'

Again that half-smile. 'You can call me Aishwarya.'

'Listen . . . Aishwarya . . . if you were to meet a man, a good man as unlike your husband as you can possibly imagine, one who will give you back your dignity and your feelings and your life and love you to the utter exclusion of everyone and everything else—would you go with him?'

'You mean if I were to meet someone like you.' She glanced at him. 'How sweet. Can I ask you a question in turn?'

'Yes?'

'Suppose you were that man—it's all right, I know you're married and you miss your wife, relax—suppose you were that man, on what conditions would you take me?'

'Take you? What . . . what conditions do you mean?'

'Everything is a bargain, Dr Chandran. What would I have to give up in order to buy this protection, this dignity?'

'You'd give up nothing. I'd shelter you—if it were me, you understand—provide for you, keep you safe from men who wanted to exploit you . . .'

'Would you let me dine at the best restaurants, pick out diamonds four or five times a year, shop in Singapore, buy Chanel?'

'I wouldn't forbid you, but of course I couldn't possibly pay for . . .'

'Then think again whether I need a male provider.'

'But . . . but you're paying for this with your blood.

Literally.'

'Everything has to be paid for. I pay with my body, you pay with your brains. You can no more choose your clients than I can. The same bosses tell us what to do. The same spies keep watch on us. They're probably listening to us right now.'

'What! But . . .'

'Relax, they'll keep our secret. They'd only interfere if we did or said something anti-national, as they quaintly term it. They won't find any arcane code in our conversation.'

'I shouldn't have drunk so much.'

'The road of excess leads to the path of wisdom. Although wisdom is so often synonymous with death. Sadly.'

'Death? Before you came in and woke me up, I was dreaming of my own death, of my own *murder*.' He shuddered. 'It was so real.'

'We're all going to die, Dr Chandran. Some of us are more realistic about this than others.'

He dug the heels of his hands into his eyes. She stubbed out her cigarette, walked round the back of his chair and spread her long fingers over his neck. He jumped. 'Relax. You need this.'

He was silent for a while, as her expert fingertips found the knots of tension in his flesh that he had not known existed. She slipped off his jacket, placed her hands lightly on his shoulders. There was only the thin fabric of his shirt between her and him. Her fingers began to move gently, with incredible wisdom, persuasive and soothing. Slowly the individual bones of his spine released their death-grip on each other and curved like a tired snake. His head hung on the end of their knotted rope. Her fingers travelled down, around his shoulder blades, then up and over into the hollows at the base of his neck. He shivered. Then he said softly, reluctantly, 'I'd rather you didn't, please. It reminds me of Viddy.'

She took her hands away. 'Viddy is your wife?'

'I'm sorry.'

'You're the client. The client is always king.'

But the base of his skull ached with sudden poignancy; the half-released tension was like a pent-up sneeze. He gave up. 'All right. Do it. But no farther.'

'I'm not trying to seduce you,' she sounded amused. 'Believe me, no one is more pleased than I when I don't have to.'

'So this is money for nothing?' he asked bitterly.

'I'm rendering you a service, aren't I? You have an excessively mechanistic view of prostitution. Do you know who Ambapali was?'

'I'm afraid I don't move in your exalted circles.'

'I'd be surprised if you did; she's been dead for more than two thousand years. She was the famous courtesan of Vaishali, for whom kings paid half their wealth for a single night. She didn't just lie on a mat and spread her legs. She was a mistress of the sixty-four arts. To do my job well, I must offer more than sex. I have to find the right context for my client, discover his fantasy woman and wear her face for a night. I even took a distance course in psychology to make sure I was getting it right. But there's no substitute for practical experience.'

Gopal grunted. Her fingers were sending him back into the deep abyss of brandy and sleep. *I should ask her to stop*, he thought, but an unspoken greed in the depths of his heart said, *Yes, but not now.*

She seemed to divine his mood. 'Want to tell me your story? That would be a fair trade.'

He roused himself somewhat. 'There's not much to tell. I was born in a small town in Kerala; a similar sort of background to yours, I guess, except my father was a petty official. I've always wanted to be a scientist; I was science-mad from the start. Our school was pretty ordinary but we had this one physics teacher, he was kind of eccentric. Most of the time he was okay, but if he took a liking for you he'd give you the hardest time in the world, push you to the limit and beyond. He never took "I can't" for an answer, if you ever said that to him he'd look at you like a tiger, then he'd push and push and push till you solved the problem or fell senseless on the ground. Even after I went to college in Trivandrum he'd meet me in the holidays, quiz me on the work I was doing. He pushed me to apply to Cambridge. I didn't think I had a chance, but he said I should at least try and remove all doubt. I was surprised when they accepted me, but he wasn't. I wonder what's become of him.

'Well, Cambridge changed my life. It was a whole new world. It was scary, like you'd go grocery shopping and meet three Nobel laureates arguing over where to get a beer, but it was mind-expanding as well. Viddy . . . my wife, she always said London was better, that was where she grew up, but the blacks and the neo-Nazis and skinheads on the streets scared me. That's why I came back, I guess, when I couldn't get a position in Cambridge. It was Cambridge or nothing. Vidura was unhappy; I'd ripped her right out of the life she knew and put her in a gilded cage, but there was no option . . .'

'Wasn't there?'

He was silent. Then he said slowly. 'You're right. I was offered jobs—school teaching, software. I could have stayed, if I'd had the guts. Viddy and I would have been dirt poor, but . . . we'd have been free. I've always told myself I came back to give Viddy a comfortable life, but that's a lie. I was scared. The West was too much, too big, too different. I just took from it what I could take, a thin layer of polish, knowing how to hold a sherry glass, that sort of thing, and ran home as fast as my small-town legs could carry me. And I told myself it was patriotism, noble-heartedness, readiness to serve my country. What a tragic, barefaced lie. I was just a burned child, running home to mummy. I was jealous of Viddy's English friends, jealous of her ease in that life, of her unerring knowledge of which streets were safe and which weren't, whether a drunken greeting called across the street meant well or ill. I wanted her dependent on me, clinging like a good

Indian wife, needing me to pay her bills and buy her things and organize her life around me. And you know what? I've succeeded. That's exactly who she is now, she's like a little gadget that makes my house run, cleans my child's shit, browns my toast in the morning exactly how I like it. I've destroyed her.'

'You remoulded her as your fantasy woman. What she's done unwittingly with her whole life I do consciously for a night, at a price. Believe me, it's the ground rules of all women's lives. They can only choose how and when and for whom they'll become a mirror.'

'That's bullshit,' he said savagely. 'And don't compare yourself with her.'

'Think, Dr Chandran. Why do you feel guilty that your wife has become your mirror? Why not accept it? Doesn't it show you how much she loves you, that she's spent her whole life mirroring you, only you? That she hasn't become someone like me?'

'Vidura never, never could become someone like you.'

She was silent. Her fingers slithered up and down his spine, making bioelectric arcs jump from ganglion to ganglion. 'Relax,' she breathed. 'Don't let your anger tear you apart. Let it flow away like water. There . . . it's almost gone now.'

'Mmm . . . How did you learn to do that?'

'Many of my clients live stressful lives. It's my job to find what works best for them. And a knowledge of basic anatomy helps.'

'You're wasted in this life. You could have been . . . I don't know . . . a scientist . . . with your mind . . .'

'And no college degree? You're sweet, but unrealistic.' She loosened his tie, then her fingers slipped lower. He felt a gentle tug. With difficulty he opened his eyes. 'Strange,' she said softly. His discoloured tie lay across her palm, the Signal Red jewel glittering in the centre of it. 'This is surprisingly tasteful. A gift from your wife?'

'Yes. It's red glass. Signal Red. I'm working on it. She . . . she had it made for me.'

'She must love you a lot.'

A bitterness made him say, 'Too much.'

She gently unclipped it, and held it up to the light. The red star awoke in its depths; she twirled it, making the star flash on and off. 'You know laser-sighted guns? When they lock on to a target, all you see for a moment is a red dot of light flash on the place where the bullet will hit.' The shaft of the pin gleamed between her fingers. 'When I woke you and you stood up, this pin flashed, right there in the centre of your chest. For a second I almost expected you to crumple at my feet.'

A clink. The pin lay before him on the glass table, dark once again like old, cold blood.

'I need to sleep,' he mumbled. The muscles of his eyelids seemed half paralysed.

'Do you need help?'

'No thanks, I can . . .' he got unsteadily to his feet. 'I'm sorry . . . if I have . . . uh . . . the fault is all mine . . .'

She stood in the middle of the room, tall and darkly shimmering. Her arms against the dark cloth seemed more than skin: some new light-bearing substance. Images of her trembled in his eyes. A faint smile lit her face; a diamond flashed in her ear. 'It's a rare man who worries about being chivalrous to a prostitute. I am privileged to have met you, Dr Chandran.'

'Good night.'

When she was gone the room seemed unbearable. He went out and leaned against the balcony parapet. Cool damp air swirled about his hot forehead and cheeks. It was a long way down. He stretched out his arms, willing the wind to blow away the chemical fog in his head. He could see his own fingers in front of him but they seemed to feel nothing; they were balloons of alien flesh tacked on to the ends of his arms.

For a long time he stared into the abyss. Then he staggered back into the room, fell across the bed and was instantly asleep.

CHAPTER EIGHTEEN

Gopal stared around him in sick incomprehension. The flood of light from the open veranda doors seared the back of his skull. His joints creaked as he hauled himself off the bed and staggered to the bathroom to retch weakly into the flowered porcelain commode. There was no drinking water left; his mouth tasted foul. He brushed his teeth but it had no effect. Pulling off his rumpled, stained clothes he stood for almost twenty minutes under the cold jet of the shower, trying in vain to wash away the patina of poison that coated every surface of his body. Scraps of words and images bloomed in his head as he stared at his own splayed hands on the pink bathroom tiles.

Who was she? Was she a spy? Had he said too much? Were they coming for him even now? His heart thumped.

They mustn't find me like this. At least let me face them with some dignity.

His nerves at once oversensitive and unresponsive, he dried himself, shaved clumsily, and dressed. As he repacked his suitcase he pieced together his tattered recollections of the night. There were many holes. Had he really said all those things? *Oh god, oh god.* Memory lanced into him every other minute.

Screwing up his courage, he rang room service and ordered breakfast. Then he sat on the bed and tried to calm his panicking mind.

He was appalled at his lack of judgement in getting drunk. What could he have been thinking of? Perhaps he had dreamed it all—the night, the woman—under the influence of brandy and loneliness. Then his eyes fell on the overflowing ashtray on the veranda. He sprang up and emptied it down the toilet, pulled the flush again and again till the last butt disappeared.

Breakfast arrived. The thought of eating revolted him. He drank only the orange juice. The phone rang, making him jump. It was Prasad.

'Overslept, did you?' He could hear the leer behind the words. 'We're all down in the lobby, waiting for you. You'll miss the coach if you don't hurry.'

'I'll be right down.'

Did they know? Why had Prasad sounded like that? Assailed by a fresh wave of fear, he scrambled downstairs.

The journey back passed in a blur. He kept to himself, not joining in the others' boisterous conversations; they were like a pack of schoolboys returning from an excursion. He sat in his own private gloom and recalled again and again his words of the night. Slowly, the mental fog cleared. He couldn't reconstitute the whole conversation, but the feelings that had pushed their way into the words he'd said were still there, still broadcasting their messages in the back of his mind. He became his own judge, attacking the internal witnesses of his own dissatisfaction. *What right have you to feel your life has come to nothing? Aren't you the envy of your profession, with more success ahead of you? Aren't you achieving what you've wanted all your life?* And within him a sudden hard point of hatred and anger blossomed, grew a voice. *No,* it said, *no.*

Why not?

Hadn't he believed in the redeeming power of excellence? Hadn't he striven to be the best? What should he have done otherwise? Where had he gone wrong?

He tried to cast his memory further back, to retrieve files from the basement of his mental record. Anu had said something . . . something about negotiating a space. Drawing boundaries. But how could you do that when you worked for the government? You had a heavy responsibility: safeguarding the lives of millions of your fellow citizens. How could you draw lines for yourself when so much depended on your insight, your diligence, your commitment to your work?

He shook himself. *I'm being silly. My masters aren't just the Director and the Centre. They're the entire republic of India. That's who I'm serving, and I should never forget it.*

But what do I do if some of my masters, the ones who give me orders, are hurting the rest? These people by the roadside that I see in a flash as we pass, ordinary farmers driving cattle or working in the fields, can they walk into my office and say, make us a better plough, find ways to keep our children healthy? No? So how are they my masters?

'Chandran!' Prasad roared. 'What's got into you? Not talking? Too much brandy last night, eh?'

The grim tapestry of his thoughts fragmented. 'Leave me alone,' he mumbled.

Prasad plumped himself down beside Gopal. 'I think we did well,' he confided. 'That guy in the loud checked shirt asked me all those questions. They're definitely interested.'

'How do you know he was one of them?'

'Don't you know? They always pretend to be dumb. And then they provoke you by saying you're work's all rubbish. They try to get you riled up to see what comes out.'

'I think you're reading too much into it. They're always some people like that at seminars.'

'Ah, but you learn to recognize these types. Usually after talking to them for some time you realize they're not as dumb as they want you to believe. Every time someone asks me a patently stupid question and then hangs around for fifteen minutes the old antenna starts beeping. Why, didn't anyone like that come and talk to you?'

'I couldn't say.'

'Come on, Chandran, you weren't drunk yesterday morning.'

'Does it matter?' Gopal burst out. 'We're just animals in a cattle market. Don't kid yourself that we have a choice.'

Prasad stared at him with raised eyebrows. 'I didn't expect that from you of all people,' he said coldly. 'You've been acting strange; don't think I haven't noticed. And they'll have noticed too. Fear of heights, Chandran? It's a bit late to decide you can't handle it at the top; jumping off now is going to be really painful. Watch your step.' Before he could reply, Prasad had got up and moved to the front of the bus.

It was only as the bus entered the gates of the Centre that he remembered he had left the Signal Red tiepin on the table in his hotel room.

★

'Look, Baby, daddy's here. Say hello to daddy. Hello, daddy! Look, she's waving at you.'

'Yes, but she waves at everyone, all the time. Why do you call her "Baby"? She's got a name.'

'Yes, it's little Widdums. No, Baby, daddy has to wash his hands before he picks you up. What's the matter, Gopal?'

'What? No, nothing, just very tired.' Gopal realized he'd been leaning with his forehead on the mirror above the washbasin, his skin pressed to the cool glass. 'Mind if I go straight to bed? It's been a hard few days.'

'Go ahead. It's time for Baby's nap anyway.'

The guest room where Anu had stayed was now the baby's room. Vidura slept there now; the baby often needed feeding at night and she didn't trust the nurse to wake her. He had the master bedroom all to himself. He lay down expecting to pass out, but after the first few drowsy minutes the infernal engine in his head started up again. Vidura was singing to the child in the other room. He lay on his back and studied the ceiling, listening.

Vidura's happy, he thought. *That's what really matters. If I've accomplished that, I've done what I set out to do. My suffering doesn't count.*

It's wrong of me to want her to come in and talk to me. She's totally wrapped up in the child. After all these years of loneliness and waiting, at last she has a focus, something on which to spend the treasures of her heart. If I'd known that it really mattered so much to her, I'd have put in the adoption papers long ago. We'd have two now. She'd have spent her time being a mother, someone with a function, responsibilities. Being a wife was never enough of a challenge for her.

And what about me? What challenge have I been fighting to fulfil? Yes, I've tried to be a creator too, but my *children are monsters that fill people with fear and dread.*

In the next room the baby cooed. Vidura laughed. Gopal felt a sudden wrenching bitterness; at her, at the woman who had asked him to call her Aishwarya. It was so easy for women. Their biology determined their lives. Sex, children, beauty; it was all laid out in their genes, their bodies, the configurations of their flesh. Only men had to invent a role for themselves, choose a career, determine a goal. A woman merely married, and let the drama of egg and sperm plot out her life for her. Or she offered to men a diversion on the road to their chosen targets. She never mapped out the road; she merely waited by the kerbside to flag down a traveller.

Anu would kill me if I said anything like this to her. But it's true. It's all right for women to condemn violence because they have no access to it. They don't have to contend with the responsibility of being a potential preserver or a destroyer. Their weakness shields them from moral dilemmas. Things can be black and white for them.

He wondered about the handful of women scientists at the Centre. He always found them rather frightening. Most of them worked on top-secret projects, the details of which were only ever vaguely alluded to. They never talked about work, and the lights shone in their labs till late into the night. His colleagues joked about their total lack of sex appeal. He found their single-minded dedication to duty rather unnerving.

'I thought you were sleeping. Do you want tea?'

He started a little. 'Yes, please.'

He came downstairs as she finished making it. 'So, how was your trip?'

'Lousy.'

'I'm sorry. Was it very boring?'

He realized that it had been, in a special way. It had had the special tedium of terror, when a second seems infinite. 'Yes.'

'Oh dear. Well, at least you won't have to go again for a while.'

'How have things been at home?'

'Wonderful. Do you know I think Baby's teeth are coming? All day she just chomps and chomps on her fingers, or on mine if I let her. You can feel the little tooth buds inside her gums. But she's being very good about it; she never cries or complains.'

'Well, that's good.' He yawned.

She looked at him carefully. 'You're still tired. Couldn't you sleep? Was my singing disturbing you?'

'Oh no. It just feels odd to sleep in the daytime. I suppose I should go up to the Centre and put in an appearance.'

'Okay, but come back soon. I'll get the maids to make dinner early so you can go to bed if you want.'

'Right.'

She cleared away the tea cups and went upstairs to check on Vatsala.

★

'Sir, may I come in, sir?'

'Agniv! My god! You're back!'

'No, sir.' Agniv shook his head sadly. 'I have come to say goodbye.'

Gopal came round his desk and held Agniv's shoulders in both hands. 'Don't look so woebegone, young man. Tell me all your news.'

'You are not angry with me, sir?'

'No, I'm not. You've been through a difficult time. Have a seat and tell me all about it,'

'There is not much to tell.' Agniv sat down and clutched his new briefcase in the old way. 'I am working in a private college in Delhi now, sir. My brothers did not let me come back, and then I . . . I had to find something.'

'Is it the money? I can get a scholarship for you. We'd like to have you back if it's at all possible.'

Agniv shook his head slowly. 'I know about the scholarship, sir. Anu Aunty told me. But . . . I don't think I should come back.'

'Why not, Agniv?'

'I . . . am not right here. I feel more better . . . I mean better . . . as a teacher. I am taking a course in spoken English, sir. Isn't my English improved?'

'It certainly is. Good for you. Do you have a place to stay in Delhi?'

'I'm staying with a friend. Sir, I felt very bad, I could not come and tell you . . .'

'Don't worry, Agniv. I could see you were deeply troubled here. It's better that you've found something you like doing. It was wrong of me to try to change your mind. I'm happy for you.'

Agniv looked down sharply. 'You have been very kind to me sir,' he said in a choked voice.

'It's my duty. I'm your guide, aren't I? This place wasn't right for you. It would only have got worse if you had stayed. And once you were in employment here, it would have been very hard for you to leave.'

'That is what I also thought, sir. I did not want to bring disgrace on you.'

'Disgrace?' Gopal looked at him in wonder. 'You know something, Agniv? I envy you. And I admire you, that you stood up to me when I was trying to persuade you to carry on against your better judgement. You did the right thing. Never listen to anyone who wants to turn you from your true path. If I'd had one-tenth of your strength of character, I'd be a happier man today. I'd give anything to be your colleague in your little private college, but it's too late for me. I'm glad you're doing something you enjoy and want to succeed at.'

Agniv looked up in wonder. 'Sir, I . . . I thank you, sir.'

'Did you think I was going to scold you for wasting your talents? Don't be silly, Agniv. This country needs good teachers as well. Those kids will get the best guidance from you. Teach them to inquire as well as work. Don't think that research only happens in big places like this. There are other ways of innovating. Teach your students to change the world, Agniv. I know you can do it; you live in the real world, unlike some people here. There are tons of problems out there that technically trained people need to solve, but no one is doing it because everyone wants to be Einstein. Remember that little history book I gave you? We need some Thomas Edisons as well.'

'Yes, sir.'

Gopal smiled. 'But I'm getting ahead of myself. Tell me what courses you're teaching, what sort of resources you have. Is there any chance of doing research? What are your colleagues like?'

A shadow seemed to clear from Agniv's face. With enthusiasm he began to describe his new job, the students, the course design. Gopal listened with a sweet sadness buried deep within him. He knew everyone at the Centre would call him a fool for letting a good researcher slip through his fingers. But Agniv was free; Agniv was walking towards the light. There was one guilt less for him to carry.

'Sir, but what will be happening to you now?' Agniv asked

towards the end of their conversation. Gopal shrugged. 'Whatever is my fate.'

'Fate, sir? Sir, you scolded me once when I said "fate", you remember, sir?'

'Did I?' He smiled sadly. 'Fancy that. Yes, I didn't believe in fate before, but now I think we make our own fate, and I made mine long ago.'

Agniv shook his head slowly. 'Sir . . .' He stopped, took a deep breath and tried again. 'Sir, I wanted to be like you . . .'

'Like me, Agniv? No, you didn't want to be like me. You're grown up now, a teacher yourself. Admit it: I am what you wanted to avoid becoming.'

'No, sir!'

'Don't try to hide my mistakes from me. What you're really saying to me when you say you wanted to be like me, Agniv, is, "Don't stop being my idol, don't dash my illusions." But I know what I've done, and what I wanted you to do. Neither was right. You're not my student any more; at least we can have that much honesty between us. Okay?'

Agniv hung his head and blinked rapidly.

'Go in peace, Agniv. Have a good life.' Gopal made an effort to smile, to push away his unread list of errors. 'You can only choose for yourself, Agniv. We can only choose for ourselves.'

It was late afternoon when Agniv finally left. Gopal sat still for a long time afterwards, thinking about fate. He asked himself, what was it that Agniv had, and he did not, that had led them on such different paths? He had always prided himself on never taking the easy way out. Why then had he not suffered and questioned and chosen as Agniv had? What had brought him here instead?

He felt a sudden distaste for his room, his desk, the piles of paper that lay haphazardly everywhere. He got up to turn off the lights and leave.

A faint knock sounded on the door. Somewhat irritably he called, 'Come in.'

A small, dark man entered.

'Dr Chandran. I am S. Murthy. I have come to brief you on your upcoming transfer.'

'Transfer?'

'Indeed. You have been selected under the Defence-Oriented Research Act. We have made arrangements for the immediate transfer of you and your family to a new project.'

Gopal stood thunderstruck in the middle of the floor. 'By immediate do you mean now?'

'In a maximum of three days' time. You know that this is a highly sensitive operation. We will request you to maintain A-1 security on every aspect of the transfer. Luckily you do not have school-going children, so it will be easier to effect the transfer. May I sit?' The man sat down without waiting for a response. 'Now let me outline for you the logistics of the operation. You, your wife and child will leave here by Tuesday, taking with you the minimum necessary. I'm afraid you cannot carry any personal mementos or other objects that will be identifiable. You will all be held for a while in an undisclosed location while we erase all traces of you from the records. Then you will be placed at your final workstation and given a new identity and background, which you must maintain as the truth at all times, even in private discussion within the family. This is for your protection, Dr Chandran. You will be a keystone person in the project and we must make sure that anti-national elements cannot track you down. You will of course be our honoured guests and you may reassure your wife that all technicalities will be taken care of and the transfer effected as smoothly as possible.'

'Will you leave us with nothing?'

'You will be amply rewarded and compensated for the inconvenience, Dr Chandran. I regret the necessity of doing this but hard experience has taught us that we can take no chances where people's lives may be at risk. I need hardly add that you must inform no one, not even your closest family, or your wife's. Should anyone come to inquire, we will put out a cover story explaining your disappearance. You will be briefed about the details and location of your new project while you are staying at our secure location.'

'This has been decided?'

'Very favourably, Dr Chandran. Our observers' reports on you are satisfactory.' The man stood up and extended a hand. 'Congratulations. The great value of your work and of your personal capability has been recognized by the Chakravyuh authorities. You are a fortunate man. Now if you will excuse me, I have further business elsewhere.'

'Suppose I say no?'

Murthy looked at him in astonishment. 'Whatever can you mean by that, Dr Chandran?' he said, and left.

CHAPTER NINETEEN

Gopal pressed the doorbell and leaned against the wall. It was six in the morning. He prayed that she would hear it, that her sleep broke.

The door opened a crack, brought up short by a chain. 'Who is it?'

'It's me, Gopal. Let me in, please, it's important.'

A shocked pause, then the door was opened and shut behind him. He leaned on it and shut his eyes. She looked at his face in amazement, at the growth of stubble, the lines of exhaustion. 'Gopal? Where's Viddy? What's happened? You look like . . .'

'I've done a runner, Anu. I'm a fugitive from the Centre, maybe from the law. I don't know. I don't know anything any more. I've . . . I've selfishly come to you for help, because you're the only one who understands.'

She was silent for a long moment. Then she took his hand and led him inside, made him sit down on the only chair in the bare living room. 'When did you last eat?'

'Two days ago. I've been hopping on local trains, flagging down trucks and bullock carts, walking. All the time I was thinking, I'll never make it. Someone'll cut my throat for the money, or . . . *they'll* catch up with me.' He closed his eyes.

When she came out of the kitchen with buttered toast, bananas and eggs he was fast asleep. Holding the plate with one hand, she gently shook him. 'Eat, then crash in my room,' she whispered as his eyes opened. 'We'll talk later.' He did as he was told; she lent him a kurta and pyjamas to wear and he washed, changed out of his filthy clothes and lay down on her narrow single bed. 'You can sleep all day,' she said. 'I'll come back early from the Institute, say three, okay?'

'Okay.' He was asleep again before she left. She locked the front door behind her. As she left she paused for a moment and looked up at the window. Was he safe there? She had no way of telling.

★

He woke with the sense of empty peace that comes with convalescence. The events of the last few days seemed like a dream, their horror now nothing but a flourish of unreality left behind by a fever. The bedroom window was a square of city darkness, pinpricked with the distant glow of streetlights. He heard Anu pottering in the kitchen, got up and went to see what she was doing. She had changed out of her sari into a light blue *bandhni* salwar kameez with her hair tied in a ponytail. 'You must be starving all over again. Just give me a few minutes.'

He wandered around the flat. It was large, but almost empty. There was only the bed next to a trunk full of clothes, a chair, a mattress on the floor in the sitting room and a portable sound system. No TV, the old Westinghouse fridge with the tarnished front panel, and in the kitchen a couple of saucepans, an armful of jars, a pressure cooker and a gas burner. That was all. Then he noticed a lamp like a transparent fountain sitting unobtrusively in a corner. He flicked the wall switch and watched it come alive, throwing a moving skin of coloured sparks over the blank white walls.

'That's my only luxury,' she said, coming out of the kitchen. 'It was a gift from my friend Akiko Tamura, a scholar working on women in the home; she came last year to do a comparative study. I'm visiting her in Okinawa this winter.'

'How can you live with so few things?'

She shrugged. 'I don't need them. Of course, I don't spend a lot of time here; only eat and sleep, really. I like to watch my lamp in the evenings; it helps me think. You missed lunch. I've made a sort of high tea; want to eat now?'

They sat cross-legged on the mattress and ate toast with *kabuli chana* and tomato salad. Only when Anu had cleared the dishes and come back to sit down again did she say, 'Okay, shoot. Start at the beginning and leave nothing out.'

'The beginning?' He smiled sadly. 'I've been trying to decide where the beginning is. But I haven't a clue. I was hoping you could help me. And I don't have much time. I don't know when they'll catch up with me. I should leave now, only . . .'

'Shh, don't talk of leaving. You've come here for answers. Let's at least try to find them. Then when you know where you want to go, you can leave.'

'You're taking a terrible risk . . .'

'You're just a friend visiting me. What's the harm in that?'

'But I don't know what . . . if . . . they suspect. In any case I'm supposed to take permission to leave the Centre. They told me . . .'

'Told you what?' He shook his head, the words refusing to come. 'All right,' she said gently. 'Let's try and work backwards. What made you run?'

'I don't know! It was like . . . I can't explain it, some sort of shadow that suddenly loomed in front of my face, and I had to run or let it swallow me. It's been building for a while now; ever since you visited us . . . no, no, since they railroaded Mani Sheth. That's what started it; having to watch that sorry circus in such helplessness and anger. Mani scared me sometimes with the weird things he'd do, but he was the only person in that damn Centre I trusted. And then he betrayed me and left me to fight on my own.'

'But it was you who refused to see him.'

Gopal dropped his head into his hands. 'I know. I thought

if I looked at him it'd happen to me. As though rebellion is catching.' He laughed bitterly, his face hidden. 'And look where it got me. You warned me, didn't you? God, I wish I'd never set eyes on the Centre. You know, Anu, some part of me knew as soon as I walked into the place what sort of life I'd lead there. But I just kept my head down and wished the knowledge would go away. And after that . . . well it was too damn late.'

'Why did you push it away, Gopal? If you knew, why didn't you leave when you could?'

'And admit to Viddy that I'd been wrong? I made her give up her citizenship to come here. Would she ever have forgiven me?'

'Wouldn't that have been better than this?'

He groaned. 'You think I haven't asked myself that in the pit of the night? I've ruined her life. Nothing that can happen to me would be worse than that.'

'But you're in danger now. How will Vidura carry on if something happens to you?'

Gopal spread his hands, then let them fall into his lap. She watched him for a while. His chin sunk down on his chest, his eyes closed. After a while she asked gently, 'Are you tired, Gopal?'

He turned a look of such anguish on her that she almost drew back. 'Anu, tell me what to do. Otherwise you're looking at a dead man.'

She took a deep breath. 'You've got to tell me more, Gopal, if I'm to help you. What's been happening in the past few weeks, what are your options, that sort of thing. I can't read your mind. You've got to try and make some sense of this for me.'

'Okay.' With an abrupt burst of energy he got to his feet and began pacing the room. The light from the lamp slid eerily over his features. 'You're aware that the Defence-Oriented Research Act was passed some time ago?'

'Yes.'

'Do you know what that means?'

'I can guess. A parallel set-up invisible to any kind of scrutiny, with unlimited resources and total security, where Prasad can work on his nightmare powders to his heart's content?'

'Exactly, him and a round dozen of people who are sitting on projects whose deliverables will be so horrendous that no one has yet dared to give them the go-ahead. Until a few days ago I was hoping it was all moonshine, even after the Director told us to be on our best behaviour at this conference in Pune last week. It was basically a meat market for the defence honchos to earmark faculty for the new secret research programme—Chakravyuh. I . . . I didn't realize just how serious they were about it until . . . well . . .' He stopped pacing and looked down at her, 'Anu, can you keep a secret? I mean, this is a personal thing. Nothing happened. It's just that I don't want to upset Vidura.'

'What are you talking about, Gopal?'

'Well, on the last evening there was some misunderstanding, probably because I got totally sloshed on the free brandy, and the organizers sent this . . . woman to my room that night. I told her there was a mistake and I didn't want her, but she asked if she could sit with me for a while . . . we got talking . . . I can't begin to describe her. She was beautiful and corrupt and intelligent and perceptive. She was evil . . . she was addicted to pleasure and she didn't mind if she paid for it with agony. I've . . . I'd never met anyone like her before. She told me her story; I asked her to. It was harrowing. I . . . I'm sorry, I still can't think of it without shivering.'

'All right, just tell me the implications.'

'I saw myself in her, Anu. I've been courting death just as she had, or said she had. What else is it when you know that you're heading for a terrible fate and yet you do nothing to avoid it, you live for the moment?'

'Is that what you were doing when I visited you?'

'Yes, damn it, it was so hideously easy then to just not think.' He sat down beside her with a sigh. 'But that woman showed me this: in the noble cause of science we scientists have always gone with whoever had the most funding, the biggest facilities, the most unquestionable authority, like prostitutes going with the richest john. I'm no different from that woman, Anu. I was greedy for money and an easy time of it, and afraid, afraid of all those brains in Cambridge, solving the mysteries of the universe while I struggled with my little problems, afraid that I didn't have it in me to compete in their world. If you're not the best in a place like that, you're dead. Science is brutal with reputations. All our work deals with what's there and you can't invent what's there. We're always racing against each other, to be the first with something, to win, and once you've *been* the first with it then it's finished, and you have to look for something else to be the first with or fall behind. It's not like that in the arts. If you write a book or a symphony, it's yours forever. No one else can write it better and wipe your name off the title page.'

'But you weren't doing that kind of science at the Centre. Your intention wasn't to publish but to develop specific technologies.'

Gopal shrugged. 'That was my fear steering me—away from the endless race of academic science to a safe world of determined goals, where I could simply work without fanfare or worry. In defence science you don't get given anything, so nothing's in danger of being taken away. What I did could have been done by anyone with the right training and a modicum of intelligence. Agniv could have done it . . . would have done it better, probably.'

'Gopal, do you regret that you chose to be a scientist?'

He shook his head. 'No. But I regret my silence . . . Anu, why are we all so blind? Isn't there one scientist in the world who has stood up and said, we won't be coddled or dictated to or locked up in big rooms full of hardware? Why must we always be bought and sold by the money men, the governments or companies or whatever?' He dropped his head into his hands again. 'I'm not making sense am I? I thought when I came back to India I would be doing good by working for my own government. Surely it must be right for a scientist to serve his homeland?'

'Do you regret returning?'

'No, I believed then—and still believe—that it's possible to do good science here. But here there's . . . something, some sort of huge network like a spider's web, that's everywhere, and ties you down even while you think you're free. It's in everything, people's voices and looks, the particular way they say "thank you" when you tell them they can have a few more days to complete their project, the way they squabble over points of order and terrorize their research scholars. And underneath, like the soil beneath a field of flowers, there's a stratum of thought and being and feeling that's totally alien and it's going to defeat you. You can't put roots down in that soil; it doesn't have what you need to live. And yet . . .'

'And yet?'

'It can't only be out there in the West that great things can be done. It can't be, can it? Is it true that we can't live in our own land, because we're too intelligent, or too committed, or too hardworking, or too modern? Is this place only for those who must be . . . I don't know, bosom buddies of Rahil Vidyadhar or something.'

'Why does Rahil Vidyadhar annoy you?'

'He's always implying that if we don't think like him, we're nothing. Ridiculous! And yet I've seen . . . that it's true. Maybe bad thought drives out good, but the Centre's coming more and more to be his mirror. It's like people *want* to believe in him. Even the Director.' He shuddered. 'I don't want to work for people who think like Vidyadhar. He can actually look at someone and decide they're not human. And some of the men find that a relief. If the people they're targeting aren't human, they don't have to feel guilty. My god.'

'You thought he was a harmless clown when I last met you. What changed your mind?'

'The way other people in the Centre hang on his every damn word. He tells them what they want to hear. They thirst for his words and that frightens the hell out of me.'

'Is that why you ran?'

'Partly.' He ran a nervous tongue over dry lips. 'There's more. When I got back from the Pune conference this man came to see me. He said I'd been selected for Chakravyuh, that Viddy and the baby and I would have to leave within three days, shed our old identities, become cardboard people out of a file and go to live and work in some prison they'd faked up to look like a town. It'll be totally secret, they kept saying I could do "what I like". I know now what that means. Whatever little chance we had to fight for that tiny space you talked about in your articles, that'll be gone, too. We'll be slaves, each to the degree that we excel. Why did we ever swallow that garbage, Anu? I saw that man's smug face and I just knew I had to run, if it was the last human thing I did. It's either that or become a brain in a vat of ether.'

'But if you positively refuse to work under this scheme they can't make you join it. They can't reach into your head and pull your knowledge and your expertise out of it.'

'No, but they can tie my hands. The Director made it clear that it was Chakravyuh or nothing. He practically threatened to make another Sheth out of me. And now that they've selected me there's no going back. Listen, Anu, you know lots of people in this city. Do you know anyone who . . . who could get me a fake passport, anything like that? Or maybe . . .'

She looked slightly amused. 'Do you really think everyone here has connections with the underworld?'

'Anu, I'm desperate. Just tell me which area is a good place to search, I'll find a broker myself. Please. You know it's my life I'm pleading for.'

She considered for a long moment, tracing the pattern of the cover on the mattress with a finger. Then she said, 'No, Gopal. If you try to escape with the help of criminals, you'll be at their mercy. If your passport broker has any inkling of who you are, and believe me he'll have it out of you in an instant if he so much as suspects, he'll ship you to the highest bidder. Would you like it if you were forced to work for a terrorist ring? You don't have the resources to fight such people. They're professionals; they'll see through any cover story you try to cook up. Don't fantasize about it; that sort of thing only happens in movies.'

'Then what do I do?'

'Go back. Go back and become Mani Sheth.'

'I can't do that!'

'Why not?'

His face was ashen. 'Look, I'd still be on the campus, I'd be coming in to the office every day, sitting at my desk and staring out of the window. Can you imagine what sort of an empty, yawning vacuum there'd be inside me? I'd . . . I'd go stark raving insane. No, Anu, I can't do it. Anything but that.'

'But Gopal, why must you give up? If you've really understood the moral implications, then . . . why not try to make amends? Isn't that the responsible thing to do?'

'I can't make amends for what I've done.'

'You can speak out. Look,' she urged as he shook his head in slow bitter arcs. 'Science is in crisis all over the world. Everyone's pretending that it isn't and that there couldn't be a better time for science to flourish, so it's getting worse. Can't you see? There's a high wall between you and me, a wall that's been created by the way we've been taught to see each other. There are people like you on the inside, who know what science really is. And there are people outside who don't, and among them some are your masters. They don't care about science; they just want to wring the fruits of science out of you and throw the skin away. You're a black box to them: money goes in, science comes out. You might as well be a genie in a bottle. Science can't survive if people with power think it's magic. Magic is dangerous; it has to be captured and commanded. It's irresponsible; it can do anything. Do you see what I'm saying?'

'People are stupid if they think science is magic. Anyone with an elementary education knows better.'

'No, they don't, Gopal, not given the kind of science that's being done today. People think science can do anything. And it's not about education, it's about values. It's about who controls science and for what, and it's about a nice little walled-in settlement of rationality trying to hold out against a society that's gone nova in the irrationality spectrum. How long will your wall hold? Is it protecting you now? Can you work without real understanding from people outside your wall? Listen, I can't tell this to the world and make it stick, I came in from outside the wall and you saw what happened to me. *You* have to speak, Gopal. *You* have to tell the world what's going on. Only then will . . .'

He gave a short bark of laughter that seemed to tear his throat. 'Can you imagine what will happen to me if I speak out? Straight into the interrogation room. They'll smash me for what I know and burn the rest.'

'So you'd rather run from them and risk so much more? Look, you won't be spilling technical secrets, you'll be talking about abstract things. You can do it without provoking the authorities. You and Mani together. Can't you?'

'No, Anu, *no*. They're not idiots. If I say, "Oh, I'm not divulging any technical stuff, I'm only striking at the ethical basis of state-directed science" I can just imagine Rahil Vidyadhar binding me to his heart with hoops of steel.'

'You're still not listening, are you? Gopal, why are you so intent on destroying yourself?'

'Because I deserve it.'

She sighed, and was silent for a long time. Then she said softly, '"What art thou, Faustus, but a man condemned? Thy fatal time doth draw to final end.'"

'I'm not Faustus, I'm Frankenstein. And the monster is after me. It's going to pursue me till one of us is destroyed. I can give in, and make what it wants me to make, or I can refuse and let it do its worst. Either way I'm doomed.' He rubbed his hands over his face. Then after a while, his head still bowed, he murmured, 'Logically, there's only one clean course of action left.'

'What? . . . Oh.' Then she said in a low voice, 'Seriously?'

'Yes, seriously.'

'You would really prefer to . . . cease to be rather than be Mani Sheth?'

'I'm a coward, Anu. I now know that Mani's much stronger than me. He knew where things were headed and he did what he had to do. I'll never be able to make amends for how I treated him. I've spent my life shying away from the moral implications of everything I've done, thinking up clever justifications, attacking anyone who tried to open my eyes, yes, even you. I can only apologize and say that I'm getting what's coming to me now. And, in spite of everything, I have to thank you, because you started the process of opening my eyes.'

Anu blinked. Then she took his hand in hers and said softly, 'Apology accepted. Want coffee? We'll talk about it later.'

★

Gopal walked through the streets. It was late at night, but this was the city and there were still people about. He had a few hundred rupees in his pocket, all Anu could get him to accept, and he was back in his old clothes, now washed and dried. He had nowhere to go.

He had ceased to wonder what would happen to him now. It was futile. His body might go on living, but the life of his mind was essentially over. There were no thoughts he wished to think, no tasks he wished to undertake, no destinations he could imagine reaching. He realized how little all his achievements actually meant to him. He didn't want to make the effort, but he knew that if he tried he would not be able to find a single moment of triumph that would surface out of the darkness for him now. There was nothing about which he could say: whatever happens to me from now on, I have done this. There was nothing that was not tainted. That was true of his work, but he knew now that it was also true of Vidura and the life they had shared. It was all connected, like an intricate machine, like an organism. Poison one part of it, and sooner or later the venom eats into the rest.

He was past wondering how it had come about. He knew only that it was irreversible. There was no cure. There was only a faint curiosity to see how it would end, a morbid wait for the tale of himself to conclude.

He walked on. It had rained. The roads were slick. Here and there were puddles. People scurried by with umbrellas, not sparing a look for him as he soaked patiently in the rain. He walked on as the moon was revealed and hid by the wind's caprice, far above the tawny lights of the city.

He came to a wider road that went straight on and, like a robot or a mechanical toy, he turned into it. Soon he had reached the station. He went inside with the smooth unhurried movements of a sleepwalker. A train was just coming in; he bought a ticket at random and boarded it. There was enough space at this late hour; people didn't have to fight for seats. He found a corner by the door and watched the city go past. He was already on the outskirts of the city proper, moving north from Anu's flat; there were gaps of darkness between the huddles of light that marked neighbourhoods. Far in the distance the faintly luminescent sky showed the humps of hills against its margins; then, as the train slid farther into the darkness, they merged into the night.

He got off at a station. Walking was a relief, and the air was cool. The sight of people made him shrink into himself;

he turned away, sought out the less travelled roads. Beyond the station's clutter of houses there was a deep hush. He walked on, uncaring of the dark and the insect susurration in the woods on either side.

There were tall trees around him now. The city was losing its hold on him; he was in a much older place. Under a dim light bulb he came upon the mouth of a path that bore the cloven marks of goat and cattle feet. He followed it, into the sparse undergrowth. The path wound between huts and rubbish dumps, now silent except for the night birds' cries. Beyond the ragged settlement there were a series of deep square pits, their edges shining faintly in the fitful moonlight: illegal stone quarries, by the looks of them. He passed them and, brushing aside the twigs and leaves that barred his way, began to climb the hill.

From somewhere far away in the night came the cough of a leopard.

He smiled to himself and raised his face to the cool night breeze. A strange joy coursed through his veins. There was a sweet fittingness in being here, in the midst of wilderness, ready to be the unremarkable meal of a beast. No science, no knowledge could find him here, to save or kill. He was alone and defenceless as the first man had been. He slipped off his shoes and threw them as far as he could into the underbrush. The touch of earth and sand on his shoe-softened skin was startling, revelatory. He walked on up through the thorns, to the summit of the hill.

The moonlight showed him the rock face when he was some hundred yards away. He stopped and regarded it. Vertical rectangles of darkness sliced its flat plane, one, two, three side by side. He came a little closer and saw that they were alcoves, standing behind pillars carved into the living rock. Steps led into the sanctuary, centuries old. He laid a hand flat against the rock. The warm licheny roughness like a beast's hide was how it must have felt to the monks, two thousand years ago on such a moonlit night.

The breeze was rising. It rattled the leaves against the pillars of the entrance. Clouds scudded across the moon. He slumped down on the threshold and leaned against a pillar. A hint of rain blew through the air, wetting his lips.

He closed his eyes. A great weariness dragged at every limb. The sound of his own heart beating in his ears distracted him; he wished it would cease its noise so he could listen to the night sounds of the forest. A bird called; insects sang in their alien voices. An owl glided overhead on silent wings. A star pulsated on the edge of a cloud, sending a message through earth's uneven veil. The clouds danced with the wind. A jackal loosed its high-pitched manic laugh and was answered by another, and another.

'Good evening, Dr Chandran.'

He looked up. A dark figure stood before him, a small black box in its hand. 'Don't move, Dr Chandran. I wish to talk to you.'

Gopal forced words from his dry throat. 'Who the hell are you?'

The figure sighed. 'Never mind. I'm here to help you. You've done a very foolish thing.'

Gopal sat up slowly. 'I know you,' he breathed. 'You're that man who came to my office. You're that . . . that Murthy.'

'That is correct. Mind if I sit?'

Murthy took up a position on a boulder. 'Dr Chandran, you have been sitting here for several hours. I can see that you are deeply distressed, your body is full of stress hormones and you appear to have thrown your shoes away. We must have an explanation.'

'God damn it!' Gopal's shout rang across the forest. 'Kill me! I'm a traitor; I've run away from your precious Chakravyuh. Are you stupid? Since when did your kind ask for explanations?'

Murthy's face was temporarily lit by a faint glow from the box. 'Dr Chandran, I have been carefully tracking your movements for some time. Initially when you ran I admit I thought you had turned traitor. I don't need to explain to you that the suspicion alone of your being a turncoat was enough for me to order your termination. But there was a thin margin of error, and I wanted to be sure. Your whereabouts and your mental state suggest to me that you have broken down from internal causes. I do not think you therefore need to die. But I must ask you to calm yourself. Your adrenalin levels are rising dangerously.'

'What . . .?' Gopal stared at the box. 'What the hell is that thing?'

'It's a fairly simple receiver. It tells me your location, your vital signs and the levels of key mood-altering hormones in your body.'

'How . . .'

'You will remember that our Dr Golwalkar gave you a course of tranquillisers after your wife's . . . mishap, no doubt? Well, not all of them were tranquillizers. One was a robot, the MATA, Mesenteric Analyser and Tracking Array. It's a tiny device of sensors and transmitters, which deployed within minutes of being swallowed and embedded itself within your system. It draws the tiny amount of power it needs from you yourself. You cannot go astray, Dr Chandran. It is lucky for you we are watching you all the time or you would have perished on this hillside. We have known of your emotional turmoil for some time now. Present events were not entirely unexpected. We let you run, or rather I let you run on my own responsibility, because I felt if you were allowed to work your doubts out of your system you would come around much more efficiently than if we had to use persuasion.'

'Persuasion?'

'You are perhaps aware that Dr Vidyadhar has developed a number of motivational drugs and techniques for such cases? We would have had to refer you to him for treatment.'

'I'd rather you shot me in the head.'

'Oh no, Dr Chandran, we will not do anything without your consent.'

Gopal's hands clenched in the soft powdery dust. 'That robot tag? That was done with my consent?'

'That was for your good, Dr Chandran. It has in fact saved your life. You do not seem to know that there are dangerous animals loose on these hillsides.'

'I can see that.'

'You are lucky we got to you first. Now I must ask you to return with me.'

'No.'

'No?'

'I'm resisting arrest, or whatever you people call it. I won't go back to your high-tech prison. I'm damned if I will.'

Murthy regarded him. Gopal saw the moonlight flash silver in the corner of his eye. 'You should reflect, Dr Chandran,' he said softly, 'that we have your wife and child.'

Gopal shuddered. Murthy peered with satisfaction at his black box. 'But you need not torture yourself unnecessarily. You are of course beyond hope as far as future research is concerned. You cannot join Chakravyuh; you have proved that you do not have 100 per cent commitment. But you must return to the Centre. You are far too valuable a commodity, even with your motivation destroyed. You must not be allowed to fall into the wrong hands.'

'Look, can I make a deal with you?'

'A deal? Dr Chandran, I hold all the cards.'

'That's what you think. Will you hear my proposal or not?'

'Well?'

'If I kill myself, will you let Vidura and the child go free?'

Murthy snorted. 'You no doubt imagine yourself a brave man.'

'I'm serious, you louse. You're worried about the contents of my brain, right? Won't my death solve your problem?'

'Why do you want to die, Dr Chandran? Here is a world full of people fighting to stay alive, fighting with cancer, with

AIDS, with horrible wounds and poisons, and you are saying you wish to die? Why?'

Gopal's face in the moonlight was ghastly. 'Because you've destroyed my life. This thing inside me that's telling you all my intimate secrets, it was built by someone like me, someone who worked for months in his lab like a monk to delicately, beautifully craft this device. And here it is, doing its job just as he envisaged. No doubt he thought he was making a great contribution to defence as well as medical science. Just imagine knowing the physical state of a soldier the moment he's brought into the field hospital; no tests, no vital minutes lost. No, it's better than that, you'd know the physical state of the men in the field itself, are they injured, are they being poisoned by chemical weapons, are they hurt, are they afraid and about to run out on you? A brilliant idea. And here it is, telling you all about me. Thank you, Murthy. You've proved to me what I've suspected all along. It wasn't just your black box that was receiving signals from your little device. How fitting that it should be there while I've run all over the countryside looking for answers. There they were, nested inside me like an embryo. Or a tapeworm. Part of me knew, part of me was certain I couldn't escape. But how wrong you all are. You think I can't step out of my own head. Well, I can! What use are my brains to you without me to run them? If I can't think I'm not worth a thing to you.'

'Dr Chandran, I must warn you to calm down . . .'

Gopal twisted his body and smashed his forehead on the pillar. Blood sprayed from split skin as he reared back and crashed into it again, leaving a dark star in the moonlight that he struck again and again, making it grow. 'Stop him!' Murthy screamed, and sprang forward as the undergrowth erupted with dark shapes. Gopal was on his knees now, and the dull thuds of his attack on the stone's indifference rang through the caves until he was stilled.

★

Dear Anu,

What can I tell you, darling, about what's been happening to me? It's been a nightmare. The night after you called me, they brought Gopal back to the Centre; I couldn't get anyone to tell me what was the matter with him or even if he was alive, and it seems like it was touch and go for a long time. All I could do was hope and hold on to little Vatsala. There was no way I could explain to her why I was sad; for her sake I pinned a wide smile on my face every day. That hurt very badly. I couldn't help asking myself over and over: was it my fault? Was there anything I could have done? And I thought, yes, there was. I could have tried to understand Gopal as a man—not just as a husband. I never have; I understand that now. I've always accepted his explanations of what was happening with him and why: totally the wrong thing to have done, I now know. I kept quiet and let him play daddy, out of laziness, maybe, or fear. I didn't care enough to ask those questions you warned me of long ago. I was so worried that it was I who was going crazy that I never noticed it was Gopal all along. It took a lot of work to face up to that. I nearly didn't make it.

For a long time after that I wondered why I was alive. All that stood between me and madness were Mani and Nalini Sheth. Nalini came and visited me twice a day; she even had me stay with them when it was clear I couldn't cope with both the house and the baby. And I can't tell you how awful the rest of the people have been. Now I have a tiny inkling of how it must have been for the Sheths. I'm consumed with shame that I let Gopal talk me out of standing by them. Nalini's been like a sister to me. I'll never be able to pay back my debt to her. If only I could have been for Gopal what she is to Mani, maybe none of this would ever have happened. But it's no use crying over spilt milk.

Last week we were allowed to see Gopal for the first time. I went with the Sheths; I didn't know what to expect and I feared the worst. But he opened his eyes and recognized me; thank god, thank god. And he knew Mani as well. There were tears in his eyes when he looked at Mani. That told me everything was going to be all right.

They say he'll have to have extensive medication and physiotherapy to counteract the effects of the stroke. When I think of him collapsing on the train from Mumbai I feel so guilty. And to think that as we were talking on the phone such a terrible thing was happening to him! Thank god there are kind people left in the world, who looked after him and brought him to the Centre. He owes his life and I my happiness to them.

Don't feel bad about it, dear. You couldn't possibly have known what would happen. I'm only grateful it wasn't worse. And you set his mind at rest; he was coming back to his life here, he wasn't going to run away. So you did the right thing, Anu darling. I'll always be grateful to you.

Dr Golwalkar says he'll probably be well enough to come home in two or three months' time. I'm having the carpenters put handrails all around the walls, like they do in old age pensioners' homes in England. That'll make it easier for him to get about. He's even talking a little now; Mani told me he said 'I'm sorry' very clearly last time he went to see him. We're going to do everything we can to get him back to normal. The only thing I'm a bit worried about is that the Director hasn't said whether he can continue at the Centre. I asked Mani what will happen and he just laughed in a funny way and told me not to worry. He said, 'Neither me nor Gopal is going anywhere.' He should know, I suppose.

Well, do tell me all your news. And thank you again for helping.

Love,

Vidura

EPILOGUE

  Access Code: Red Ten
  Priority Code: Alpha One
  Report Code: T/1/58-S410
  From: Central Control Authority
  Re: Current status of Subject S410, principal investigator: VarGeom Flat Panel Display, AHAN ultralight armour, Sanjaya Nano-vision TRS, BioGlass, Virtual Layer Instrumentation III, Signal Red, Flexible Digiteye, NOVO-FDDP, X-Helmet; contributor to: Intranaut VI-A, Project AL-TPI, Low Radar Profile Coatings, Project O48890, Project R234510, MATA system, Q-Photon I. For list of past projects where Subject was PI see attached report.

<<Text>>
Assessment of Operative C318: Under influence of alcohol Subject reported disenchantment with interpersonal relations, described career and achievements as 'hollow'. Lacked faith in supervisory authorities but stopped short of open criticism. Displayed distaste for wealth and financial reward, unlikely to be turned by offers of money. Reported paranoid fantasies of own murder.

Report of Operative A109: Subject was tracked to Borivli National Park, apprehended, sedated and returned to Centre. Showed extreme nihilism and death wish. Dr Golwalkar carried out simulation procedure SS009. Subject's relations were informed he had had a stroke. After SS009 tests, showed expected short-term memory loss, weakness and disorientation. Violent behaviour normalized.

Actions: Subject is burnt and removed from all projects with immediate effect. Medication will continue. Subject no longer fit to work. Retained within Centre and kept under vigilance. Loss of social prestige has occurred. All contacts to be logged. </Endtext>>

Read more in Penguin

The Village of Widows
Ravi Shankar Etteth

The murderer began to laugh. He was confident that the police would come up with nothing . . .

When a diplomat at the Madagascan embassy in Delhi is stabbed to death in mysterious and quite possibly scandalous circumstances, the ambassador calls upon his old friend Jay Samorin to help find the murderer as quickly and discreetly as possible. In his somewhat unorthodox approach to solving crimes, Samorin crosses swords with the police officer in charge of the investigation, Deputy Commissioner Anna Khan, recently transferred from Kashmir where her zealous pursuit of suspected terrorists had threatened to cause an uproar. But it transpires that each has an intensely personal reason for their obsession with murder: Samorin's father, a pilot and war hero, was hanged for the murder of his mother, while Anna Khan's husband was killed by the Kashmiri Mujahadeen. Forming an uneasy alliance, the gifted amateur and the jaded professional start to untangle a shocking web of corruption, prostitution and callous medical malpractice. It is a trail fraught with danger, tainted by the older, deeper mysteries that lie outside the more tangible boundaries of a criminal investigation—a trail leading back through the darkest recesses of their own lives to that elusive, haunted place known as the Village of Widows . . .

Fiction
India Rs 295

Read more in Penguin

Cardamom Club
Jon Stock

An electrifying, sinister read, packed with unexpected twists and thrills

What is the Cardamom Club? Why does it still operate in India? Is it responsible for brutalities at odds with a modern, progressive India? These are some of the sinister and disturbing questions Raj Nair is confronted with when posted to Delhi. It's his first time in India, his first job for MI6 (his cover is his job as the resident doctor at the British High Commission), and not everyone is pleased to meet him. Ambitious and patriotic, he is soon forced to question his own loyalties, particularly when his father is arrested in Britain on spying charges. Raj realizes he is up against a secretive, colonial organization working at the very heart of Whitehall: the Cardamom Club. Can his father really be a traitor? And will Raj expose the Club before it destroys him?

Fiction
India Rs 250

Read more in Penguin

Stillborn: A Medical Thriller
Rohini Nilekani

'The foetus was suspended in a wide-mouthed dusty glass bottle with an aluminium seal . . . Neglected, vulnerable, ashamed. A dead human being . . . Stillborn.'

Recovering in a Bangalore hospital from a road accident, Poorva Pandit, a journalist, overhears a bizarre story about a contraceptive vaccine research, unwanted pregnancies and a missing malformed foetus. In MR Hills near Bangalore, Anshul Hiremath, returned NRI and doctor, has set up a research centre to test the efficacy of his new vaccine for contraception. But word soon leaks out that some of the tribal women on whom the vaccine was being tested, have become pregnant, and one of them has delivered a deformed stillborn baby. Even more strangely, the foetus disappears from the lab and turns up mysteriously at an NGO camp nearby. Following the trail for a story to break out of her ennui, Poorva begins to uncover a chain of incredible links. She realizes that Anshul is just one of the players in this international game where scientists and researchers are playing for incredibly high stakes and will stop at nothing to be the first to produce the ultimate contraceptive.

Drawing on the latest developments in the field of immuno-contraception as well as the imminent adherence of India to the GATT agreement and changing patent laws, Rohini Nilekani's first novel is a nail-biting, unputdownable, racy thriller.

Fiction
India Rs 200